A Bouquet of Darts
Reed Stirling

Print ISBNs
Amazon print 9780228631309
Barnes & Noble 9780228631316
Ingram Spark 9780228631323
BWL Print 9780228631330

Copyright 2024 by Reed Stirling
Editor JD Shipton
Cover artist Pandora Designs

Dedication

For Kevin & Sherry K

Acknowledgements

"For I must tell you that we artists cannot
tread the path of Beauty without Eros
keeping company with us and appointing
himself as our guide."
— Thomas Mann

"Eros is everywhere. It is what binds."
— John Updike

Table of Contents

Day One
a plethora of potential mischievousness

Weesp:

Amoretto Algea rocks gently at its berth near the Vecht, a river with historical significance that meanders into and around Weesp south of Amsterdam. All is subdued, voices remain low, meager lighting casts faint shadows. No one is about except for the crew, four in total, headed by Captain Jan Van der Oor. Most of the boat and bike guests have retired to their berths for the night, in all likelihood puffing up on their pillows any expectations they might entertain for the next day's cycling and the sites they will visit.

"Mister Raymond Rudiger is going to be a hell of a problem," announces Finn Bonger, tour guide and general go-to guy on the Amoretto Algea. He yanks out a chair from its place at the crew's table in the dining area and drops into it. He sighs heavily, miming exhaustion. The others seat themselves as well.

"Which one is Rudiger?" Simon Oliver wants to know. He removes his ball cap with the Everton logo, wipes his brow, and replaces the hat that he sports with considerable pride when not wearing his pleated chef's hat, the one he wears with considerably more pride.

"Raymond Rudiger is the little guy with the big mouth," Finn Bonger explains. "Short, stalky, with muscular legs. A hodgepodge of tattoos on the arms. Spiderweb tattoos on his calves. Fancy riding gear with expensive labels just for the preliminary bike assignments earlier. Trying to impress, maybe."

"Bald headed," Captain Van der Oor adds. "Shiny."

"He's got a lusty leer," Finn Bonger continues, "pointed ears, and he comes across like the perfect horse's ass that he is. Demands special treatment."

"Another *pijn in de kont*," Captain Jan Van der Oor declares in his native tongue, voice like a rasp running across a rough surface. He strokes his beard then grimaces. All that identifies this man as captain of the *Amoretto Algea* is the peaked cap he wears.

"Meaning what ?" Simon Oliver wants to know.

"Pain in the ass," Finn Bonger offers, and the two others nod in agreement. Dirk van Kesteren, deckhand and general goffer, laughs out loud and then apologizes, red-faced.

Captain Van der Oor gets up from his seat, looks out the large starboard window which gives on to the quay, and with right index finger doing a characteristic digital dance, he counts the heads of four guests straggling back to the barge. They are making their way gingerly up the gangplank to access the main entrance which is situated by the reception desk, and with minimal conversation or consternation they hang room keys on the appropriate hooks. Captain and crew watch the foursome disappear down the hallway leading to their respective quarters, the aforementioned Ray Rudiger picking up the rear.

"And only one day out of Amsterdam," Captain Van der Oor states matter-of-factly.

The comment is punctuated with a toothy bit of concession to the obvious. An up-turned lip and a sucking sound follow. The crew reads the captain's expression with complete understanding. They know he's playing his part. He looks back to the starboard window, grimaces, and, seemingly pleased with himself, proceeds to say, "Nobody tripped on the ramp."

He reaches across to the bar, grasps a bottle of Irish whiskey, and sets it on the table with a bang. Dirk van Kesteren quickly procures four glasses. Ritual. Part of the process of getting together the first night out and comparing notes.

"Gentlemen," the captain says after pouring full measures of the whiskey, "as you heard me say before, BS from guests comes with the territory."

"*Proost!*" Dirk van Kesteren calls out.

Simon Oliver, chef, chimes in with "Cheers!"

"What about the family at table five, the Picketts?" Finn Bonger asks, having swallowed his whiskey in a single gulp. He taps his glass on the tabletop as though demanding an immediate response to his query from anyone who might provide one.

"With the twins," Captain Van de Oor adds. "Big fellows, athletes."

"Intimidating louts?" Simon Oliver asks.

"I think not," the captain replies. "They certainly do not intimidate me. Nor would they intimidate any of you. I would not allow it."

"Know who is intimidating? I'll tell you who," Simon Oliver goes on to say with observable annoyance. "Pickett senior. I found him nosing about my kitchen facilities."

"Name's Dexter, Dexter Pickett," Finn Bonger says, tapping his glass on the table once more.

"When I confronted him," Simon Oliver explains, "this Dexter Pickett character mumbled something, in Dutch or maybe it was German. Said he got disoriented, yeah?

Boats can do that to him, he said. Ridiculous excuse, innit? I told him we speak English, all the crew of *Amoretto Algea* speak English, especially me as I'm English. My Dutch is very limited. So English, as a favour to me, yeah? At this the wanker just sneered and left."

"Odd," Finn Bonger says. "He strikes me as a sly guy. Shifty eyes. He had the comforting look of a smiling Lee Van Cleef training a gun on you."

"No reason for him being there, in my kitchen. After my priceless knives? No one touches my knives. So what was he looking for?"

"Recipes for bitterballen or perhaps your mutton stew?"

Everyone laughs at the captain's joke and watch him as he picks up the bottle of whiskey again.

"*Ja,*" Dirk van Kesteren says, "with you on board, Chef Simon, all English for us is better, especially if we want good grub."

"Thanks, mate. I'm a well-practiced scouser from way back in Liverpool. Remember, though, it's my last run with your lot."

"Off to new parts," Captain Van de Oor says. "All is confirmed?"

"Got my ticket booked, Maastricht to Paris."

Having poured again, Captain Van de Oor asks what else is on the minds of his crew. Any potential conflicts of a serious nature? He recalls the double murders on a boat and bike excursion from a year ago, in Belgium. No one has any intimations about possible trouble, just an awareness of how difficult it is at times to please everybody.

"The Pickett woman, Bonnie," Finn Bonger begins, "has something to say about how things onboard could be better. Right at the reception desk, with others still signing in, she complains about towels and wants to know if there will be enough hot water for showering. Mostly she is unhappy about their room being below deck, below the water line, as she puts it. I tell her she and her family were the last group to register, and therefore were the last to get assigned rooms. She'd appreciate being on the main deck if a change with another party could be arranged."

"Good luck with that," from the captain, who knocks back dramatically his splash of whiskey. He shakes his head and then grins appreciatively.

"At least she didn't complain like Ray Rudiger about table seating in here," Finn Bonger contends. "He can be very insulting, that guy. He's full of self-importance."

"Rudiger, again?" from the captain.

"Yes, Rudiger again," from Finn Bonger.

"So, the tosser's gone and lost the plot already, has he?" Chef Simon says. Finn Bonger and Dirk van Kesteren readily nod agreement. "We've got six more days with him. Maybe during that time he can prove to be a half-decent bloke, yeah? Maybe even heroic. We can only hope."

"A long shot, that hope," Finn Bonger responds. "You know how I like to ease into my introduction with a little humour, about regulations, cycling procedures, and the route for the next day's excursion. A little tongue-in-cheek, as our beloved Chef Simon says when he keeps secret what he is preparing in the galley."

"Cabbage or aught, yeah?" Chef Simon teases.

"So I say to the group: 'Don't show me your pictures and don't tell me your dreams! No high fives, knuckle knocks, and no hugs. Captain's orders.'"

"That went over well?"

"Got a few laughs, Captain, but nothing from Rudiger who maintains his long face. He's still angry with me about dining room arrangements. I assure him it's for the ease of all the guests. Tables are organized according to family group, or language, or in some cases nationality. The usual explanation."

"Then what?"

"Then he says that he's not accustomed to being told where to sit. That he tells people where to sit. Made a successful career of it. Did I understand that?"

"Wanker!" from Chef Simon.

"Then with a couple of fingers," Finn Bonger continues, using two fingers of his right hand to illustrate his complaint,

"Rudiger gives me that eye-to-eye gesture that means he's going to be watching for me to screw up. While I eventually get around to describing some of the attractions on tomorrow's route, I notice he's not listening at all. Why? Because he's eyeballing the young women from table three. They're cousins. Isla and Candace Troyes. Actually, he's leering at Candace. In fact, he —"

"He does the same," Dirk van Kesteren interjects, "when I am fitting the bikes for everyone. But he complains like so: 'This bloody bike's too large. Can't reach the fucking pedals.' Something like that. I check and tell him he asked for a large, electric-assist bike and show him the request form with his name. 'Just have the lad lower the seat, dear,' his wife says. She is very patient with him. He points his thumb behind his ear and says to me, 'what she said.' She is a very nice person."

"Yes, she is a delightful woman," Finn Bonger agrees. "Her name is Ruth. She's quite vivacious. Seems enthusiastic about the cycling tomorrow."

"When I bend to fix the seat," Dirk van Kesteren continues, "and ask how low, Rudiger pulls down on my ponytail and says, 'that far, buddy, exactly that far.' I am embarrassed. I know my face is red now. I do not want to be foolish in front of the group. The two young women are looking at me. So, me, I know about Mister Raymond Rudiger."

"Wanker!" Chef Simon says again, and then goes on. "I understand the appeal of the young women and the interest they can generate. Drop dead gorgeous, so they are, especially the blond."

"Got that right," Finn Bonger readily says. "Remember the Argentinian trophy wives parading around in their bikinis on the upper deck?"

"What I remember most about that group is the outrageous demands and assumptions their wrinkled husbands made of me and my crew."

"What I remember most about this group is the large tip the women gave me."

"For services rendered, Dirk?"

"For help with the bikes, no more."

"So why are you blushing, Dirk?"

"Your false accusations."

"Just taking the piss, mate," Chef Simon says and laughs.

Finn Bonger adds to the cajolery in asking, "Provided a little extra help with their seats, Dirk?"

"No, not even once."

Finn Bonger flashes a smile, then turns to Chef Simon and with a raised eyebrow says, "What someone in your position would call a side dish, right Chef?"

"Compliments of the kitchen, yeah?"

"Or like dessert," Captain Van de Oor suggests and gets a laugh.

"Sweet," Chef Simon concedes, acknowledging the captain with a glass raised. "The boat and bike routine, whatever the additional attractions you blokes joke about, beats my stint as cook on a wind blasted platform off the Scottish coast with a crew of yobs. Two weeks on, two off. Working here is more dependable, yeah? Weather watch is only a minor concern. My gig on the rig was DC, during Covid. Despite the tricky protocols, we still managed to serve hearty, excellent meals. We had quality food to work with. We also developed a new way of indicating time. BC meant Before Covid. AC meant After Covid."

"That could catch on," Dirk van Kesteren says.

"Never."

"Maastricht is only five days away but it might seem like an eternity getting there," Captain Van de Oor states. "Someone like Professor Wolfgang Albrecht makes it easier. Remember, gentlemen, the object of our efforts is enjoyment for all the guests. Physical, social, culinary, cultural, all in agreeable company despite nationality, ethnicity, religion, or sexual orientation. Individuals like Raymond Rudiger and Dexter Pickett offer us a challenge in achieving our goals. Go about your duties with a smile."

"Right, sir," Dirk van Kesteren says, gathering together the empty glasses.

Looking about furtively, Finn Bonger in all earnestness declares, "Men, I have a premonition that we're being overheard right now, right here at our table."

"Not your so-called ESP again, Finn! I thought we concluded it's unlikely. Just a kind of wishful thinking, innit?"

"Agreed, we reached certain conclusions. I've put up with your mockery on more than one occasion. Same now."

"What is it this time, ghosts of the Argentinians?"

"No jokes, please." Finn Bonger's voice is firm, directed. "This is my fifth excursion with you, Captain, but this is the first time I sense something is amiss. Like being eavesdropped on."

"Dexter Pickett lurks again," Chef Simon jokes, "he's right behind you, Finn."

I want it understood right from the get-go, dear reader, that I am not partial to the name of the boat, this converted barge called *Amoretto Algea*. The word *Amoretto* bears too much of an allusion to that little usurper-wannabe about whom I have definite opinions which you will come to read about in due course. On the other hand, the pain implied in *Algea*, whether emotional or otherwise, is acceptable in that it is germane to my purposes, and these are, except for one or two instances, not entirely nefarious.

A word on Finn Boger's comment about eavesdropping: his premonition is perfect, in fact, it is absolutely on the mark. I can personally attest to its accuracy. I can also attest to the fact that, in another era, this young man could have passed for Adonis. I am certain the lovely Aphrodite in her glorious, ersatz standing would agree, as would others engaged on this boat and bike excursion, like the young women from New York. I have seen the guest list and heard Captain Van de Oor and Finn Bonger counting heads and organizing table groupings for meals.

Yes, I've undertaken to oversee this adventure along the byways and waterways of the Netherlands but not only for my own amusement. I also intend that you, dear reader, may amplify your knowledge of what goes on behind the scenes in the realm of the enflamed human heart. What delights me in particular is the conjunction here onboard of two favourites, a confluence of time and place that is totally fortuitous, although my influence as active observer could be defined differently in modern scientific terms. These favourites are Mick Mallory from table four and Ruth Rudiger from table one. Both have over the decades professed a detailed understanding and great appreciation of just who I am. Such awareness on their part cannot go unnoted, if not, in effect, rewarded.

What the crew mentioned about Candace and Isla Troyes from table three is also quite accurate. They are indeed enchanting. I overheard Professor Wolfgang Albrecht from table four observe to a father and son duo as they shared a cordial on the upper deck that Candace and Isla are the personification of beauty and truth. Father and son, Cole and Drake Cantlay, table three as well, seemed indifferent to the comment, the son more than the father. The elderly Wolfgang Albrecht did not go into any detail but I comprehend absolutely his reasoning. He must at some point have conversed with these two charmers to arrive at such a conclusion. The concept in all its binary implications remains for me a challenge in that I see beauty in light of truth and truth in light of beauty.

Professor Wolfgang Albrecht's assertion derives, of course, from a well-explored philosophical aesthetic. As to particular application, it requires that I take you briefly to the Rijksmuseum where I hang about periodically to evaluate renderings of my august self, old and new. I am motivated to make these museum visitations because interest in my abilities has waned in recent centuries except for the fascination that artists in all genres have. Last week I cruised the Louvre in Paris and just a few days ago three significant venues in London, including the central attraction in Piccadilly Circus.

I came upon these engaging young women first in Room 226 of the Rijksmuseum, commenting on Gerard van Opstal's miniature ivory from the middle of seventeenth century that depicts putti and satyrs engaged in a bacchanal of sorts. Candace said she favoured the sculpture, found it beautifully rendered. She admired anything in the Flemish Baroque style. I saw her point but wished she could have elaborated on her observation that she felt giddy looking at it. She certainly gave me that impression. Isla, on the other hand, though impressed with the detail in such a demanding, miniscule work, objected to having so many Cupids floating about. She called Opstal's effort "a plethora of potential mischievousness" and was convinced that the artist had to have been laughing up his sleeve when seeing to the final touches. I admired Isla's take, her need to give an honest opinion of an objet d'art, a sculpture, in this case, that leaves me miffed about how time can distort precedent and twist fact.

One of my greatest attributes is the capacity to eavesdrop unseen on selected individuals or groups of individuals: that is to say, I can operate unnoticed for what and who I am. They go about their business ignorant of how I can affect their next move, their very being, in fact. Delightfully encouraging, however, are the more astute among them who have occasionally indicated awareness of an ultra-presence, an über influence that they can describe only in vague terms, a premonition, for instance, a subtle but detectable movement of air, or nothing more than an instinctual response to something beyond the tangible. So, when

Candace asked Isla if she'd picked up on the scent of roses, and did she think it emanated from the sculpture, I had to snicker. I'm renowned for my great love of roses. Very perceptive of Candace. Very laudable. Much like with Finn Bonger and his awareness of an extraordinary presence in the room when he and the crew were discussing matters. My eminent presence, of course. More power to them, I say, to both of them.

Surveillance of Candace and Isla Troyes in Room 19 of the popular Rijksmuseum a short time later offers perspective on that troubling effect of time vis à vis received truth, on what can be considered contentious, and maybe with the correct outlook on what proves me correct. Again. A large, seated Cupid in white marble from the eighteenth century is the focus of their attention here. Again, I do not intentionally side with one over the other but do agree with what I believe is verifiable, or at least verifiable in my larger world. I refer here to Isla's point of view.

Étienne-Maurice Falconet's Seated Cupid is nicknamed l'amour menaçent, menacing love. This, understandably, I appreciate fully. I get it. I absolutely do, considering. So does Isla who points out to Candace the artist's intention in evoking a sense of secrecy — the gaze on Cupid's face, his finger raised against his lips. She calls it "a statement of potential mischievousness carved luxuriously."

Wow! Talk about rendering one giddy!

Candace agrees with the sly impression Falconet creates but is more impressed with the sensuousness of the piece, its fleshiness, "like something,' she confesses, "achieved in a classical Bernini sculpture. Absolutely beautiful. What a gorgeous Cupid, god of love and desire. I just love it. Don't you? I'm giddy about it, for sure. Imagine, Isla, this very work was created for Madame de Pompadour, King Louis Fifteen's mistress. A well-recognized, historical romance. I'm all for it."

Isla replies: "Yes, sensuous, tactile, wonderfully rendered. But I don't love it as you do. Such a large representation of such a small character. I see it as a misinterpretation of ancient tradition. Aesthetically it's pleasing, yes. Philosophically it's not truthful. Cupid vs Eros, Latin over Greek. An artistic hangover from the somewhat religious flirtation with the somewhat angelic putti of the early Renaissance. And didn't you, when criticizing one of my sonnets, insist that Cupid was the son of Venus? Retrospectively, that would make Eros Aphrodite's son. That's not the way the ancients drew it up."

Perfect. Could not have stated the truth more beautifully. Candace is deserving of my attention. More so, Isla.

At this juncture, let me explain my position in all of this. I operate in the here and now, always have done so and always will do so. My responsibilities lie in being, to quote with acknowledged irony Paul of Tarsus, "all things to all people." To this universal embrace I add the following: Let love and desire motivate those most in need. Important at this point for you to understand, dear reader, is my ability to be everywhere, my flights to all quarters of the globe over all periods of contemporary time, such is my quasi-omnipresence. And although I am quite able to leave tomorrow and arrive today, indeed, within my immediate domain, it's quite doable, given Greenwich, the twenty-four hour clock, and longitudinal demarcations of time. Ubiquity, however, is not within my remit. Instantaneous travel yes, ubiquity no. Furthermore, the past is not accessible save for remembrance, nor the future, because I operate totally in the present, a dynamic fifth dimension where time fuses with infinity. And I do get around. We all get around in one guise or another although our collective raison d' être has been called into question over the centuries since the birth and spread of Christianity; we survive metaphysically despite a reticence on the part of many mortals to accept our resemblance to humanity in general, a correlation from much earlier between the profane, the mundane, if you will, and the divine. We blame such regression on the ambitions of the Emperor Constantine and his cursed, saintly mother. Nonetheless, ours is a continuing universal and numinous presence no matter the influence of any countervailing base beliefs, worldwide or otherwise.

As mentioned, dear reader, I do get around.

Before arriving in Amsterdam and joining the boat and bike excursion on the Amoretto Algea, Raymond Rudiger and his wife Ruth spent several days in London, the first part of an extended European vacation. They were celebrating forty years of married life. They had reservations at an upscale, conspicuously five-star hotel just off Leicester Square. Piccadilly Circus was a mere five-minutes away from their luxurious West End comfort zone, his comfort zone in all its irony, to be precise, and this was where our mutual appreciation of a signature attraction overlapped for a short period of time. What I overheard as I hovered above them—an absolutely fortuitous encounter, I assure you — pleased me in one sense and incensed me in another. Granted, eavesdropping is a speciality of mine along with other significantly useful gifts. Not to be too categorical about the issue, let me clarify its meaning from a superior vantage point. I claim this in all modesty, with all the humility in human terms that I can muster. Ages ago my peers defined this aptitude quite specifically as "paying acute attention to matters métier-related" and thereby obviating in the definition any connection to voyeurism because that furtive eyeballing supposes the exercise of sordid or tawdry inclinations as in the pseudo-sexual gratification achieved through pornographic gawking, and obscures scopophilia when understood as legitimate aesthetic appreciation, the love of intensely regarding beauty. And again, with perfect clarification in mind, let me declare here that I make no claims to being omniscient. No, not at all. Though I speculate from time to time, I only reveal what I see and report what I hear. Like my celestial peers, I enjoy "lucidity of perception" which is no more than the ability to put two and two together about some event of note, or about someone of interest, and come up with four, enhanced, of course, with perfect hindsight. Like my celestial peers, I have access to a cosmic calendar but make use of it infrequently. For the most part, the stars and the moon guide me in my terrestrial dealings, be they diurnal or nocturnal. Unlike some of my celestial peers, however, whose foresight far surpasses mine, I make no claim to any prophetic ability, that is to say, an ability beyond knowing what the effects of any action I take will be.

This was not the only time I floated within earshot of the Rudigers. During these earlier sessions I developed a deep sympathy and fondness for Ruth. She evinced a great understanding of the vicissitudes of love in all its multiplicity. He, on the other hand, proved himself to be a libertine, more aspirational than actual, a wannabe wanton of rakish renown, but no more than a Lothario given to self-aggrandizing pretense. That said, I turn your attention, dear reader, back to the historical attraction in the centre of Piccadilly Circus, the famous aluminum sculpture that is poised so very artfully in the middle of the Shaftesbury Memorial Fountain.

His tourist brochure held firmly in both hands, Ray Rudiger read out loud so that Ruth could hear his words above the din from jostling visitors and assorted street performers. "The memorial was created to honour the good works of the Earl of Shaftesbury. It goes on to say here that Alfred Gilbert's design is intended to advance reflective and mature love over frivolous cupidity. Considered too risqué for its time, it was temporarily renamed The Angel of Christian Charity. The name now widely accepted is Eros, which is more appropriate, wouldn't you agree?"

"I agree it is known as Eros," Ruth answered. "But my information maintains that it is not a statue of Eros at all, but of Anteros, the god of requited love who punishes those that scorn amorous advances and such like. I think we are obliged to distinguish one god from the other."

"Right. His parts are covered. That's not like the Eros I know."

Though an inconvenient truth and indeed a slight to me in no uncertain terms, what Ruth proclaimed is accurate, absolutely so. Again, I could not take umbrage with her for naming the work for what it really is or for what it was originally intended to celebrate. A self-indulgent character at bottom is Raymond Rudiger but he did attempt, perhaps in ignorance, to allow me my place of prominence in the popular imagination. However, when he went on to call the statue "ridiculous, aesthetically wanting, and misleading in every regard," I got vexed bigtime, momentarily at any rate. From time to time I adopt contemporary idioms to express my reactions to statements or events that displease me. Likewise for situations that inspire positive response. Wow! comes immediately to mind. Identified as Anteros or not, it matters little with respect to the sculpture's function as a social and cultural statement. Regardless of the intended purpose of the whole enterprise in the middle of the circus, the statue is a beautifully rendered and staged work of art, and in his rather facile evaluation of the work, Ray Rudiger proved himself a charlatan, a philistine incapable of getting beyond appearances. To give credit where credit is due, however, he was insightful in drawing attention to particulars.

The statue: Anteros appears to be angled in full flight, his wings spread wide above and behind him. Bow is steady in his left hand while his right hand is positioned as though he has just let fly an arrow. If an observer had the impression that this godly figure is about to launch himself after the arrow just sent off, that would be an accurate impression. If pursuit is the point intended in the representation, then a sightline that follows the arrow's trajectory is necessary. Look, then leap, as they say. Logically enough, the sculpted figure wears no blindfold. On this very point, Rudiger proved himself astute in sussing out a detail that fails to keep with traditional interpretations.

He said, nudging Ruth's elbow, "I thought Eros is supposed to be blindfolded."

"True. Eros has frequently been depicted that way. Love is blind, according to common belief. I can substantiate that, dear, can't I? And sometimes love requires you to turn a blind eye, doesn't it?"

"Let's not get into that. We're celebrating here, Ruthie."

"We are," Ruth agreed, "and I don't really need to hear about your youthful adventuring in Soho, not again. Last night was reminiscence enough."

"Well I never promised you a rose garden, Ruthie. Isn't that how the old song goes?" Rudiger stood firm with arms folded across his chest. With such an assumed pose, he put me in mind of Silenus but without the wisdom he evinced when berating the young Dionysus for messing with the wine.

"True," Ruth agreed. "And I never received a bouquet of roses, let alone a rose garden. Forty years is quite a spread."

Of the blindfold syndrome, let me briefly say this. The blindfold is an attempt on the part of mortals to explain the randomness of an encounter. They understand that there is no definite answer as to why love hits when it does, no real psychological insight into its apparent spontaneity. Hence, the application of metaphors, of symbols. Hence, allegorical intuition, not always precise in its revelations.

Private reminiscence apparently put aside, at least for the moment, Rudiger consulted his tourist brochure again. "Very ironic, it says here, that the statue was located on the shores of Soho. All about a play on words. A pun on shaft, the arrow, being buried along the thoroughfare somewhere. Confusing, to say the least. I suppose the meaning is that everyone knows where a man's shaft can get buried in Soho."

"Think what you must, dear," Ruth said, looking up at the statue. "Nice spread of wings. Now there's a weaponized action hero if ever there was one."

More power to Ruth, I say, indeed, more power to her. She possesses a lovely soul, so she does, and has made that plain on many occasions. She reminds me of my Psyche, sans wings, of course, those beautiful butterfly wings, those perfect symbols of spiritual transformation. Psyche, a rival in beauty to Aphrodite herself and by whom she was cursed. Fated in her own right to marry an ogre and survive the relationship for forty years, Ruth is a model of moral beauty. Moreover, she understands intuitively the forces that compel me to act the way I do, and for this I am in a sense indebted to her, that is to say, indebted to her as far as being indebted to a mortal goes.

Earlier in the evening of the first day out of Amsterdam, and before returning to the *Amoretto Algea* to eavesdrop on the crew's mandatory bitch session, I whisked myself along to the Wispe Brewery. The popular tourist attraction, formerly Sint Laurentius Church, is situated by the canal running through central Weesp. Let's just say this: the minions of Dionysus have taken possession of a space that once housed pulpits and wooden pews, where clamorous imbibing rituals have supplanted those of a more sacrificial nature. Dionysus riotously hailed the transformation of grapes into wine, not the extravagant transubstantiation of wine into blood as was once celebrated in these premises.

From the canal verge a paved walkway leads to an imposing cathedral-like entrance. Overhead elongated Gothic windows with leaded, stained glass inserts lead the discerning eye up the length of the steeple to the geometric plate tracery, a multi-foliated flower design. Above that, smaller arched windows, and above them, two more, smaller yet, both sets churchy in appearance. Upon entering through the double doors this evening, visitors like those from the *Amoretto Algea* would be immediately aware of how busy the establishment can be, especially on a Saturday. Loud voices, much laughter, din.

Seated at a table on the second level, JJ and Angela Jones in the company of the Rudigers of whom, dear reader, you have by now some knowledge. Both couples identified themselves as western Canadians when signing in with Finn Bonger at the Amoretto Algea reception desk. Their placement at table one in the dining room confirmed what they share in common, language and nationality, and from what was revealed in subtle ways at that first evening meal, they could make claim to similar levels of respectability, to say nothing of social and financial achievement.

The Joneses hail from Vancouver: JJ had a successful career as a city planner; Angela had been a social worker before becoming "a proud mother and an excessively indulgent grandmother." The Rudigers call Calgary home: he had recently retired from an executive position in a global oil company; she had been "a high school counsellor before turning her talents to a less stressful occupation." What both couples find compelling in their new association is that all four are connected to cycling clubs in their home areas. They know the meaning of gran fondo and randonneur and find amused comfort in that fact.

In the Wispe Brewery they continue conversing about retirement issues and to-do lists in the face of threats like Covid-19.

"I gave the codes to all my accounts to my daughter, Amber," Ruth explains.

"You did. Hell's bells, woman, why not to me?"

"You were always too busy with your business concerns, dear."

"Nonetheless, Ruthie..."

"Contrary to local opinion and that of some of our politicians," Ruth goes on to say, "we did suffer in our province because of the pandemic."

"You continue to make too much of this," Ray Rudiger states emphatically, tapping a finger on the table. "What she said, folks. But always more than a little overstated about the resistance to getting vaccinated and so on."

"We had issues in BC as well," Angela says, glancing quickly at JJ.

"Absolutely."

"Snow free winters in Vancouver," Ray Rudiger muses, angling his head. "Must be nice."

"A total misconception. Snow flies a good two or three times each winter sending unprepared drivers into ditches. And later into expensive repair shops."

Loud applause followed by a series of celebratory hoots echoes from down on the main floor and briefly interrupts the conversation between the two couples.

Diffused yellow light gives colour to their faces, now animated with looks of surprise.

Turning his gaze from the arch immediately over their heads that has caught his attention— it connects pillar on their right to pillar on their left— JJ offers a comment on the well-appointed, altar-like taproom bar below.

"Though I prefer a glass of Merlot," Angela confesses, drawing her focus away from the glass in her hand, "I do like craft beer. Occasionally."

"I'm sure you'll enjoy this blond," her husband JJ assures her, holding up a bottle of Wispe IPA to the light. "It's hoppy and fruity, whether blond or amber."

"I prefer blond," Ray Rudiger states authoritatively. "A gentleman's preference, so I've heard."

"So, what motivated you to sign on to this cruise?" Ruth asks.

"Like all at this table at this stage in our lives, I've got limited time left. Therefore, this cycling adventure in the Lowlands that Angela and I have long considered. Life makes no effort to follow one's to-do list, however, as has been proven many times over."

"Hey, I've been meaning to ask you, JJ, what's with the JJ?" Ray Rudiger asks pointedly.

"Short for Jean-Jacques. My maternal grandmother was Belgian."

More discussion follows about ageing and the loss of physical aptitude despite being comfortably well-off and determined efforts through physical activities to ward off setbacks.

"To keep ahead of the curve of decrepitude," is how Ruth describes the endeavour.

In listening to their discussions over dinner on the *Amoretto Algea* and here now at the Wispe Brewery, I find that Angela and JJ Jones are considerably more reserved in describing their varied accomplishments as a family, eschewing what is boastful or vaunting. Raymond Rudiger's probing questions about material wealth and all the trappings thereof are answered honestly but without unnecessary elaboration. Despite the marks of prosperity they could not successfully downplay— they are attired in label-worthy duds but without the ostentatious labels such duds carry— modesty guides both JJ and Angel in all their replies. With them, prosperity is not on display. Apparently attuned to their reticence to reveal too much in any supercilious way, Ruth changes the subject from monetary accumulation, in fact, she changes the subject several times to the displeasure of her husband, initiating discussion on such wide ranging subjects as cycling gloves and helmets, feeling perfectly at home on the *Amoretto Algea*, the time differential between Western Canada and the Netherlands leading to the subsequent indecision about when to phone grandchildren, and the taste of the Wisp IPA blond, which she finds herself savouring. The last idea she introduces, before husband Ray indelicately takes the lead, is how efficient Dirk van Kesteren was in helping Finn Bonger organize the bikes for all the guests despite hassles from this one and that one.

"I intended him no harm," Ray confesses, then allows a pink sliver of tongue to lick his lips.

"Such a bashful young man but so enthusiastic," Ruth says. "He reminds me of—"

"JJ," Ray Rudiger breaks in, "what did you make of that Bonger guy telling us in his introduction he didn't want to see our photographs or hear our dreams."

"Just his way of keeping things light."

"And no high fives either," Rudiger continues. "He had to be putting us on, wouldn't you agree?"

"I suppose so."

"All he needs to complete the picture is a blackboard. You know, the 'chalk and talk' method of conveying information. The term is one our daughter once used to describe a lecturer at college.”

“I think Finn was just trying to be humorous,” Angela opines, “to have us all relax. The thing is, I trained very little in advance of this boat and bike holiday. To be perfectly honest with you, I was a little anxious knowing I had fifty kilometres to cycle tomorrow, even though Finn assured me, when I was getting my bike seat adjusted, that the route’s all flat and that we make frequent stops. He’s our guide, I assume.”

“Guide or not, I gave him the fingers and eye treatment which I’m sure he understood. I’m watching you, buddy! You gotta set the tone if you want the right treatment. Doesn’t matter where you are or what you’re doing.”

“Oh, Ray, you’re always so agreeable,” Ruth says, giving his arm a gentle tap. Ironic intent is evident.

“I’m agreeable when it matters. No, it’s all about setting the tone and getting respect.”

“You mean like in hockey,” JJ suggests, “where one team starts to rough up the other.”

“Right. Rub a few out. And then you can get more pucks to the net. Give it one hundred and nine percent.”

“Normally you hear one hundred and ten percent.”

“I hate clichés, JJ, I hate clichés.”

"Finn Bonger is perfectly bilingual," Angela picks up again when Ray pulls back from hating clichés and takes a long draught of his blond Wispe IPA. "He told me he'd studied to be a teacher, but then the travel bug got him. He spent two years working in England and a year touring around the US. He's still single, which might be of interest to those two American gals."

"Not that I have any objections to being at the same table with fellow Canadians, but I let Bonger know what I thought about dining room arrangements. The way he organized the seating limits getting to know others onboard, like that German professor. Wouldn't you agree?

"I take your point, Ray."

"Or that English family. The kid looks to be on the spectrum, and maybe could be, I don't know, motivated."

"Motivated how, dear?"

"To behave properly at the table, Ruthie, or anywhere else for that matter."

"To know the boy is to love him, folks," Ruth offers. "That seemed obvious with how the parents reacted. I know the scenario. Neural diversity. So did the fellow at their table and the professor, apparently. What's his name again?"

"The professor? Wolfgang something or other..."

"Isn't it interesting how so many Europeans can speak very good English? Like the Dutch and the Germans. I'm hardly able to converse sensibly with my eastern relatives in our other official language. Shameful."

"Frankly, Angela," Rudiger comments immediately in a defiant tone, "Albertans don't worry too much about that."

"Pity." Having said that almost under his breath, JJ indulges himself in a modestly dramatic sigh. He repositions the ball cap he wears. It reads BC Lions.

"My husband reserves an unobliging deference for individuals who might be considered a little slow on the uptake."

"What she said, folks," Rudiger says, pointing his chin in Ruth's direction. He allows himself a short gleeful hoot, then adds sarcastically, "Don't forget to include, dear Ruthie, in your list of objections as to how I express my opinions, those who may not have perfect English, visitors, foreigners, people from Holland."

"Did you know that Simon Oliver, our chef," Angela begins again apparently undaunted by Rudiger's insensitivity, "was trained in London's Cordon Bleu and also in France. I suppose he can say more in French than *plat du jour*. I had a few minutes with him in the lounge when he was setting up for dinner. He may be English but he knows a lot about French cuisine."

"Sounds promising," Ruth says. "*Coq au vin*, and the like."

"What she said, folks," Rudiger agrees, thumb cast sideways indicating his wife.

"Promising, as long as it's not a steady diet of best before and awful after."

JJ snickers. Angela smiles. Rudiger allows a grin of amusement and self-congratulation to shape the look on his face. He nickers like a horse and then, getting up from the table, offers to fetch another round. Only JJ accepts the offer.

"Ray likes to argue politics and religion," Ruth admits after Ray leaves their table. "I don't, especially with people just met."

"Not a problem, Ruth," JJ states with easy accommodation.

"He's not quite tuned into people being reticent to talk about their wealth or their worldly possessions, so if he..."

"Also not a problem." JJ again.

"Money talks, wealth whispers," Angela whispers.

"Exactly. But Ray doesn't quite get the concept."

"Not everyone does," JJ says.

"I must confess," Ruth goes on, "that occasionally I can pander to Ray's inflated sense of worth. As a kind of self-defence, if you see what I mean. I don't get any more respect from him for doing so. But that's life with Ray Rudiger."

"More power to you, Ruth," JJ says, his deep voice resonating with empathy. He smiles benevolently at her. He goes on to say, "I can project an air of amicable disinterest when dealing with arrogant people, obnoxious conservatives, for example, pushing hard an agenda antithetical to the public good."

"JJ's got principles, but he's no saint and he's definitely nobody's fool," Angela says, grabbing JJ's elbow and shaking it affectionately. Ruth laughs at the good-natured tease.

JJ demurs to his wife. He smiles at her knowingly. He takes down the last drops of beer from his glass, licks his lips, and then after expressing something like a murmur of satisfaction, he says, "I think Ray misread me earlier when I referenced Deny Arcand's *Testament*, that recent film of his that's satirical of recent developments in the social sphere like exaggerated sensitivity, political correctness, the extremes of woke, and pronouns for nebulous states of being."

"No, he understands that you're not a redneck."

"On this theme, I find it difficult to argue with those that say as human beings we're all connected in more or less positive ways. I don't feel connected in any way, let alone a positive one, with someone like Putin or his ilk."

"No argument there, JJ."

When Ray Rudiger returns and places two bottles of dark on the table, JJ thanks him prodigiously.

"Seven point six percent," Rudiger says all cheerful animation. Rubbing his hands together, he smiles and adds, "I managed to get a word or two in with the young barmaid.

A real looker. Said her favourite was the Tripel so that's what we got. Lovely town you got here I told her."

The conversation then turns to just how lovely a town Weesp is and how interesting the Wispe Brewery is from an architectural point of view.

"Those copper brewing kettles above the bar are quite impressive," Angela opines, "particularly with that aqua green backlighting."

"Makes me think of the Northern lights," Ruth muses. "Very dramatic. Just like at home in Alberta."

"I see this brew is having an effect on you, Ruthie!"

JJ says, "I'm impressed with how major aspects of the original were maintained in the repurposing of the structure. Like the interior pillars and the arches. They create a kind of devotional effect even as we sit here quaffing back brew."

"I'm devoted to the quaffing," Rudiger says and laughs.

"Those big stainless steel containers reflect a silvery brightness, at least I think they're stainless steel."

"Probably," JJ says.

"They're like something celestial, like stalwart guardians of good taste."

"Very poetic, Angela."

"I counted fifteen pump handles behind the bar, maybe more," JJ adds.

"I imagine them being like a choir of saints," Ruth says, "you know, this place once being a church. I suppose the palms and other decorative greenery add to that impression."

Do the three go on about the décor and the architecture of the brewery just to put Ray off? Are they being facetious? Does Ray suspect that they might just be putting him on? Possibly. Possibly not.

When the décor and architectural themes peter out, Angela comments on the route planned for the next day that would take them south of Weesp, through Utrecht, and down to Vianen, reportedly to be an equally attractive Dutch town. Expectations vary.

"I'm sure we'll visit any number of interesting brew houses along the way. The Wispe here is just the first."

"So what's it like being a high school counsellor, Ruth?" JJ asks when an unexpected lull in the conversation occurs.

"That question deserves a long answer, one I can't really get into now without bringing down the mood of the group. So a short one will have to do."

"Whatever you're comfortable with."

"There's the academic side and programs offered. And then there's everything else that might be problematic for a teenager, especially in the age of social media and all the instability and uncertainty it can cause in developing one's sense of self-worth, you know, like surfing TikTok to find peer approved solutions that will eradicate unsightly acne. Let alone falling in love with someone who either does not know you exist or does not meet with parental approval."

"Exactly," Angela agrees, nodding. "Been there, got the scars. Right, JJ?"

"Absolutely."

"So, yeah, it is like social work in various ways, which I know you both can appreciate. Many strategies are in play depending on particular circumstances. About all I can really say is that a counsellor offers hope."

"Hope does not work well as a strategy," Ray Rudiger states knowingly. "Agree?"

"I can't disagree, Ray."

"Of course not. Talk is cheap. Whiskey costs money. Or in this situation, the brew."

"True enough, Ray." JJ replies. "But look at it this way: the hope is that the betterment of one can lead to the betterment of society as a whole. A long shot, sure, but—"

"Damn right, it's a long shot."

"Schools today are very different from what they were like for us. Especially high school and post-secondary institutions."

"Yes, it's a different world. No argument there."

"In so many ways, education has been reduced to the monetization of the young. In other words, how best to serve the interests of the corporate state. That's what really generates modern life. The free enterprise system and profit."

"Get a grip, folks," Ray Rudiger suggests rather forcefully, tapping the table with an index finger. "Ruth and I have been over this a lot over the years. Look, you go into a grocery store and see the wide variety of everything available, from canned sardines to pineapples and exotic fruit, goods that would have been inconceivable fifty years ago in the middle of the prairies in winter. We live today in a very providential society in the West."

"It can be over the top, excessive," JJ observes. "Automatons in pursuit of luxury, that's what we're becoming. We leave humanity behind at every turn."

"When it comes to kids learning how to cope, well... Okay, take for instance Monopoly. Fun, yes, if you come out on top. But the game and other games like it instill aggression over peaceful co-existence, acquisition over munificence, and greed over generosity."

"Sounds like you rehearsed that line, Angela," Ray Rudiger objects, pulling a sceptical face.

"I care for my grandchildren."

"Any game or sport is based on competition, Angela. You know that."

"Precisely my point."

"Speaking of leaving humanity behind," Ruth says after a momentary pause, "I think a large population of youth is being short-changed when it comes to getting a well-rounded education. Sadly lacking is even a basic exposure to the classics and all they have to say about leading an informed life. Even the story of how fire was a gift from Prometheus to mankind might prompt inquisitiveness about origins and how a whole range of creation narratives came about. What did Socrates say? The unexamined life is not worth living."

"A bit extreme, that. Wouldn't you agree?"

"Can't disagree, Ray."

"I appreciate you, JJ. I really do. Now tell me, where did you get those sexy shoes. What did they cost you? Big bucks, I bet. I've been admiring them ever since standing next to you at the Amoretto Algea sign-in."

Right. I'm okay with the sexy shoes and with what Socrates said about the unexamined life. I'm okay with Prometheus, a big-hearted early starter, the perfect exemplar of forethought and divine generosity. No complaint there, but Ruth might have included in her impromptu lesson how love and desire are registered in the human heart. I expect she will eventually and I will get over my disappointment, temporary though it usually is. I could be accused here of being jealous of her allusion to Prometheus' heroism, his sacrifice, but with jealousy being destructive in so many ways and especially among Olympian divinities as the records show, I choose not to dwell on that negative emotion. Let the idea pass.

Nonetheless, I am a personage, a luminary, rather, of considerable complexity and vision and, dare I say it, very directed in my creative purposes. And so, dear reader, I must continue with relevant disclosures. In today's idiom, I am an influencer. An influencer nonpareil, as they say in the upper echelons of academe where I roam periodically when symposiums are underway. Regard what I report on these pages as a species of admission, an ad lib deposition, a one-off *apologia pro vita sua*, to borrow a phrase from the lexicon of confessional literature amassed over the centuries in the West.

If you haven't yet reached anything definitive regarding what I am all about, you're probably still thinking, "Who is this insufferable character, this garrulous, ungodly character constantly running off at the mouth with a propensity to go on and on, and constantly interrupting the narrative?" A fair enough question. Given that we have several days together with the Amoretto Algea crowd, I'll answer that question and prove myself more gregarious than garrulous and, more important, godly. Therefore, please do pardon my frequent insertions, emendations, and asides. Admittedly, my cadenza cravings are monumental, particularly as the denouement looms, so, I advise you, be prepared.

Okay, by now I assume you've got it. I am Eros, god of love and passionate, physical desire. Obviously. I've been depicted as a cunning trickster, and I confess I do indulge in a little amorous playfulness from time to time. I've also been accused of being cruel, toying with victims and causing them considerable confusion. That criticism is not entirely unjustified. There are many definitions of what that confusion entails, often described in exaggerated terms by those affected, the attention seekers, the self-serving, the wounded. But don't ever confuse me with Cupid, that creepy little usurper from the Renaissance who is no more than a pasty-faced putto that religion and unregulated history has allowed to dominate the popular imagination. I am the original, the only real and authentic god of desire. And let's just leave Aphrodite out of the picture at this early stage in the narrative.

As to the functions of the divine elite among whom I rate myself highly, let truth prevail. We Olympian stalwarts and all attendant deities have kept abreast of developments within our collective understanding: Aristotle's *Poetics*, the rise and fall of the Roman Empire, the spread of aggressive religions and the Dark Ages, Bruegel (*père et fils*), the Renaissance and the Enlightenment, global exploration and jet lag, Descartes, the Industrial Revolution and World Wars, Vaudeville, atomic energy and its bi-polar application, Tourette's syndrome, technology, New Age sensibilities, echolalia, the decline of decimals and the rise of digits, spermicide gel, fauvism, jargon, memes, stealth wealth, scopophilia, and what icing means in the game of hockey. In all eras, whether desire-based cultural activities or needs-based ones, we exercise free rein. We are cognizant of everything that is in vogue and everything that is not. Athena and even Apollo motivate us the way political party whips motivate their members. As our beloved goddess of wisdom declared at a grand banquet to thunderous response from all quarters, "We are the earliest manifestation of A I." However, I see AI as a growing challenge to my role in the service of mortals. It has, in a sense, hacked into my domain of influence and now threatens to replace my time-tested arrow-to-the-heart method of inducement and manipulation. Understandably, ambivalence as to how AI best serves our various assignments prevailed at that assembly of immortals, several raising concerns about being totally supplanted, the loudest coming from Hephaestus, aka Vulcan, although Zeus declared, when all were heard from, as long as he retained possession and use of his thunderbolt, he welcomed innovation.

Day Two
farm fresh cheese

Weesp to Vianen:

A you-brew-it coffee machine stands against a wall on the periphery of the dining area in the *Amoretto Algea*. Bonnie Pickett complains to Angela Jones about its location as "less than convenient" when they line up with others for breakfast at eight o'clock. At seven, the coffee machine suits Mick Mallory perfectly well. He retreats with his café au lait to the lounge where comfortable sectionals are arranged in two semicircles. In the kitchen, Chef Simon and Dirk van Kesteren are busy with prep work. Hearing their chatter over the clatter and clang of activity brings a smile to Mick Mallory's face as he begins checking and answering his emails.

Mick Mallory with tablet in hand writes to his daughter that a young woman called Isla Troyes is so like her in a number of ways. From what he's heard about her at the first dinner from those at his table and others on the boat and bike tour, she's a poet.

"Fascinating," he types in, pauses, takes some coffee, and then continues composing. "I was assigned a place at table four in the dining room and have enjoyed the company of Wolfgang Albrecht, who is approximately my age and whose English is near perfect with just a slightly discernible accent. He's a cycling enthusiast and listens to the blues when the need for relaxation from the pressures of academic life get to him. He is a professor at some German university, the name of which I've lost, at least for now. He cycles to and from work each day.

At my table as well are Otto and Elsa Müller, also German and also capable of excellent English. Interesting connection for me with my GM association because Otto is involved in car manufacturing here in Europe. He's a design engineer with BMW. Elsa runs a florist shop in Dusseldorf, the city where they reside. She has the same infectious laugh that your mother had. Uncanny. Or do you think I'm still projecting? I'm sure you know what I mean by that. While enjoying our first dinner, a savoury lamb stew Maastricht-style as announced by Chef Simon, the four of us skipped through topics of mutual interest, the waterways of Holland in particular, about which the Müllers knew a great deal. Otto is a high energy guy and is a rabid randonneur."

After hitting the send key, Mick sips more coffee and then allows the darting shapes on the ceiling, from light reflecting off the surrounding waters, to distract him as though his thoughts, like the darting shapes, have led him elsewhere.

I first came across Mick Mallory when he was touring around the continent with a sidekick. Years ago, as time would have it. It was just after I'd left a rather rollicking afternoon with Dionysus and the satyrs way out in his wayward grove. The Lassithi Plateau in Crete provided me with the kind of tranquility I needed, that is to say, tranquility at a safe distance from politics as usual up on Olympus. Mick Mallory and his buddy were exiting the Dikteon Cave, long reputed to be the birthplace of Zeus. A traditional interpretation of the site but not without arguments questioning the accuracy of the mythological claim, and yet of sufficient interest to attract a range of visitors: ordinary tourists with their expensive guides, the curious with a penchant for exotic stories about miraculous births, spelunkers on holiday from their usual hands and knees peregrinations, or just plain young adventurers like Mick Mallory. The very fact he had some awareness of the theory about the cave impressed me as he held forth with the story of a primeval struggle for dominance among the immortals— how Zeus savagely dethroned his progenitor Cronus in the same way that Cronus savagely dethroned his progenitor Uranus. Mick knew about the birth of Aphrodite and about how other gods of my generation reflect human dispositions, drawing on me as an example. He was definitely informed and very complimentary, detailing to his travelling companions not only where but how I fit into the whole heavenly scheme. I made a point of following his exploits, periodically checking in on his progress as an aspiring individual intent on making his way in the world. When he first saw Delores, I decided to do both him and her a big favour. I reached into my quiver and the rest, as humans often phrase it, is history. So yes, it behoves me to say that I have history with Mick Mallory. I came across him again when circumstances in his life were far different from what they were when he was carefree and on the loose as a student. It moves me considerably seeing him here on the Amoretto Algea lost in reverie as Professor Wolfgang Albrecht approaches with his steaming coffee.

Early morning greetings exchanged, the professor proceeds to explain why Anna, the love of his life and just as keen about cycling as he, was unable to accompany him on the boat and bike excursion to Maastricht.

Mick says, "It seems you are very philosophical about being without someone close to you and who shares so much with you."

"Philosophical, yes. Philosophy is my métier."

"That's humorous, Professor." Mick snickers and smiles.

"*Ja*, Anna and I travel much together, ever since we are younger."

"I get that. Absolutely. Youthful adventuring. Loved it."

"Tell me, if it please you to do so."

"This episode comes immediately to mind, Professor. Young, for sure. Rucksacks on our backs, my buddy and I sauntered into Chania's Old Port searching for cheap fare and found it. It was a magnificent old city that the Venetians built up and it appealed to us most dramatically. It had a beautiful harbour where fishing boats of every description wove in and around a very distinctive breakwater and lighthouse."

"I know Crete and Chania," Wolfgang says. "Faros, the lighthouse is called. It stands at a slight angle by the opening to the sea. Anna and I have walked out to it."

"Exactly."

"Angled so," Wolfgang says, projecting an arm upright. "Very memorable at sunset."

"Right, right. Ethereal light, exotic flavours, searing sunsets. I remember reading that about Chania. From a tourist guide or a novel. I kept a journal where I would express ideas like the sensation of warm winds on your face as you anticipated a new island while standing on the deck of a ferry in the Aegean."

"Anna keeps a journal for all our trips together."

"Absolutely essential. Sometimes I'd include what my buddy said about a place we'd visited. Sometimes he would write jokes in the margins of my journal, a less than respectful scribble, for instance, about Botticelli's Birth of Venus hanging in the Uffizi Gallery, Florence. Lenny kept me grounded. He made no pretence about being a Byron or Shelley. In Crete we explored archaeological sites of interest. The Minoans. Zeus's cavern. Even Matala on the south coast of the island and the celebrated caves, the hippy haven that was no more. A must see, but we got there more than a decade too late."

"Anna's father," Wolfgang says, unable to hold back a grin, "was there in 1969. We have many stories from that time."

"When planning excursions with Delores, I made a habit of reading excerpts from that old rag of a journal with its dog ears and coffee stains, like my reactions to the work of some of the Pre-Raphaelites in the Tate Gallery in London or evaluating in contemporary coin the worth of the Cretan Bull of Minos. Delores is no longer with me. A tragic event in the life of my children and me. And so, a couple of years after her death, not all that long ago, actually, I reached Crete again. Alone. Alone with a new notebook. Clean sheets of a psychological nature, so to say."

"*Ach*, I do not wish to ... what would you say in English? Pry?"

54

"I'm gradually coming to grips with my new status, including the careless behaviour of a notorious tycoon at the core of it all. That second trip to Crete helped. Maybe later I'll get into it. Not now, Wolfgang."

In the grand theme of lost love, Mick Mallory is under divine influence from perspectives other than mine alone. Anteros, god of selfless love, of reciprocal love, who punishes those who reject love; he nullifies the madness of hormones gravitating round a sudden physical urge, the essence of which I know so very well and, depending on my mood, inflict on unsuspecting victims, not all of whom can be identified as innocent. Recall, dear reader, the statue in Piccadilly Circus described earlier, yes, that Anteros. Pothos, another of my esteemed brethren from among the Erotes, is the god of passionate longing and desire for one who is absent. Additionally, I have watched Hymenaios, god of marriage, shake his head with sad understanding when contemplating Mick's tragic situation. Though he does not prance around the world singing of his fate, Mick Mallory does on occasion describe his love and the pain in all its manifestations that its loss has caused him. I equate the story of Mick and Delores to that of Orpheus and Eurydice but without the grandiose musical score, Mick's descent into psychological and emotional hell notwithstanding.

At approximately seven-thirty Ruth Rudiger arrives in the lounge. She wishes Mick and the professor a good morning, and with coffee and book to hand, leaves them to carry on in the privacy of their surroundings on the port side. She slides her pyriform body into an armchair with wide armrests, starboard side of the lounge. Comfortably seated, Ruth sips slowly her coffee, reads, and every once in a while, glances over expectantly to the dining area entrance. The concept of six degrees of separation where Ruth Rudiger and Mick Mallory are concerned is a bit of a stretch. I, Eros, am what bridges their separation and I mean here, at this time, on the *Amoretto Algea*.

Just before eight o'clock, Elsa and Otto Müller join Mick and Professor Albrecht who are already seated at table four.

"Breakfast is self-serve, *ja*?" Elsa says, pointing at a small stack of trays to the right of the entrance.

Definitely so. Available is coffee, of course, and much to choose from several neatly arranged counters: jugs of apple and orange juice, a selection of cereals, prunes, fruit, buns, sliced breads, jams, croissants, cakes, assorted cheeses, meat cuts deli style, and scrambled eggs with rashers of bacon in a large aluminum platter.

"We must get in the queue, *Liebchen*," Elsa decides, rising from the table.

"*Ja, ja,*" Otto agrees, watching other guests move slowly along, loading plates with breakfast choices, and then heading over to their respective tables.

Observe, patient reader, the seating arrangements decided with deliberation by Finn Bonger that bothered Raymond Rudiger to the extent that he had to resort to confrontation to make known his discontent about such logical arrangements.

Table one: Canadians JJ and Angela Jones, Ray and Ruth Rudiger.

Table two: the Birtwistle family, Nigel, Lizzy, and their son, Benny; with them is Conor St James. All Brits.

Table three: Canadians Cole and Drake Cantlay. Opposite, Candace Troyes and her cousin Isla Troyes, Americans.

Table four: Professor Wolfgang Albrecht, Otto and Elsa Müller, German nationals; seated with them Canadian Mick Mallory.

Table five: Dexter and Bonnie Pickett, and their adult, identical twin sons, Tim and Tom. Americans.

Finn Bonger has entered and moved to a position near table six, which is immediately across from the bar. He rings a small bell.

"On your table is a paper bag for each of you. This is for when you pack your lunch from the breakfast foods, the cheeses and cut meats, apples and oranges, and so on."

"But not the scrambled eggs, is that right, Finn?" Dexter Pickett calls out and gets a laugh.

"There's no bloody scrambled eggs left," shouts Ray Rudiger who has just arrived on the scene. Laughter again, louder.

"You can have mine," offers Ruth, now comfortable in her chair at table one. Laughter, but diminished.

The last of the guests to line up is Drake Cantlay. He grabs a tray and nudges forward, following Ray Rudiger who is decked out in bright cycling shorts and an equally bright top advertising the annual gran fondo through the foothills of the Rockies.

"And I wish to remind you," Finn Bonger continues, "we leave at nine from the quay. It is good to be ready to go. The route for day one is flat but interesting. We have several stops before arriving back at the boat."

As Finn Bonger outlines in some detail where the route will take them and the approximate times when the stops will occur, what remains of the queue wends its way through the various breakfast and lunch offerings, Drake Cantlay the last in line. Tray in hand, he heads over to table three but stops bemused in front of the Birtwistle family occupying table two. Ray Rudiger is sitting across from Candace and Isla while Cole Cantlay is shrugging his shoulders in dismay. Drake Cantlay at this point is the personification of betwixt and between. He frowns and looks over to the empty chair at table one and to Ruth who appears equally nonplussed and then back to his chair adjacent to his father's at table three.

"Where you gals from?" Ray Rudiger asks, drawing attention from all the tables. Silence, except for the sound of young Benny's fork scraping.

"New York, New York," Isla replies, then turns to Finn Bonger who has taken a few steps forward.

"The Big Apple. How sweet it is," Rudiger says and stirs a spoonful of sugar into his coffee as though that action will anchor him in exactly the spot where he's decided to be, the spoon now raised in his right hand like the sceptre that a newly arrived monarch wields with unabashed self-interest. "Sweet and lovely, just like you. Ray Rudiger here, at your service, if you know what I mean. Funky, funky Broadway."

I must inform you, dear reader, that I detect at this juncture in the morning procedures on the *Amoretto Algea* the influence of Hedylogos. Who, you are entitled to ask, is Hedylogos? He is another of my Erotes associates, god of sweet talk and flattery, and he is inspiring Ray Rudiger with blandishments intended solely for the ear of Candace Troyes. From what I have discovered about this young charmer, she is no stranger to being called prepossessing, lovely, and even eye-candy by those lacking a thesaurus, but she appears to be embarrassed at such uninvited attention from such an obnoxious individual at such an inauspicious time. I am amused at the confusion Rudiger is causing but I am also impressed with how diplomatically Finn Bonger is able to manage the situation. Rudiger is unapologetic about his intrusion into someone else's space, but he retreats to table one without too much resistance or insult. My antipathy for Raymond Rudiger is increasing.

"Wanker," Chef Simon says, standing by the kitchen entrance and casting a sceptical eye over the disruption. I hear him but, apparently, no one else does, least of all Ray Rudiger.

Drake Cantlay takes his seat, mumbles a word to his father, and then acknowledges the smiles both Candace and Isla direct his way. Candace asks if anyone else has picked up on the scent of roses. Evidently, only she has. She dismisses the idea as fatuous. Breakfast rituals at their table and at the other four proceed as captain and crew intended.

What is it, dear attentive and perspicacious reader, about Candace Troyes that evokes such attention? Please permit me, being who I am, to explain; all my amplified powers of observation and superior viewpoint allow me to comprehend completely the whys and wherefores of her undeniable allure. That you must accept unquestionably.

When not here on the *Amoretto Algea* consuming what remains of her croissant and engaging in a chit-chat about cycling protocols in Holland, she works for a

Manhattan cosmetics firm. Schooled well, she is now a respected practitioner of applied beauty, an initiate in the rites of female enhancement procedures. To say that Candace is more than a lovely, shapely specimen of womanhood is to understate her emergence in the world: she is classically beautiful in every sense of the word, statuesque in all regards. Her long blond hair is tied today in a ponytail that hangs down through the back adjustment of a ball cap sporting a red, heart-shaped logo. Candace has startling gray-green eyes that an aesthetically charged Botticelli might have fashioned; in fact, she strikes me as one who could easily have glided off one of his canvases except for the fact Aphrodite herself has claimed that honour on several occasions in one shape or another, each critically acclaimed and provenance accredited. Surprising, it surely is, that a jealous Aphrodite has not marked Candace Troyes out as a mortal to be dealt with severely. Various accounts reveal that the imperious goddess has often drawn upon yours truly to do her bidding. Can you believe it, the god of love in the role of a sharpshooter from a mythological hit squad. In any hypothetical case involving Candace, I'd favour her, not an envious goddess.

In moments of reflection, Candace might project a stand-offish demeanour even as her sultry nature projects the opposite. She is absolutely engaging, her voice mellifluous to any ear within hearing. At her table, Drake and James Cantlay give evidence of being so enthralled, but not completely, it must be noted, no, not by a long shot. However, most observers would agree that Candace attracts attention, her beauty absolutely spellbinding. The famed sculptor Praxiteles, who carved out a most charming and captivating statue of yours truly, would be inspired by her undeniable beauty to create a work as moving as mine is.

At this juncture in the morning of the first cycling day, let's not leave the more demure Isla Troyes out of the picture. What of her? Isla looks to be in her mid-twenties as well. Plain in her appearance, she makes little attempt to change that appearance. She wears no makeup: her face looks bedimmed, her features paradoxically accentuated by lack of cosmetic definition of any sort, so unlike her cousin Candace who is quite capable of producing the opposite result. A brunette with a saddle of faint freckles over her upturned nose, she possesses washed-out blue eyes that might lead one to suspect her absent minded gaze is permanent, but she is more given to the interior life of the spirit, from what I have noticed about her and heard her say, than the world of superficial distractions. She is well-spoken when engaged, amplifying her carefully chosen words with manipulations of her loosely manicured hands, her fingers long and delicate. There is a husky note in her voice that listeners of the right generation might associate with cinematic queens of the 1940's. A poet with romantic sensibilities that regards form and structure as essential in creative expression, Isla Troyes is very imaginative and very insightful when it comes to articulating truth. Witness her reaction in the Rijksmuseum Museum, so full of brio and alacrity, when she debunked Candace's take on Cupid as the darling of rapturous derring-do and referred to the little culprit as no more than a cut-rate, tawdry spectacle for St. Valentine's Day and in the process giving me my full due. In my view, which is extensive, almost borderless, Isla's adherence to precedent and established fact is most admirable and worthy of reward. And as I observe the Cantlay father and son duo listening to her, I determine that they find in her an agreeable conversationalist with more than a little knowledge about cycling through the Lowlands. As she informs them, she's done it all before.

If these portraits of Candace and Isla Troyes in any way sound familiar, let me advise you, dear reader, they should be. After all, as Isla points out, both of them have been here before.

Just after nine o'clock, those cycling this first day, all but Dexter Pickett, have gathered on the quay, ready to depart. Lunches have been packed, water bottles fit in place, stark red panniers hooked securely on bike racks. Finn Bonger and Dirk van Kesteren are at pains yet again to fit guests to the bikes requested; they make sure that batteries are completely charged and explain the mechanics of electric assist to those unfamiliar with the feature. Conor St James from table two has already set out on his own, Finn Bonger having given him strict instructions about getting back on time to the boat which will depart the dock in Utrecht at precisely three-thirty. I have no choice but to leave this loner to his own devices, and these include a detailed map of the route and GPS connection. I hover over the group, noting Candace in particular because of the stir of hormones she appears to be causing in Ray Rudiger. She is attired in attractive form-fitting cycling gear. So is Isla. Most, but not all, wear cycling helmets. Most, but not all, are wearing appropriate sports clothing for a biking trek that will cover fifty kilometres. The Birtwistle family lacks what might be considered sartorially appropriate but they do have yellow helmets on their heads, aslant. Angela Jones takes a series of photos and a few others follow suit. Otto Müller explains to Mick Mallory that he has an app on his smartphone that can be used as a tracker of elapsed time and distance covered, duration of stops, a map outlining the route, and vital statistics if set to record them. Mick nods approval.

Before leading off, Finn Bonger makes another announcement about cycling protocols: "In negotiating a traffic crossing or a narrowing of the path, advise the cyclist following. Cry 'Pole' when approaching one used as a lane divider. Go Slow in the vicinity of bollards and chicanes. When spread out, the rider second in line will dismount and point in the direction of a turn. Single file is preferable, especially today, a sunny Sunday. Cycling clubs go by each way very quickly."

"I've heard them called mamils," Isla calls out.

"What?" Lizzy Birtwistle asks, placing a protective hand on her son's shoulder.

"Middle-aged men in Lycra bonding over craft beer," Isla explains. "Groups of them do whizz by. They're fast but not reckless."

After the laughter subsides, Finn Bonger asks, "Tim, Tom, as agreed, one of you is set to ride sweep?"

"No problem," one of them answers and takes the yellow vest and walkie-talkie handed to him by Dirk van Kesteren who is helping to expedite departure.

Drake Cantlay says to Candace and Isla who look on the exchange somewhat dismayed, "No point in trying to distinguish one from the other. I don't even try. They've got school colours on, I think. Some college."

Tim and Tom Pickett are dressed in identical sportswear. I suspect dressing in such a manner is a form of humour enjoyed universally by twins intending to be humorous. It is certainly easy to mistake one for the other, but I noticed small tell-tale birth marks on them, near the left ear on Tim and near the right ear on Tom. Though guests might be stymied about their appearance and the fact they act in a similar fashion externally, I can observe the traits of two very distinct personalities. I'm sure their mother, Bonnie Pickett, would agree. After all, this is not the first set of twins I've had to deal with over the centuries. Recall, dear reader, the intimate connection of brothers illustrated in the story of Castor and Pollux, heavenly reminders of how love exacts sacrifice.

From his perch up on deck of the *Amoretto Algea*, Captain Van der Oor sweeps his hand through the air and smiles appreciatively at the assembled cyclists. I read his gesture as indicating that the day's activity will be graced with cooperative weather. And so the group sets out, Finn Bonger at the head, the Pickett twins at the rear, and yours truly floating effortlessly along casting an eye over everyone involved, from the experienced cyclist to those aspiring simply to get from A to B without plunging disconsolately into a canal, exhausted and no longer keen to carry on. For your added information, dear reader, this is not the first time I've surveyed tourists on bikes negotiating their way along Lowland fens and waterways. Believe me, I've been here before. Often.

Leaving Weesp and the occasional luxurious yacht moored along its central canal, Finn Bonger leads the group, single file as requested, over to the path that follows the meandering Vecht River. They traverse rich farmlands, stop briefly for shots of windmills of various size and function, proceed along dikes demarking polders and marshy lowlands. The file of cyclists, everybody keeping pace, even young Benny Birtwistle pounding away on his pedals, secure in a position between father and mother, contracts around bends and then expands on the straight flats, so like a snake uncoiling purposefully. After an hour's determined pedalling, Finn Bonger heads the troupe into a farmyard, many making for the shade of large poplar trees.

"The cheese factory, at last," Lizzy Birtwistle says to son Benny who had begun to complain a little. "A site for sore eyes, so it is."

"Stinky, innit?" Benny says, holding his nose. "What kind of cheese is that? What kind of cheese?"

"It's not the cheese, son," Nigel Birtwistle says. "This is a farm with lots of cows."

"Lots of cows. Cows. Cows. And more cows."

Finn Bonger announces that for those interested, the owner, whom he now introduces to those that have stepped forward out of the shade, like Otto and Elsa

Müller, will lead a twenty-minute tour of the barns and the renowned cheese making processes employed on the premises. All are invited to visit the tourist shop and order refreshments or buy selections of cheese. Tables and comfortable chairs are located on the back lawn. Washroom facilities are inside. They have a forty-five minute timeout. Of the group, about half take up the offer of a tour, the other half take up the other offer and make ample use of the washroom facilities.

Sitting together at a table on the back lawn, Bonnie Pickett explains to Lizzy Birtwistle who has commented on how big and strong and so much alike her sons are: "Identical, yes, near perfect specimens."

"Like two peas in a pod," Lizzy says, nodding affirmatively.

"Or like two pennies," Bonnie Pickett adds, placing the phone she has been toying with on the table and then rubbing finger and thumb of her right hand together. "Or better yet, two crisp hundred dollar bills recently printed with only one serial digit to distinguish them."

"In for a penny, in for a pound, as I've often heard repeated, mostly while serving at our meat counter. Nigel and I work in a family-owned butcher shop, so we do, he more than me."

"So tell me, Lizzy, what's Lizzy short for?"

"Elizabeth. I was named after the queen."

"That's like Americans naming their sons Jefferson," Bonnie says and then lets out a raspy croak.

"Brilliant, innit?"

That said, Lizzy Birtwistle glances over to where the bikes have been parked and sees that Benny is standing with his father who is digging into his pannier. "The lad's plugged into his MP3 player," she notes, "which means he's adjusting well enough. We took this biking adventure on for his sake. To maybe help him cope better."

"In coping with twins, it's been double down all the way into their maturity. And college, of course, which is a bit of a gamble. They eventually got over their rivalry. They bond well nowadays, fully aware of their likeness but also of their own uniqueness. They're athletes. Used to be, we nicknamed them Push and Shove because, let me tell you, that's what they engaged in particularly during their pre-teens. Push for Timothy and Shove for Thomas. They've undertaken this bike and barge thing for our sake. Well, more to get Dexter out of his shop."

"Lovely."

"Dexter said he bashed his knee this morning coming out of the john in our cabin. Doesn't know what he's missing, does he? So you bought some cheese. Let me tell you, I prefer American cheese. I also prefer crisp bacon, don't you?"

Over at another table, Isla Troyes is sitting with Mick Mallory and Wolfgang Albrecht, a cold drink in her possession, and has casually mentioned that she and her cousin Candace undertook a biking adventure similar to the present one. The professor asks when that might have been. Last year, she tells him, and looks over to where Candace, having just exited the shop, stands contrapposto by the bikes. She slowly scans the tables in the garden area.

Candace Troyes so positioned presents the very image of a poised Aphrodite. Think, dear reader, a classical Greek statue. Think again, dear reader, Venus de Milo fully attired and, of necessity, fully armed. Let it be known here that my feelings on the subject of Venus versus Aphrodite as the universally identified goddess of love remain ambivalent. Yes, indeed, what's in a name if not what others attribute to the one named? Much that can be determined about origins, that's what.   And let it be perfectly clear and stated without contradiction that my feelings regarding Aphrodite as Aphrodite also remain ambivalent. And let it never be forgotten that Aphrodite came upon the scene as a refugee from the island of Cyprus, and as mistress of emotional mayhem took over all the intricate workings of love as hers alone to supervise, leaving endless generations of mortals so hoodwinked by her beauty that they built temples to her honour where cultish veneration was practised by votaries of dubious distinction. Aphrodite's rise to power was a total shell game as one intuitive romantic poet called it.

Isla waves Candace over.

"Yes, do please join us," says Wolfgang, fitting a packet of cheese into his pannier. Mick places his helmet and water bottle on the ground by his feet.

"So, I hear you both have done some biking like this last year," Mick comments.

"The Triple B adventure— that's what they called it on the *Iphigenia*, the boat we were on. It turned out to be quite the adventure."

"We'll tell you about it when we have more time," Isla says, finishing off her drink.

At this juncture, Finn Bonger signals that the cycling will resume in five minutes. Those mulling about, like the twins, and those at various tables begin reassembling by the bikes. Candace asks those with her if she were the only one experiencing the flowery scent, "sort of half chrysanthemum, half rose," as she describes it. "Somebody's perfume, aftershave? Eau de cologne?"

"Nothing on my person to take special notice of," Mick Mallory says. "Just sweat that too often proves deodorant proof. Wolfgang?"

"*Nein, nein.* What you are smelling, Candace, goes above the odours of the barnyard. *Eau de parfum des vaches.*"

Though joking about the cows, the professor speaks the truth. The aromatic effluvia of the lower estates of human and animal, or stink in the vernacular, are not traditionally associated with my presence. Roses, nothing but roses for transcendent Eros, thank you very much. Kudos once again to Candace.

As I hover above the group's imminent departure, I focus on the figure of Tim Pickett standing tall and muscular like a warrior from ancient Sparta. Very stimulating for me is the way his smile widens as he contemplates Isla Troyes mounting her bike. I am moved considerably by what I see: he rushes into the cheese shop and moments later exits, securing a package in his pannier. He hurries to get into position ahead of his brother, the sweep. At this point I reach into my quiver and extract a gold-tipped arrow. Tim is right in my line of sight, a look of triumph still registered on his face. My aim is true, and it always has been, as the chronicles of time record. Well, for the most part at least it's always been true. I won't distract you here about the Leda kerfuffle, nor counter that with details of all the successes I can lay claim to, but I will eventually get there. So, dear reader, for the present just concentrate on the effects of my action, an action that conveys in vivid imagery the sudden infusion in both the physical and spiritual sense of all that I epitomize. I employ language here, limited though it is being a human institution, language that best conveys the notion of sudden and swift penetration into the core of one's existence, be it that of a mortal or of an immortal. Take note: the bigger they are, the harder they fall.

The sensation of getting hit in the heart is real. As Hesiod explained: "It loosens the limbs and weakens the mind." The interval between the arrow being launched and the effects taking place is negligible. In most cases, a magnificent confusion arises in one's total being. In simple terms, the one struck is hooked, raptured in a benign frisson.

Thus, when the group resumes its cycling, Finn Bonger leading and Tom Pickett in the role of sweep— there is no mistaking Tim for Tom, absolutely not, not now. The truth is that Tim has left Tom at the back of the pack and slid in behind Isla and ahead of Candace. No doubt about it, his heart pounds inordinately, his limbs feel odd, and his brain races to figure out why. Moreover, anyone watching can see that he can't keep his eyes off Isla's undulating bottom. Breaking constantly becomes an intricate part of the pedalling cadence that has taken control of his efforts to keep up with her. It looks as though he is making every effort not to cause a rear end collision although he probably really wants to involve her in one. From all appearances, Isla is as yet totally unaware of his pursuit, but Candace looks a little perplexed, no doubt uncertain of what one of the twins is doing joining in the line where he wasn't before. I must confess, the rhythms now in play between Tim and Isla amuse me greatly. Although the cross currents they are causing are of a more mundane nature, their evolving relationship takes me back to the good old days.

Now a point to consider. You know perfectly well, my cherished and informed reader, how things fell into place for us. The crux of the matter is that when our existence finally became known to those entrenched in pockets of civilized life, humans, to be specific, organizing themselves into kingdoms, we immortals were inclined as a collective to acknowledge their perception that we were in so many ways the amplified image of them. But can you imagine, dear reader, immortals setting out on two-wheeled conveyances for exercise and pleasure? Demi-gods and heroes like Perseus and Heracles, okay, maybe, to keep in shape, but Titans and Olympians? No. Especially the goddesses, with the possible exception of Artemis in her hunting tunic or chiton-clad formals. I must admit, Candace and Isla would look superb in similar garb.

Having left the cheese farm well behind them, the Amoretto Algea cyclists proceed at an acceptable speed via Zanpad on the bank of the Vecht River. Finn Bonger appears to be in his element. Angela Jones hums as she cruises along while JJ whistles, the tunes rendered not exactly from the same musical score. Drake Cantlay pumps the pedals in a low gear setting as though he were making his escape from some encampment not sanctioned by law or polite society. There is a strain on his father's face but he keeps up. Young Benny Birtwistle has ceased complaining, not that any but his dear mother would hear his complaints or tolerate them if heard. Ray Rudiger waves a hand at the many mansions located along the opposite bank and comments about their munificence and extensive lawns. No one in his immediate vicinity appears to be interested in lawns. Tim Pickett still pushes hard between Isla and Candace. Amused by what I am witnessing, I pose the following questions to you, dear reader. Is Tim's pounding heart beginning to ache? Is his mind searching for ways to be accepted? Must he double down in his efforts to attract a positive response from the shapely, demure one ahead of him? At the rear of the pack Tom Pickett is wearing a very wide grin.

The designated lunch stop is at the Breukelen Bridge, a narrow access across the canal to the Breukelen townsite. Here in a tree-lined, open area paved with cobblestones vehicles from three directions merge and proceed slowly. Finn Bonger points to a post with multiple road signs and distances marked and then points to his watch. Sets of benches are located on the periphery of the intersection and make for excellent viewing of the passing traffic and yachts in the adjacent canal. It is also an excellent location for respite, or lunch, or both, as is the case on this occasion. Finn Bonger announces that they have thirty minutes for lunch and that meeting the Amoretto Algea at a specific time is paramount.

On one bench are Candace, Isla, Ruth and Ray Rudiger. And next to them, the Birtwistle family, Nigel, Lizzy, and Benny, the boy plugged in once more to his MP3 player. He bops back and forth, back and forth. On the opposite side of the intersection are Mick Mallory, Professor Wolfgang, Otto and Elsa Müller. And next to them, JJ and Angela Jones, Cole and Drake Cantlay.

Sitting on the third bench on that side in the company of Finn Bonger are the Pickets, Bonny and Tom. Tim has hesitated in joining them. He is bouncing from one foot to the other in a confused adult version of young Benny's gamboling. Tim digs into his pannier and with a loud sigh he pulls out a round package labeled with the cheese farm logo. He waits for a car to pass, and then another car to pass, and then a third, which to him was going way too slow, judging by the expression on his face, and then, after nearly tripping over his bike stand, he virtually stumbles across the intersection heading for Isla's bench. He introduces himself to her while nodding at the others who are now watching and listening intently. Isla is taken aback when Tim presents her with what he describes as "farm fresh cheese."

"I...I... I don't know what to say."

"Thank you would not be out of place," suggests Candace, bright-eyed.

"Thank you," Isla responds, looking from Tim's smiling face to the wrapped packet of cheese in her hand. She appears to be overcome with uncertainty.

"For your enjoyment, lovely lady," Tim says, "and your friends."

"That's very considerate," comments Ruth Rudiger, who is following the exchange with delight. "How very generous of you, young man. A truckle of cheese, is it?"

Ray Rudiger is now standing up. His head comes to about midway between Tim's shoulder and elbow. "What she said," Ray puts in, motioning to his wife, "but leave the poor girl alone, Bud."

"Oh, Ray" Ruth says, "let the young man do his thing."

Seeming reluctant to cause strife or further embarrassment to Isla, Tim quickly retreats to the other side of the intersection, his face bright red like the red of his pannier. Tom slaps him on the back and hands him a water bottle. Applause from the other benches echoes.

Let us get beyond this cheesy interlude at the Breukelen Bridge and pick up again on the ride of the day as Finn Bonger guides the group towards Utrecht. Focus on Tom Pickett. As sweep, how can he not become increasingly aware of the different ways riders ride their bikes? Some cycle with confidence and awareness, some of whom are actually able to throw comments back and forth about what they pass, while others seem awkward in their struggle to maintain balance and keep pace, let alone view anything beyond the wobbling front wheel of their own bike. Human effort is varied. Inattention, consequential. Achievement, capricious.

With Finn Bonger leading and Tom Pickett following up at the rear, the *Amoretto Algea* group proceeds into the heart of the old city, Utrecht centrum. In a tight queue, the cyclists pass numerous crowded cafés, but there is no stopping at any of them except for when Tim Pickett in his position behind Isla apparently loses control of his bike and flings himself out of line to land in a heap before a table of four drinking coffee. Apologies made to both those at the table and to those ahead and behind waiting no doubt in states of mind ranging from mild amusement to real concern, Tim joins his twin at the tail end of the line. Still audible over the general murmuring is the sing-song voice of young Benny Birtwistle crying out, "Not good. Not good. Not good."

Continuing along busy thoroughfares but with few traffic stops and starts, the group rendezvous with the barge moored at a quay located on the east side of the city. In virtual silence, best understood as humorous but brotherly imputation, Tim and Tom Pickett assist Finn Bonger and Dirk van Kesteren with getting all the bikes on board. Nothing specific is said at this juncture about Tim's infatuation with Isla, who disappears immediately upon turning in her bike. Candace, on the other hand, engages the brothers for a short time, ending the exchange by expressing gratitude for the cheese, the implication being that she and Isla will certainly savour it. Then she retreats up the ramp in pursuit of Isla.

Like Candace and Isla, other guests have retreated to their quarters. Downtime, they call it. For mortals, physical exertion has its aches and pains but also its rewards, or so I have been led to understand. A few other guests have repaired to the upper deck with liquid refreshments of various kinds as the Amoretto Algea courses down the Amsterdam-Rhine canal towards its berth for the night in Vianen. I leave these stalwarts to their camaraderie and good cheer. I leave them to their drinks and the enjoyment of passing views— cows on sandy tracks of land watching with large curious eyes. I leave them finally to the amazement they express at the workings of the Prinses Beatrixsluis, the lock that gives access to the Lekkanaal, and to their comments regarding the massive commercial and industrial barges plying the same waterway. I leave them to go check on Candace and Isla, refreshed now in their berth on the upper level.

Sleeping quarters and general accommodations on the *Amoretto Algea* are ample, considering all aspects of what guests require once signed on to the bike and barge adventure. Brochures online and in colourful hard copy assure those interested that their every want will be satisfied. Ensuites are tight, according to Bonnie Pickett, but functional, though at times lacking sufficient hot water, according to Bonnie Pickett yet again, especially after people return to their rooms after cycling. Beds, apparently, are comfortable. As to their wants and needs, Candace and Isla register no complaints about their situation, none that I know of at any rate.

"Those twins," Candace says, posing before a mirror, "not just jerking us—mostly you— around, are they? And everybody else on the barge? Isla, what do you think?"

"Maybe it's just a game they play," Isla answers, interrupting for a moment her efforts to dry her hair.

"Yeah, okay. Like, I had a few words with their mother in that cheese shop we stopped at. Called Bonnie. She told me the twins are both on their college football team. Tim's a tight end, and whatever that means, I just can't imagine."

"It's a position where you run and catch the ball," Isla explains. "On offense."

"Bonnie said Tom is a rush end. Again, I'm clueless."

"Defensive position, I think."

"Bonnie said that ever since they were kids the twins rumbled. The one with the ball impeded by the one without the ball. Offense and defense. Like that. Got them good scholarships."

"I'm still confused over which one of them is coming on to me," Isla says, returning the hairdryer to its place on a shelf. "Tim, right?"

"Right," Candace says. "At least I think that's right. Like, I asked one of them at the bikes, Tim I thought, who he was. And he said 'I'm Tom, not Tim.' Then he smiles devilishly."

"Then what?"

"Then he says, 'there's love in the air' and smiles again."

"So I ask him, 'You sure it's not you who brought the round of cheese over to Isla?'"

"And he says what in reply?"

"And he says that it was Tim. That Tim's fallen for you. He means you, Isla."

"So I'm not just imagining things?"

"Apparently not. But it's all so odd. Fortunately, as far as potential romance goes, there's two of them. And Finn Bonger."

"Sure, but I feel like I've pedaled my way into a Shakespearean comedy of errors and I'm getting a lot of unsolicited attention."

"Yeah, right. So far all the attention I'm getting is from Ray Rudiger. Like, whoa, whoa, mister."

"Ray Rudiger is perfect as Shakespeare's Caliban," Isla suggests after a moment's thought. "Think about it."

"Yeah, that works."

"And those ugly tattoos of his."

"Creepy."

After a pause, Candace adds, "Like maybe the cheese sent to us, well, to you, is the new football that Tim and Tom are playing with. Or maybe fighting over and we don't know it."

"So what do we do? Play offense or defense?"

"Very confusing."

As to the twins, having showered and spruced up appropriately in their cabin, Tim and Tom make for the upper deck. Each has a mug of beer in hand.

"So tell," Tom says. "Start with the cheese shop."

"Man, I don't know what hit me. Whatever it was, it hit me hard. Like one minute I'm fine, enjoying the scenery and everything, then bam, I'm off my rocker eyeballing the chick."

"Looks pretty sexy in her cycling gear. Great hips."

"It was more than just appreciating a shapely form, believe me."

"I'm listening, bro."

"It's like going up to catch a high-thrown ball and taking a vicious hit right in the gut. The physical contact I feel is immediate. It's like the ground under my feet gives way and at the same time my whole body is being pounded into a pulp. Head's spinning. Ball drops, of course, and I expect to get whacked a second time."

"As they say, you might as well catch the ball because whether you do or not, you're going to get hit."

"Look, man, I'm trying to describe to you what happened to me back there at the cheese farm. I'm serious."

"Sorry, bro. Are we talking real pain here?"

"You feel crushed, ripped apart, absolutely winded, popped like a balloon. Not just physically but mentally. Your stomach's suddenly in knots. Your heart's pounding and your ears are ringing. You're totally confused because all's you're doing is looking at someone."

"So it's not really painful, like getting pulled injured out of the game kind of painful?"

"No. Not at all. Your mind's in a muddle and yet somehow you feel elated, like you're walking aimlessly through a rose garden. And the confusion, which can be delightful, I must admit, lingers on and on."

"So, a kind of mental lapse, then? Loss of control? I mean, giving her the cheese at the bridge. Very mystifying."

"Impulse. Pure impulse. I needed to make an impression."

"You did. And you really made an impression at that café in Utrecht. How'd that happen?"

"I saw a florist shop right by the café and thought a bouquet of roses would ingratiate me to the girl. Instead of a lump of cheese, I mean. Roses are symbolic, right? I don't know what possessed me. I sort of lost focus and hit the curb and it was head over heels. Like losing the ball again. Only it's more of a heartache, man, a big heartache."

"Lucky you just got off with a few scrapes and bruises from that fall."

"Finn Bonger treated them. He's got first-aid."

"Some story, bro. Locker room material for sure."

Thus, dear readers, Tim's novel explanation of what he experienced when a dart from the god of love hit him in a vital part of his being and completely unhinged him. Football! You just can't make this stuff up.

Before dinner gets started, Finn Bonger rings his bell and calls for attention. He congratulates the group for the fine outing that marked the first day of cycling. He also expresses his gratitude, with apologies to Tim Pickett, that no serious incidents occurred to mar expectations and adds that the route to the walled city of Heusden the following day will cover forty-one kilometres. He provides a few details about what can be expected in terms of natural attractions, windmills in particular. Chef Simon enters and with no lack of pride describes what "delectable concoction" he has prepared to take the edge of the hunger that all guests likely feel after a day out in the open air. House salad with special dressing (a secret recipe), stamppot with kale and smoked sausage, and apple strudel as dessert. Applause follows him back to his kitchen. Finn Bonger proceeds to help Dirk van Kesteren serve the meals.

At this juncture, dear reader, let me introduce the myriorama effect; that is, by a series of shifting foci, I offer you an entertaining glimpse of what's going on at each table, my intention being to create a composite of conversations taking place simultaneously. Think personalities and voices rather than pictorial display cards being shuffled and re-aligned. Follow?

"A dish fit for the gods, innit?" the butcher Nigel Birtwistle announces to his wife and son at table two after digging into the stamppot.

Careless words.

Understandably, taciturn Conor St James responds. "I'm not at all fond of kale in whatever dish it is presented."

At table one, Angela Jones says, "I think that young man injured himself when he fell off his bike. Notice the bruises?"

"He's smitten," Ruth Rudiger says. "Probably doesn't feel anything but desire."

"Don't play with your sausages, Benny," Lizzy Birtwistle says. "Eat them. They're very tasty."

Bonnie Pickett at table five points an instructive fork at her son and says: "Pull yourself together, boy, and stop playacting."

"I'm not playacting, Ma. Isla's so beautiful, so beautiful in her own way. That's the truth of it."

Dexter says what's happening with Tim is a mystery. Not at all typical of how Tim romances young women.

The conversation at table four centers on national celebrations, typical pastimes, and naturally enough, given the olfactory high that the stamppot on their plates induces, national dishes.

"I think you could say that sauerbraten is best known in our country," says Elsa Müller, who is decked out neatly for dinner. Pearl earrings glimmer.

"*Ja*, I think so, *Liebchen*," Otto says, skewering a sausage with his fork and then cutting into it with his knife. Wolfgang expresses agreement.

"Do you see what Candace is wearing? Ray Rudiger asks. "Trying to get us all excited, is she?"

"She's very plain, in my opinion."

"But, Ma, she's so nubile."

"She's what?"

"Pass the salt, please."

At table three, Cole and Drake Cantlay listen intently to what Candace and Isla are saying.

"Caliban is giving me the once over," Candace says. "Again."

"Notice how the twins with their big eyes have changed seats with their parents."

"The better to see you with, my dear."

"Honestly, Ray, you get excited if you think some gal's winked at you."

"Tasty. Tasty. Tasty."

"It's not a supper club, for Christ's sake," Ray Rudiger maintains, "it's a barge. We're all casual here, right JJ, despite your quiet finery and Angela's noisy but pricey bangles?"

"Right, Ray. Very tacky."

"You don't admire the casual luxury of my away wardrobe, Ray?"

"Very bespoke."

"In Canada, what dish?"

"Well, Otto," Mick Mallory says, "I'd have to say poutine is well known in all parts of the country. It is now, at least. I could be wrong in saying it's our national dish."

"What is poutine?" Otto Müller wants to know.

Back at table one, Angela Jones says, "So after being a high school counsellor, Ruth, you decided to write a help column for the local paper, is that right?

"Yes, that's right. I suppose one could call me an agony aunt."

"You'll have to tell me what that's like."

"Basically it's cheese curds and gravy served on fries. In the province of Quebec, where the delicacy originated, it would be on French fries."

"You're wasting good food, Tim," Dexter Pickett says, probing his son's plate with a fork.

"Man, would you stop stealing my sausages!"

A loud silence breaks over the whole dining area for a moment, but then the dinner time din picks up again when Bonnie Pickett's cackle rises to a pitch.

"Ah, yes, poutine," the professor says. "Like what is served in Paris, *ja*?

Otto and Elsa Müller smile appreciatively, and the professor breaks into a hearty laugh.

"Busted again, bro."

"It's not all a game of Blackjack, okay. I've told you what it's like."

"Tasty. Tasty. Tasty."

In the service area beyond the coffee machine, Chef Simon says to Finn Bonger and Dirk van Kesteren, who are preparing to clear the tables, "No real damage. The dazed bloke will sort it."

And so, dear readers, dinner on the *Amoretto Algea* progresses at a reasonable rate until dessert is done and Finn Bonger and Kirk van Kesteren begin clearing tables. Mick Mallory and Professor Wolfgang ascend to the upper deck carrying pints of Belgian beer that Dirk pulled for them. Otto and Elsa Müller call it an early night as do father and son Cantlay and the Birtwistle family. Candace and Isla also retreat to their quarters. Conor St James heads out for an evening stroll about the area.

Responding to Bonnie Pickett's request, Dirk van Kesteren reaches behind the bar to retrieve the aluminum case containing poker chips and playing cards available at any time for the use of the guests. Table five is cleared. Joining Dexter and Bonnie in a game of blackjack are Tim and Tom, although Tim needed a great deal of cajoling to play a few hands. He declares that the only reason he's hanging around is the off chance that Isla will appear and he intends to buy her a nightcap and engage her in meaningful conversation.

"Busted!"

"That's it," Tim exclaims, brushing his cards aside. "I'm out."

"Still mooning like an infatuated fool," says Bonnie, sweeping her hand over a spread of chips. Dexter guffaws. Tom looks away. A heavily sighing Tim takes his leave.

And that, dear readers, just about sums it up, the activities of the day ending with a whimper and not with a bang. I leave the rest of the night to the machinations of Oneiros, my long-time accomplice, and retreat for the nonce into the firmament.

Day Three
all x's and o's

Vianen to Heusden:

Early A.M. of day three on the *Amoretto Algea.* Mick Malory and the professor sit in the lounge sipping coffee and conversing much as they did the morning before. Ruth Rudiger with book and coffee has taken the same seat she did previously. In answer to Wolfgang's observation about enduring love and compatibility, Mick offers the following answer. "The basis of our long relationship was not only unconditional love but also friendship, well connected friendship."

Gesturing with a waving hand, Wolfgang says, "Ach, you are describing well how it is with my Anna."

"Camaraderie between husband and wife in the truest sense of the word. That's what Delores and I enjoyed for all of our time together. Then... well... you know."

"I would not want to lose Anna," Wolfgang concludes, his bushy brow knotted. He reaches for his coffee and sips audibly.

"Losing Delores the way we did caused me and my son and daughter all kinds of suffering. Especially me. Loss of a loved one makes a hole in your heart that has to be filled."

"Mick, if you wish to tell me about it, do so, please. If not, I understand completely."

"I have no problem doing that, Wolfgang, I've had therapy."

Having said that, Mick takes to scanning the lounge as though seeking something to fix his attention on. Moments later, he refocuses on the professor. He takes a deep break and begins anew.

"A few years back Dolores sustained serious injury while recreating at her sister's country retreat in what we call cottage country. She was paddle boarding her way slowly out from the shore of the waterway when a wave struck, overturned the board, and launched her headfirst crashing into the corner of the dock. A few inches this way, a few that way, and the results of the impact might not have been fatal. She died in hospital."

"Tragic, Mick, very, very tragic. A great trauma for all of you. Yours is a story of love, loss, and regret. *Schicksal, ja.* Fate. I think so."

"Tragic, for sure. But so much more. Unfortunately, I was away on business at the time. I went out of my mind when I heard. Guilt, you see. Try as you might, you cannot control these swift emotional shifts that mark your entry into a space of dream-like improbability. Along with the grief and remorse and guilt, I experienced an overwhelming desire for justice."

"Justice?" Wolfgang asks, a quizzical look accompanying his question. "An accident, was it not? A rogue wave?"

"Rogue, sure, but it's not that simple."

"How so?"

"Long story, much of it dealing with grief, much of it dealing with revenge and murderous intent. There were ethics and morality issues I had to sort through."

"You had help, you say. Your system provides what is necessary when trauma strikes, ja?"

"Yes. My therapy began a year or so after Delores' death, when I was completely lost in a world of negativity. The scheduled sessions continued for some time."

"This benefitted you?"

"Did I get whole? Cleared to get back to normal life? Difficult to answer in absolute terms, Wolfgang. Very difficult."

"One's life is a work in progress. I believe this is so. Grief is part of the process, ja."

"Grief led me to excessive drinking, consuming copious amounts of comfort food, befriending crows and foxes, shoplifting. What else? Right, I could not complete sudoku and jigsaw puzzles."

"Perhaps these activities were merely failed coping mechanisms?"

"Very possible. But if they were, they were baffling and more frustrating than helpful. Very confusing."

"Of course."

"Even with months of consultation I found it hard to get every dark impulse, every regret, every instance of rage if not under complete control then at least put into perspective."

"What held you back?"

"Anger. Hatred. I got way beyond grief and guilt. Anger charged me, I told my counsellor, it gave my life without Delores a sense of purpose."

"Why hatred? At life itself?"

"No, not that really."

Again Mick breaks off from the narrative that holds the professor's concerned interest. He sips the last of his café au lait then sucks out the creamy remnants from the bottom of the cup. After taking another deep breath, he continues.

"You wanted to know about the wave? Yes, in a sense it was a rogue wave that tumbled Dolores. More a case of operating a boat under the influence, you know, DUI, on the part of Silas Flower, a well-known media personality and high-flying tycoon. He caused the wave. He was with a sidekick of his and two young women, yahooing and squealing loudly as the boat raced along. Signs in this particular part of the channel read No wake! They were travelling well beyond the posted speed limit."

"So, you sought justice?"

"I did get around to that. Eventually. In the early going, it was always twilight for me, always verging on darkness despite any benefits from grief counselling. The same on days of bright sunshine. Morning mirror horrors reflected a range of self-destructive behaviours, not all of them little ironic twists like feeding crows out the back. I languished in that enduring sense of loss. The point was, Wolfgang, before too long it became apparent rather dramatically that the only honest and realistic way out of the madness that had beset me and for which I had sought professional help through therapy was to assign Silas Flower the role of evil antagonist. I saw him as arch villain, poser, fraud, and my lovely wife's killer."

"So, more than grief motivated you."

"Exactly. That's exactly what I'm saying. Grief counselling based on psychodynamic therapy had its limitations as far as it applied to me. Retribution in the form of revenge, that's what came to dominate my world. It was like my mind was consumed with a kind of sacred duty to the goddess Nemesis. Vengeance — justice with extremely sharp edges. As I reported to my grief counsellor, what I wanted most was to see Flower not dead, but to see him suffer physically, mentally, emotionally, and financially. Suffer the way he caused me to suffer. But enough of this for one day, Wolfgang."

It strikes me as very likely that during this time of great emotional upheaval in his life that Mick Mallory was definitely under the dark and devastating influence of Eris, goddess of strife and discord. She rarely needs assistance from her nasty daughter Até, but in Mick's case, she got it. Recollection of what he suffered reduces Mick to tears. It would appear that he needs a moment or two to pull himself together.

Wolfgang shakes his head sympathetically, drains his coffee cup, and as a kind of pull-back from the intensity of the conversation so early in the day, he nods to Ruth. She hasn't been intentionally listening, or so it seems, but she could not have missed much of what was said if what was said proved to be more interesting than what she read. Soon enough, the queue forms for the breakfast pickup and the tables get filled according to plan.

Breakfast holds the usual rituals, the difference in this go-round being that pancakes are on offer. An occasional yawn can be heard over the disturbance that young Benny Birtwistle causes with a series of slurps that comes across in bursts of three. Orange juice. Tim Pickett, his concentration riveted on Isla, drops a fork several times. Tom and the rest of the table express amused embarrassment. Conversations are muted, desultory, somehow out of tune with what Finn Bonger announces in a brief statement as the potential highlights of the day. In due time, lunches are packed and exits get taken. The sighs of unrequited love hang in the air.

Setting out on another biking tour follows the pattern established previously, Finn Bonger leading and Tom Pickett riding sweep, both in yellow vests. The forty-one-kilometre ride will take the group from Vianen to Gorinchem and on to Heusden where the *Amoretto Algea* will berth for the night. Conor St James heads out on his own for a second day with detailed instructions about where and when to meet the barge. As for the rest of the group including Dexter Pickett, no specific arrangement regarding position has been designated, so cyclists align themselves where they want, usually in accordance with family or table groupings, but not necessarily so, as in Tim Pickett's case. The sky this day is overcast, much like Tim's countenance, although he does appear to be fraught with nervous energy that is expressed with aimless gazing about.

From the quay in Vianen the group makes its way through the verdant countryside where thatched roofs of rural cottages compete with windmills for the notice that might result in a passing comment or two. Otherwise, it's predominantly flat vistas, drainage ditches, cows, sheep, and goats.

A break in the constant pedaling occurs in the town of Schoonrewoerd. Finn Bonger, strict in keeping to the schedule, leads the group to De Zwaan, which he designates as the rendezvous point for all the cyclists no matter how they take their break. He stipulates they have forty-five minutes, no more, and then it's on to Gorinchem via Leerdam. Candace and Isla disappear once they have secured their bikes. For those interested in visiting an historical church, Finn gives directions to Gereformeerde Kerk, a short walking distance away. Those interested are Otto and Elsa Müller, Mick Malory and Professor Wolfgang, and the Birtwistle threesome, although Benny seems to be the least interested. He wants to know where the swan is.

De Zwaan is a café with outdoor tables nestled under umbrellas. Service is quick and efficient for those who rest here and order beverages— assorted coffee concoctions with English translations are written on the menu next to those in Dutch. One table suits three members of the Pickett family just fine. Tim, on the other hand, has decided to wander about in pursuit of the obvious. Another table accommodates the Cantlays, father and son, who have insisted that Finn Bonger join them for any drink he might desire. Ruth Rudiger and Angela Jones are sitting at a third table, which is situated a little apart from the others, while Ray Rudiger and JJ have opted to tour around the town. Before leaving, Ray claimed he fancied some of the Leerdammer cheese, his favourite, which Ruth declares is news to her.

Having finished showing photos of their various grandchildren to each other, Ruth and Angela put their phones aside. With a subtle little head movement in the direction of the Pickett table, Angela makes note of Tim's return. Ruth responds with a raised eyebrow.

"The poor guy's absolutely smitten," Ruth says, rubbing her forehead lightly where helmet pressure has left an impression. Her short grey hair, remarkably, remains neatly in place. "He displays classic lovesick symptoms. And probably confused about why."

"It's like he's in a sort of trance," Angela says. "I'm surprised he didn't ride headlong into a drainage ditch setting out today. Or crash his bike again."

"Or suffer some kind of love-induced cataleptic seizure and go all stiff."

"Infatuated with Isla Troyes," Angela speculates, "that New York gal. He's so ardent."

"His wooing is rather woeful, it seems to me just observing."

"I suppose as a school counsellor and then as an agony aunt you've had experience with all the ins and outs of love, real or imagined."

"I have indeed. All too frequently it's closer to home than one would imagine." Ruth picks up her helmet, adjusts the tension knob, and sets the helmet down again on top of her panier.

"Too tight?"

"A little. As I was about to say, Ray has a wandering eye, but he's loveable in so many ways that might go unnoticed by others. Forty years with Ray has forced me to double down. Practicality over incoherent rapture, if you catch my drift. He'd be lost without me."

"I see what you mean."

"If anything ever happened to Ray, the grandkids would be immensely saddened, they'd be inconsolable. They love the old bugger because he loves them and shows it in every way possible. They just love it when he shouts 'get in the hole' when he's watching golf."

Within the allotted time, the group reassembles by the parked bikes. Slightly late in arriving are Candace and Isla who say they went searching for the glassworks they'd heard so much about. Wrong town, Finn informs them, and leads the group off.

Approaching the outskirts of Leerdam, Angela Jones encounters a problem with her bike. As she pumps her pedals and moves along, all she and those in her immediate vicinity hear is a grinding kind of bang, bang, bang, a sound that young Benny Birtwistle picks up and imitates with apparent relish. Angela stops, gets off her bike, and sets the stand. She shrugs her shoulders at JJ, who quickly hops off his bike. He looks as concerned as she. Coming up to take a look as to why the line has halted, Tom Pickett with walkie-talkie squawking tells Finn

Bonger to stop immediately and come back to deal with a mechanical malfunction on one of the bikes. A half-ring of observers offering half-assed assumptions about what broke gathers around Angela and her bike. Closer in and presumably able to assess the situation with greater understanding of cause and effect are Finn Bonger and Tom Pickett; moments into their inspection of chain and cogs and their manipulation of pedals, they back away, scratching their heads like a duo in a dumb show routine. Stepping forward, Drake Cantlay says that it sounds like the bearings in the crankcase are shot; in fact, he's pretty sure of it. The bike can still be ridden he assures Angela but offers to exchange his bike for hers if she's agreeable. She is. Judging by the number of smiles and nodding heads of the onlookers, Drake Cantlay's gesture is greatly appreciated. Candace claps her hands with little restraint and so does Benny with no restraint at all. Finn Bonger confirms that the ride can continue with a minimum of time lost, and by noon he leads the cyclists single file along cobbled lanes into Leerdam, an attractive town renowned for its glassworks that lies on the banks of the river Linge.

In the central area of the town stands Grote Kerk, a grand church with clock tower. Surrounding the brick structure on two sides is what could be termed a functioning town square replete with several sets of bike stands, and these the Amoretto Algea cyclists quickly fill. Playing tour guide for the moment, Finn notes that for those interested, several galleries and outlets are located down towards the water, Leerdam glassworks and the National Glass Museum included, both reachable by means of a pedestrian bridge across the narrow channel. He adds that a wide walkway demarks the shoreline of the town and provides access to various sites of interest to visitors, the marina being one of them. They have a one hour lunch break with enough time to explore around. Candace and Isla express interest in seeing the glass museum and head off along a lane that Finn indicates as the quickest route. A majority of the cyclists heads down towards the water.

Watching Candace and Isla saunter away, Tim Pickett declares he's going to search the town for a florist. Tom attempts to dissuade him from doing so. Dexter and Bonny insist that he accompany them and that he should put the girl behind him even if she is attired in her "alluring, form-fitting cycling gear." He complies, offering little real resistance to their jokes and jibes.

The Birtwistles opt to have their lunch sitting on a bench by the Grote Kerk. After finishing the sandwiches they packed, Nigel takes Benny for ice cream, leaving Lizzy alone. Benny is once again plugged into his music. He gambols along beside his father, a redheaded leveret anticipating the next change in their playful stride.

Approaching Lizzy from across the church square are Ruth and Ray Rudiger. Ray complains about Bonger's ruthlessness when it comes to "downtime" and then says that he's going to check out the glass museum he's heard so much about. Ruth smiles and sits on the bench, turning her attention to Lizzy. Brief introductions follow.

"Just resting?" Ruth asks.

"In for a penny, in for a pound," Lizzy answers in her singsong voice. "I'm content to be sitting alone here for a few minutes in quiet appreciation of just where I am. In Holland, for heaven's sake."

"Nice."

"I haven't the proper clothing for this kind of activity, I find. Shabby, yeah? And hot. My husband Nigel says I look dowdy. I tell him it's an unfair comparison. So many with us are experienced cyclists and know how to dress."

"Not to worry. It's what you make of it, Lizzy. That's what counts. Fancy doesn't increase the enjoyment."

Lizzy smiles appreciatively. She then says, "We're here for the lad, you see."

"He seems to be getting along just fine. Benny, is it?"

"Benny's adjusting. He's been diagnosed with ASD, so he has."

"Yes, I understand."

"On the spectrum, isn't that what they say?"

"Yes, that's the term used."

"Benny's hard to care for but we love him so much, don't we? He's as keen as mustard about certain things. His football team, yeah? Arsenal. Wears their jersey wherever he goes."

"He's not alone in that regard."

"He finds it difficult to make friends. He prefers being alone. Standoffish. Rude sometimes."

"He'll make his way just fine, Lizzy, with time. As a school counsellor, I dealt with students of different ages with similar disorders. Interaction with others, even peers, can be distressing, hard to adapt to. He appears to be doing quite well here in the midst of all these adults."

"Thankfully. He likes Finn Bonger."

"I know of only one person in our group who doesn't like Finn Bonger."

"And he likes the fellow at our table, Conor St James. There's a kind of communication between them I don't quite understand. He makes Benny laugh. Strange, innit?"

"All good."

"We were told that Benny may have his own way of learning, different ways of getting on with things, paying attention, and so on. But he's as fit as a butcher's dog, as they say."

"Physically active, I see, lots of bounce."

"What they call body language, his is strange at times, even laughable, his repetitive habits, what he does and what he says. He likes to place belongings a certain way, coins, comic books, and curious things. He arranges them in order."

"Par for the course, Lizzy. Symptoms of autism spectrum disorder."

"The oddest thing we have to deal with is that Benny can take what people say so very literally."

"That's not unusual in these cases."

"When he overheard the cook call some bloke a wanker, well, you can imagine what our Benny made of that."

"I have a fair idea. Also a fair idea who the cook meant."

"When Benny's father said he thought that pretty young thing was drop dead gorgeous...'

"Yes, Candace, one of those two young New York women."

"Benny wanted to know if she would. 'If she would what?' we asked him. And he answered, 'Drop dead.'"

"An interesting observation, Lizzy."

"Just yesterday he said he was sure he was being regarded mysteriously."

"I said it was his guardian angel looking out for him. He liked that idea. Gave the angel a name, Dante. As I live and breathe, I have no clue where he got that name from. Nigel thinks his son is possibly an idiot savant in the making."

When Nigel and Benny return to the bench, Lizzy, with all the musicality her voice can generate, introduces them to Ruth. No one looking on can miss how lovingly a mother can embrace a son and regard him with adoring spaniel eyes. Love, dear reader, of a different order, love without borders, love that engenders more of itself. All four move toward the bikes where Finn Bonger is waving.

I leave you, dear reader, at this point in the day's outing with a scene temporarily deprived of significant action: namely, most of the cyclists standing by their bikes ready to be off, a befuddled Tim Pickett contemplating Isla's shapely curves, and Candace watching Drake Cantlay's every move approvingly. Let's call this scenario an episodic interim, a timely hiatus, or even the hackneyed calm before the storm. Stasis, in effect.

Before I enlarge on what I have presented to you so far about the history and nature of my existence— I can be very inclusive in that regard, exhaustingly so— let me include this little instructive insertion here for your immediate edification. Call it a data point, a notification, no more than that. You must understand, I avoid a rank of bullets piled one upon the other without connection or elaboration. Please understand that I am extremely passionate about what I do and demand relevant acknowledgement from my reader.

Therefore, I hereby state unapologetically that chaos is in my DNA, to use the terminology that learned mortals established in their efforts to understand human biological connectivity. The reason for this categorical declaration is that by their union Chaos and Gaia brought me into being; my perpetual mandate then is to fulfill their directives unstintingly. Like both Chaos and Gaia, I am primordial, of the first celestial order. Nothing less. Hesiod, who has much to say about my genealogy, asserts that love is the primal force in the creation of the universe. I agree. How could I not? And how could you not, dear reader, agree with me? Let it be widely known that I continue to this day to benefit from Gaia's munificence, from how, despite upheaval, both natural and man-made, she sustains the life she engenders. Entropy has multiple applications, for such is Chaos' domain where, as his heir, I am permitted to roam freely without restriction or censure of any kind or from any origin. Zeus, be damned!

So, Candace Troyes. I still harbour more than a little resentment over her understanding of just who I am and what I represent. Her comments in the Rijksmuseum, where she disregarded the facts established in ancient chronicles, amounted to a gross and erroneous appreciation of the god of love, me. To be specific in my criticism of her, she believed me to be no more than a pint-size poster boy for the rituals associated with St Valentine's Day. A primordial god like me dallying about impishly in the guise of a putti accompanying an impulsive and fickle mother— the reduction is not to be credited at all, no, not at all. What I have designed for Candace will be attributed to the ironic caprice of circumstances, a spontaneous burst of passionate desire that can occur at any time in any place. And yet, can it be said that my impulse to do something about this insult, inadvertent though it might have been, is Aphrodite inspired?

No matter.

In any case, the effects of my gold-tipped arrow piercing the heart are well understood by this point in the narrative. The heart pounds, the ears ring, the scent of roses fills the air. Got it? Tim Pickett is living proof of all that. Obviously, the upshot of the penetration is an irrepressible, overwhelming feeling of need for contact with the person contemplated.

As far as being an archer goes, my closest rivals over time were Artemis and Apollo. Such a straight shooter is Apollo when compared to the likes of Dionysos although he is somewhat bent as is said of mortals who deviate from what many consider the norm. As mentioned, I did eventually get one over on him. Revenge for being slighted. Now, only the feeble-minded will want to hear a cartoonish thud-a-dud-a-dud— the sound effects of the creative geniuses over at Disney designed to entertain children. Not a chance with my arrows, be they gold-tipped or lead. Silent they are and effective.

To the point. Regard Candace expressing admiration for Drake Cantlay as they stand with the group ready to exit Leerdam. Yes, she is obviously due. Her inclinations are anything but furtive, so in a sense this one will be easier for me, the rationale for my arrow pretty much self-evident. No surprise, then, about what happens next after the action I take to reanimate the scene. I leave the details, dear reader, to your imagination. Be certain of these two factors, however: one, I rarely misinterpret the obvious, in fact, I enhance it considerably; and two, my arrow never misses its mark.

The group exits Leerdam along Kerkstraat, gaining access to paths along the Linge that lead in time to paths into Gorinchem, a charming town on the river Waal where the *Amoretto Algea* is docked. Tim Pickett is again given to kinetic jerkiness as he pedals along madly in love, his chosen position in line defined by brother Tom in a burst of laughter as "the Isla Troyes slipstream."

Meanwhile, the gold-tipped arrow lodged in Candace's heart has Drake Cantlay's name written all over it. Her riding becomes undisciplined, especially where the cycle paths curve or require right-angle turns. After several attempts to overtake Tim and Isla cruising along ahead of her, she eventually slides into the line ahead of Drake in an apparent all-out attempt to have him take more direct notice of her. She is, after all, drop dead gorgeous. Nonetheless, getting noticed is not easy when riding a bike in a single file led by a guide determined to set and keep a pace arranged intentionally to keep to a schedule. Obvious to the observer such as you, dear reader, that the benign stupefaction I have inflicted upon Candice is causing her more than a little discomfort as she pedals her ass off in rigorous pursuit of what's behind her. An additional impediment to her desire for successful interface is the rattling bang, bang, bang emanating from the crank case on the bike Drake so readily volunteered to see back to the barge. I wish her good luck. No, seriously, I really do.

Having traversed much of Gorinchem to reach the *Amoretto Algea*, the cyclists, who are fussing about in a state if moderate confusion, are required to guide their bikes down a metal gangplank to where Finn Bonger and Dirk van Kesteren are securing them on the cradling platform. The broken bike that Drake has been riding is cursed vociferously and then set aside. Soon Captain Van der Oor, watching the operation from his post on the upper deck, will hoist the cradled bikes aboard. Loading operations run smoothly enough once procedure is understood by all involved.

The clouds of early morning doubt have dissipated, leaving the sky bright and full of promise. So declares Otto to Elsa ahead of him as they maneuver up the access ramp while behind them, proceeding cautiously, the Birtwistle family, Benny waving at Conor St James looking down from above. Following Benny, a greatly distracted Candace stumbles and then trips, nearly tumbling sideways into the canal. Drake offers her a helping hand, which she willingly takes. He puts her right. Unlikely though it might seem, she stumbles again before reaching the deck and he again puts her right. Many guests head directly to their quarters, like Otto and Elsa, while a few others, like Candace and Isla, remain on deck. Appearing there shortly after are Tim and Tom with mugs of Belgian brew. Within twenty minutes of the group's arrival, loading up is complete and the Amoretto Algea pushes off, heading down the Maas, destination Heusden.

"I'm really confused," Candace tells Isla, handing her a bottle of iced tea." I ran into Drake at the bar when I was getting these drinks and try as I might to further ingratiate myself to him, he seemed all too ready to avoid me. Politely, of course, but avoid me. Guess who was sitting there taking it all in?"

"I don't know. That professor guy? Drake's father, Cole? That man is so straight. I finally decided who he reminds me of, John

Lennon but without the hair. The wire rimmed glasses, of course, and—."

"No, not Cole Cantlay, that Ray Rudiger guy with a smirk on his face. Caliban."

"No surprise there, Candy."

"Yeah, no surprise there."

"But odd, Drake's lack of response. He was keen to help you before."

"Didn't want me to slip on the ramp and fall."

"Or fall for him?"

"Usually there are signs, you know. I mean if a guy is interested."

"Yeah, but you don't need someone like Tim Pickett shuffling around you idiotically. Look at him over there, the pair of them like conspirators planning an assassination or something sinister."

"I reckon not. I'm just a mess, Isla. Can't figure things out about why I feel this way."

River traffic diverts their attention momentarily when a horn blast shakes the air. A long tanker passes on the left, creating a slight roll in the forward motion of the *Amoretto Algea*.

"You will," Isla says, when Candace looks back to her.

"I will what?"

"Figure it out. Get on top of it."

"Like, I just don't know what came over me back there in that town. Up until a certain point Drake's just an ordinary guy sitting at our table or riding along like the rest of us. Then wham, I get this crushing sensation all over as I watch him dealing with the bike noise."

"From a shaking of the head to a complete body shiver. That's what it looked like."

"That's what it was like, yes, more or less."

"So he's a nice guy that you'd like to get to know more."

"That's too tame. Stomach gets in a knot when I start fantasizing. It's like an emotional pain. I really like the guy— no, it's way stronger than that, more like a magnetic pull towards him. But I just can't get any positive reaction from him other than his courteous helpfulness."

"Nothing? No intuition coming out of it about trysts or secret rendezvous by moonlight?"

"Like, you mean really hook up with him?"

"Precisely. Passionate clutches and everything that follows."

"Know what? We've got four more days on the *Amoretto Algea*. Anything's possible."

"Google him, why don't you?"

"That might destroy the agonizingly beautiful illusion. Wouldn't want that."

"Right. What's a cruise about if not romance?"

"Oh, look at the length of that barge coming at us," Candace says, looking up the river. "Like something out of a European thriller where the protagonist jumps onboard from a bridge, hurts his leg, but eventually gets around to rescuing the girl."

Progress down the Maas slows when the *Amoretto Algea* enters the Wilhelminasluis lock. Vibrations now take on a different rhythm, slower, less insistent than when the diesel engine is fully engaged. Once through the lock, speed on the barge resumes, ensuring anyone curious enough to ask captain or crew about arrival time, that tying up in Heusden will be as scheduled. No fear of arriving late. Not with this captain and this crew. Windmills upon entering Heusden, as one observer said on a previous excursion I oversaw a few years ago, are like welcoming arms waving boaters into a safe haven.

Ray Rudiger exits the lounge and takes himself to the upper deck, leaving Ruth in the company of the Cantlays, the father having just arrived and taken the mug his son handed him and gulping down its contents with gusto. The glass placed on the low table remains half-full. Small talk among the three of them about places in Canada called home and occupations there, from which the bike and barge excursion provides escape, gives over to opinions about older European cities, Dutch differences, picturesque cycling routes, and how helpful electric assist bikes can be even on Lowland flats. Individual pedaling style merits comment as does those in the group drawing attention to themselves in one way or another. Ruth observes that romance seems to be budding here and there among the younger generation, which she admits is nice to see. She smiles encouragingly at Drake. Drake quickly consumes what remains in his mug and then excuses himself, saying he needs to take a shower before all the hot water is gone. He deposits his empty mug on the bar with a clack.

"Mr. Cantlay," Ruth begins immediately, "did I say something to offend your son?"

"Please, I told you it's Cole. No need to be unduly formal now that we're getting acquainted."

That said, Cole Cantlay watches his son leave the lounge. Ruth appears to be upset, her brows momentarily locked in a downward position.

"If I did offend," she continues, "I certainly apologize."

"I was told by your husband," Cole says, uncertainty evident, "in one of those quick little conversations, you know, that take place along the way when the cycling pauses, he said you were a counsellor."

"Well, I was. I'm still involved with counselling in a restricted sense. I suppose it depends on the type of counselling you're talking about."

"Be that as it may. As a counsellor, you would be aware of what they call conversion therapy."

"Yes, I know what it is. It's fake science. What it attempts to do is to change sexual identity to what is considered normal by the hetero community. All about gender identification, isn't it? Why do you ask?"

"You seem like a sympathetic, informed person, Ruth, so I'll tell you why I ask. In the interest of saving my son unnecessary embarrassment and stress. You see, this bike and barge adventure is supposed to be a way of putting a series of bad experiences behind us."

A lost, vague look now defines Cole Cantlay's facial expression as he appears to hesitate about revealing what the bad experiences he alluded to were exactly.

"Cole, I don't wish to intrude..."

"No, it's okay. I want to explain a few things that you will find relevant, given what's been troubling Drake since we stopped today in Leerdam."

"Only if you really feel comfortable doing so."

"I do."

"Some vestigial recall can be painful."

"It's okay. Please understand, we are from a very conservative family. My wife is particularly religious. She's very right-wing and so much more in the conservative camp than ever I could be, although I do lean to the right when elections are the order of the day. You could say, as Drake did at one point, she's hard-nosed about accepting scripture as the last word in morality. She insisted, still does, that Drake's inclinations are an abomination."

"Abomination?"

"It's like this, Ruth. Drake is mild-mannered, respectful of others, and helpful in every way. They love him where he works. As he may have told you, he's a nurse-attendant in an Ottawa old age home. He's a decent guy, rides a bike everywhere, and has proven himself to be a great cook. Very creative. The point is my wife heard or read somewhere that women of a certain frame of mind believe they can convert a homosexual man. Just what that frame of mind is I'm still clueless about."

"What you're saying is that Drake's gay."

"Yes, Ruth, that's what I'm saying."

"It's not obvious. Not that it has to be. Not that somebody being gay troubles me."

"He is. And we thought we could do things to change that. It was only arrested development, we believed. His mother said we were helping him to heal the body and the soul to fit with the biblical script. In the beginning, I didn't reject that particular idea at all."

"And now?"

"Now it's different."

"How so?"

"Let me go on. Drake is left leaning. Fine. He's aware of all the triggers used by the snowflake community out there but he doesn't pull any. He's not a member of any victimization league. He isn't a social reformer in any way. He's not effeminate, he's not flamboyant, he's just gay."

"So, Cole, you and your wife encouraged him to subject himself to something operatives of a twenty-first century Spanish Inquisition might be ecstatic about using to bring about conformity. Orthodoxy at all costs."

"Pretty much. Started in his late teens. Lasted a few years."

"I repeat, conversion therapy is nothing but pseudo-science."

"You're absolutely right, Ruth. Methods employed to effect change are, well, you'd know what they are."

"Yes, castration using chemicals and drugs, psychoanalysis, shock therapy. It's an extensive list. All supportive of confirmation bias. How did Drake respond?"

"Poorly, very poorly. In due course, I came to realize how demeaning conversion therapy was for him. The shame it aroused in him, feeling insulted as an individual, being treated like a deviant, a pervert. And the regret he had knowing that he could not please his mother and living with the knowledge that he would not, could not change."

"You obviously have had some in-depth conversations with Drake."

"They've been on-going, the result being that I am the one who has changed."

"Which is good, isn't it?"

At this point, Cole Cantlay stares off as though the object of his regard is not out there but, ironically, right on his eyeballs themselves and he is not quite seeing clearly or able to grasp mentally what he wants to say.

"'You have a moby dick, don't you know?' One of his analysts reportedly said this to Drake. I supposed it was said tongue-in-cheek as an incentive for Drake to use his manhood for purposes deemed natural and traditional and morally correct, meaning with a woman and a woman only. Hearing statements like that moved Drake to tears. It only added to the shame he felt about not getting it straight, straight according to dictates understood as absolute in our church."

"No doubt, in his worldview that mind-bender of an analyst conceived of woman as an ocean of exotic if not esoteric fulfilment. Idiot. Homosexuality is not a disease that can be remedied with inhuman treatment; in the spectrum of human sexual behaviour it's natural, like drinking when thirsty, eating when hungry, sleeping when tired."

"Through the painful process we subjected our son to, I gradually came to understand that homosexuality is a normal variation of human sexuality in general and is not based on moral choice but on natural inclination."

"Nor is it a disorder of the soul punishable for all eternity with hellfire. In my opinion, your son was subjected to abuse, physical and mental. Conversion therapy is fraudulent, and will be universally condemned as illegal.”

“I certainly appreciate all you’ve just said. I’m sure Drake would be of the same mind.”

“That’s a relief, Cole, believe me. And you seem very accepting of your son as he presents himself to the world.’

“It was hard for me deciding on a course of action that would ultimately break the family up. I mean opposing my wife. She walked out the door less than a year ago, which is very strange for someone so convinced of the sacredness of marriage, that is, marriage between man and woman. She checked out when it became obvious that the conversion therapy she favoured proved ineffective and all she could do to save face was condemn ‘our special boy’ as a sinner.”

“Odd nomenclature, I mean, odd way of mother referring to a son she’s rejected because of his sexual orientation.”

“She can’t bring herself to say gay unless happy-go-lucky or mirthful is what she is trying to describe. It’s laughable.”

“An apotropaic euphemism. Ward off the bad vibes kind of thing.”

“Ironically, my rather straitlaced sister now working in Edinburgh is very accepting of Drake. We’ll be visiting her after this excursion ends. As to what’s happening here on the Amoretto Algea, Drake's more interested in talking to Chef Simon Oliver about recipes or to Finn Bonger about the features of electric assist bikes than to that charming young woman from our table who seems to be leaning a little into his private space."

"I've noticed. Candace Troyes."

"Nonetheless, Drake can be very graceful, very sociable, and very attentive to the needs of others. He backs away from hurting anyone's feelings. He'll appreciate your knowing what's what."

"I'll see what I can do."

The *Amoretto Algea* ties up along the appropriate quay in Heusden at the appropriate time, five P.M. Three windmills stand like trademark signposts welcoming visitors to the city. Marinas grace the harbour and inland waterways with big and small yachts. Historic Heusden is renowned for being a walled city.

Finn Bonger in his pre-dinner announcement mentions what visitors might like to see should they wander into Heusden and he encourages all guests to do so. There are three gates, one of which those heading in will use. It stands immediately above the quay. The city boasts a variety of architecture styles, although much from earlier times was modernized after the war. Its history goes back centuries; fortified, it once served as a garrison town. In and around the central square there are cafés, restaurants, art galleries. Vismarkt is very interesting as is the visitor centre with its informative displays.

By this point in the narrative, dear reader, you have insight into the guests at each of the five tables and what their interests are. Effecting another myriorama for this meal in particular strikes me as a bit superfluous. As for the split screen and its numerous possibilities, I'll reserve it for later when different contexts demand close-ups that transcend mere talking heads. Sufficient for me to say that the meal presently served is both delicious and consumed with delight. However, one note is warranted here: Candace and Isla do not appear until just before the bowls for soup of the day are being removed, Candace wearing a revealing dress, her intention, apparently, to set but one heart aflutter. Drake, on the other hand, looks appeased. Over at table one, Ray Rudiger mentions he can't help noticing how seductive Candace appears in her lovely outfit.

A number of groups set out after dinner to explore Heusden. It behoves me therefore to limit my hovering, eavesdropping, and reporting. I'm quick but I'm no match for Hermes, and I've already explained to you, dear reader, that I am no more omnipresent than I am omniscient. I'm just more or less present in one place at one time and more or less cognizant that four is the sum of two plus two. Sadly, it is not within my powers of intrusion to be aware of all the *Amoretto Algea* guests once they leave the dining area, and this lack I do regret as much as I am capable of regret at all. I have amends to make, but they can wait till morning after I've retired to a state of quiescence.

Among the guests remaining onboard is Ruth Rudiger. Ray has attached himself to Dexter and Bonnie Pickett who set out to find a brewery. Not an alignment of personalities I might have imagined, Ray Rudiger and Dexter Pickett, given the antipathy between the two already evident. And then there's Bonnie Pickett's sharp tongue. Ahead of them a good ten minutes are Tim and Tom. Remaining in the lounge with Elsa Müller and Angela Jones is Lizzy Birtwistle who expresses delight in knowing that Elsa runs her own flower shop in Dusseldorf and that Angela has a granddaughter with special needs. I leave them there to enjoy each other's company.

Otto Müller hustles to catch up with JJ and Professor Wolfgang as they make their way towards the arched gateway and on into town. I cannot establish Mick Mallory's whereabouts, nor those of Conor St James who has a habit of quickly disappearing. The Cantlays could be anywhere, just not within my reach at the moment.

On the upper deck Candace and Isla sit in lounge chairs sipping drinks and conversing.

"Are you aware of a kind of fluttering up here? Like a hummingbird hovering?"

"No, nothing special. A slight breeze, maybe. As I was saying before, you can only slice and dice your feelings so far before you give up trying to figure him out."

"He's just so polite while being just so not interested."

"Candy, it's not like you haven't tried. There's been no response that I can see to your nudge-nudge and wink-wink routines, subtle though they have been. Maybe too subtle or not subtle enough."

"Say no more," Candace says. Rising abruptly from her chair, she throws up her hands dramatically and then strikes a pose that expresses absolute discontent. After smoothing down her evening dress, she then says with emphasis, "I don't expect him to break into a TikTok inspired jig when I appear in the same room with him, or launch himself into a break dance to impress me with his agility. It's just, it's just. I don't know…"

"Mind if I join you?" Ruth asks, making her way gradually towards them. "I think I know. I mean I think I know the answer you're seeking. You're wondering about Drake Cantlay's indifference."

"The answer to that would be helpful," Isla says. "Very helpful."

"Yes, please, join us," Candace says with considerable conviction.

Ruth Rudiger is definitely what mortals call a people person. Though not as well versed in the subtle doings of the Olympians as I am— how could she be?— I admit her scientific knowledge surpasses mine. It is well within her means to explain the effects of a launched love dart as considerably more than the cliché-strained idea of getting knocked for a loop. Much like you, dear reader, I need not listen in any further to grasp the significance of what Ruth is about to reveal to Candace and Isla about Drake Cantlay. I'll hover here no longer. Allow me to drift away.

I catch up with Benny Birtwistle and his father Nigel making their way down the cobbled street leading to the visitor centre. Here they voice mild expletives about how perfect in scale the model of the city fortifications is. Nigel describes the work as a fantastic diorama.

"Brilliant, innit, Benny?"

"Brilliant, innit? Innit?"

I leave them there to their many expressions of wonder, and flutter onwards. My next sighting involves Tim and Tom Pickett who have repaired to a bar overlooking one of the Heusden marinas down below the town square. They occupy a quiet corner, pints of local brew on the table before them.

The time has arrived, dear reader, to take a closer look at the twins as would-be exemplars of the enhanced male physique.

In fact, the time for such an evaluation is long overdue.

Add a little more beefcake to Michelangelo's David and you have what Praxiteles might have carved out of his block of marble and called Tim Pickett. Or Tom Pickett. Take your pick, dear reader, as the twins are like bookends. Describe one as you would the other. Both are well over six foot with muscular builds. They are trim and in shape. Calling them ruggedly handsome is to do them a disservice. Possessing dark eyes, chiseled cheekbones, and copious, curly fair hair does not necessarily make them stereotypical poster boys for male comeliness, but a critical mind might be satisfied in seeing them in that light. Had the occasion presented itself, they might have signed on to supporting roles in Alexander, a recent film depicting the life and accomplishments of Alexander the Great, or 300, which highlights in a historically significant and vital way the 480 BC Battle of Thermopylae. On the other hand, the critical mind would quite possibly describe them as fitting models for action heroes in the world of cartoon caricature. Their college scholarships might have been the result of intelligent responses, which is difficult to determine based on anything they've articulated thus far on their bike and barge adventure; more likely it was ability on the playing field that netted them their academic rewards.

"Okay, I haven't nailed it," Tim says. "Maybe she's involved me in some kind of game theory."

"That would be taking unfair advantage of you, bro. Be more forward with her, that's what I say."

"So, is this some kind of intervention?"

"Just trying to help, bro."

"Which I appreciate."

"It's not something you can talk about with Ma or even the old man. You know what he's like. 'Don't you be tomcatting around drawing a lot of attention my way.' Baiting that aggressive little loudmouth, that's attention grabbing. Anyway, the old man's got a few ideas of his own. It's always hush hush with him. Now it's a big mystery."

"What's a big mystery?" Tim asks.

"What happened to you. This Isla Troyes thing you're on about."

"Yeah, well, you never know with Pop. Always has something up his sleeve."

"Got that right, bro."

"The point is, this whole Isla Troyes thing, as you call it," Tim says, drawing in his lower lip, "is driving me crazy."

"I'm surprised you haven't charmed her already. Want me to talk to her for you?"

"That would only add to the confusion."

"Who's the one confused? You or her?"

"Listen, man, it's like I got a fever, okay. I get all emotional when I see her. Sweaty palms. Cycling gloves get wet and go stiff. Shit like that. It ain't normal."

"Not that you expect to hear violin music when you see her or when you get a whiff of her presence. Am I right?"

"Yeah. I just get tongue-tied. I'm all x's and o's and can't come up with a good offense play to run. Game plan's all screwy."

"Your mojo's definitely gone," Tom proposes, his voice heavy with brotherly understanding. "Look, just have another drink."

"Disappeared completely. Never happened before." Tim takes another drink, a long one, his swallowing echoing his declared thirst for understanding. "But it's not like she's giving me the cold shoulder exactly. She just looks bewildered in a curious sort of way when I approach her."

"She seems pretty smart though."

"Probably is. I didn't research her on Facebook or anything. We didn't hook up on some online dating service like Odyssey Romance or Mix and Match."

"No, I can't see you doing that."

"This desire thing for that girl just happened suddenly, out of the blue, like I already explained to you. Remember the words in that song Granny Larson used to sing when we were little?"

"Who?"

"Ma's ma, Granny Larson, when she thought we couldn't hear."

"Yeah, Granny Larson. What words?"

"How you've touched her perfect body with your brain."

"I don't remember any words like that. But you want more than that, don't you? I mean..."

"That's right, man. To have her feel my perfect body and whatever."

"No sweat, bro. We've got four more days ahead of us on this crazy adventure. Anything's possible."

When Tim gets way ahead of himself boasting about his sexual exploits, I decide I've heard enough. I fly off, more amused than annoyed with human self-adulation, the details of which I've heard over and over again for centuries. Back on the Amoretto Algea, I pick up on a conversation well underway involving Candace, Isla, Mick Mallory and Professor Wolfgang.

"That trip started out like this one," Isla says, "but it turned out rather tragically."

"Yeah," Candace joins in, "a big family affair, you know, on the Iphigenia, going from Amsterdam to Bruges. By the time we reached Bruges there were two murders to deal with."

"Two murders?" Mick says, expressing both disbelief and concern as he looks to Candace, then to Isla and then back to Candace.

"I read of this in our national newspaper," the professor says.

"My mother and my stepfather," Isla states rather matter-of-factly. "First him and then her. I've begun composing a long narrative poem describing events."

"I understand how devastating it can be to lose somebody you love dearly," Mick says, reaching out and touching Isla's arm. "Even more difficult when it's times two. And family, on holiday, with all the positive, uplifting events a family get-together entails."

"It was definitely a family affair for us but it wasn't all that uplifting, I assure you, with everybody on board being questioned by Belgian authorities. And suspicious glances cast at all of us in our particular circle because of how my older sister Alexsis had been proving herself to be a real pain in the ass when it came to dealing with our mother and stepfather. We were always the centre of everyone's attention on the boat and on the trails.'

"So, family dynamics came into play, did it?" Mick asks, shaking his head.

"Alexsis believed the three of us, and that includes my brother, were deceived from way back about what happened to our real father. She loved to say we were manipulated, were the victims of gaslighting. Resentment motivated her every action, her every utterance. Without getting into details— there are too many and too upsetting to recall— I'll just say that there was a scrim of lies and obfuscation we kids had to fight our way through during the growing up years. The boat and bike thing on the Iphigenia last year brought it all to a head. But two murders in the family, that was a bit hard to deal with."

"Were those responsible brought to justice?" Professor Wolfgang asks.

"Exactly," Mick says most emphatically.

"A suspect was arrested, but I have not followed up on what transpired."

"That trip had so much promise for me and my cousins," Candace explains, "but, you know, it turned out so bad. Isla and I decided to see if a new excursion here in the Netherlands could undo some of the negativity that still lingers on about what happened. We share the hope that this adventure will be more exciting for the two of us. So far, so good."

"You've certainly attracted attention on this adventure," Mick says, "Both of you, but a different kind of attention."

"Yes, in some ways," Candace says and smiles. "But also not so different from what it was like for the two of us, I mean, like when we weren't embroiled in family arguments."

"Oh, I know what you mean," Isla picks up, "that obnoxious guy who was hitting on us right from the start. He thought that because we didn't have boyfriends with us or fiancées or whatever, we were vulnerable, that somehow we'd be receptive to his sexual advances."

"Isla has this way of appearing flirtatious when she is really anything but, you know, that kind of unadorned innocent look. But you're quick-witted, aren't you?"

"Candace, let's not—"

"Know what she did to put an end to all the uninvited come-ons? She weaponized her Philip Larkin Collected Poems and totally discombobulated the scumbag. He hadn't a clue what she was talking about. We had a good laugh at his expense when he left."

"Think the same approach would work with Ray Rudiger?"

"Why not?" Isla responds quickly. "You weren't exactly basking in the glow of his ravenous admiration, were you?"

"That's rather expressive, Isla. You see how he plopped down at our table at breakfast and took over Drake Cantlay's place?"

"Very presumptuous," the professor notes.

"I didn't want to say too much about her husband when Ruth was here talking with us."

"Ruth has a sanguine nature," Mick Mallory says. "Yeah, I believe that to be the case. I see her as projecting not so much world weariness but a knowledge of how the world works in its intimate and difficult corners."

"Gets along with everybody," Isla says and then allowing herself a little grimace adds, "even with her husband."

"Fortunately," Candace adds, "Finn's a good negotiator."

"Finn seems to be popular with most of the guests," Mick Mallory adds. "Well organized. Got things down to a fine art as far as the cycling in single file goes and all the rest of it. The twins are doing their part as well."

"An interesting couple of guys, but puzzling," Isla says with an affirmative nod of her head. "I mean, what can upstage a round of cheese. It's delicious, by the way."

Professor Wolfgang: "Those boys, they thrive on competition. There are many kinds of cheese, *ja*."

Day Four
mania from the gods

Heusden to Cuijk:

Before we delve into the doings of day four on the *Amoretto Algea*, permit me to expound on matters relating to what transpired among the guests as a result of my precipitous action. I refer here specifically to Candace Troyes vis á vis Drake Cantlay. My effectiveness as a proponent of passionate adventure, I must confess in retrospect, was lacking. Not an absolute failure, just a miscalculation, the upside of which proved to be an educational opportunity, a point of reference, if you will, in understanding human sexuality. In due course I'll rectify matters. In the meantime, let me educate you, my studious reader, with some facts as to my time-honoured successes. Consult the historical texts, regard the ubiquitous artistic evidence, do basic research and you will come to understand that my accomplishments in masterful matchmaking are without equal. Not only that, they are also widely celebrated.

But first, my accoutrements and my approach. In the quiver are my barbed, gold-tipped arrows that incite in the targeted heart a multi-faceted, overpowering urge for passionate embrace; the name of the potential beloved need not be inscribed on the shaft to be effective, but often it is when I have been more meticulous in preparing for the shoot. The fletchings run straight as a die and the feathers could be described as satiny. Also available in my quiver are blunted, lead-tipped arrows. These can infuse repulsion in the target's heart but not necessarily in the absolute sense; they can bring on a low-level but effective resistance to the advances of love no matter the source. I prefer these negative-effect darts to be silver tipped. My supply of them, all darts, as a matter of fact, depends on how busy Hephaestus is. Regardless of what they are called, they have the potential to end love. The stronger the draw on the bow, the deeper the penetration and the more dire the effects.

As stated previously, I am not omniscient: I have only what can be defined as qualified knowledge of the human individuals with whom I deal. Additionally, immediate presence is of the essence as far as we gods and goddesses are concerned. For the most part, we have to be there, be right on the spot to enact our powers, Zeus and his thunderbolts notwithstanding. If you doubt my word here, scrupulous readers, consult

Ovid who was very insightful in matters pertaining to my dealings with mortals. And so, a sampling of my greatest triumphs in all spheres.

Orpheus and Eurydice? Echo and Narcissus? Narcissus and himself? Helen of Troy and Paris? Antony and Cleopatra? All my doing, let alone how randy peers from Olympus and elsewhere in the ancient world benefited from my handy work. Who has not heard of these great love affairs? Classic they are in the truest sense of the word. My arrows also saw to the bond between Dante and Beatrice, Abelard and Heloise, Napoleon and Josephine, Nelson and Lady Hamilton, and the Brownings, husband and wife. In terms of poetic inspiration and creativity, who has not been moved by the fates of Lancelot and Guinevere, Romeo and Juliet, Tristan and Isolde? Epic romances. My doing, absolutely. Furthermore, no erudite reader of literature can fail to see how my understanding of human nature was exploited by renowned dramatists and novelists in very ingenious ways. I inspired Shakespeare in *The Tempest* to have Caliban fall in love with Prospero's daughter. I inspired Emily Bronte in her writing of *Wuthering Heights* to have Heathcliff go ape over Catherine Henshaw. The list of similar works is endless, a great many, if it so please you, my savvy reader, erotically suggestive and provocative in the extreme. I leave Biblical allusions to those of you who delve into the good book, as you call it, and suggest you draw what conclusion you can feel comfortable in accepting. Then there are the great romantics that have demonstrated in their lives what I unquestionably represent: for example, Sappho, Casanova, Byron. And recall, informed reader, all those lovers in recent times who find themselves hounded by the paparazzi.

A sidebar here. Or if you prefer, a footnote. Either-or but appearing in the text as a short, thematically relevant paragraph. I found fault with Tim Pickett's boasting last night at the marina bar about being the new Don Juan, about how much more erotically uplifting he is when it comes to endowments. Being a physical hunk and knowing it is one thing, being witty about pudendal attachments is another. Tim Pickett is no match for any of the great lovers with whom I've had truck in one way or another. Nor does he have the wit of a Byron from anything I've heard him say. His bragging is very presumptuous, very hubris weighted. The bigger they are, remember, the harder they fall.

Oh, and Pygmalion and Galatea? Was I involved? Of course, I was involved in this romantic tale of entanglement as was, wait for it, Aphrodite. Allow me to provide a modicum of insight as to how the goddess of love and beauty rewards those who venerate her and punishes those who scorn her. The Pygmalion story illustrates both.

The Propoetides, Cypriot women, were contemptuous of Aphrodite. As punishment, she subjected them to live the lives of prostitutes. Pygmalion developed considerable antipathy towards these lowly creatures, these disreputable representatives of the female sex as he convinced himself they were. He chose to live in isolation where he was inspired to create an ivory statue of the female form which projected his own version of beauty. So lovely was his creation that he fell in love with it. Whose inspiration was that? Mine, naturally. Aphrodite had no choice but to approve. As a reward for his loyalty and his devotion, she answered Pygmalion's prayers and brought the statue to life which enabled love to flourish. He called her Galatea. As for the Propoetides, Aphrodite allowed them to lose all sense of shame; so hardened in their ways, even to the point of being unable to blush, they turned to stone. Read all about it. Your reward, dear reader, will be a superb lesson in the workings of Nemesis and a deeper understanding of paraphilia, specifically agalmatophilia, a theme cleverly presented in drama and cinematic forms of the modern era. In touching on the Pygmalion and Galatea tale, be it known here that I make no claim to the inspiration that produced the well-received Barbie movie.

The most challenging task I faced was when Aphrodite sent me to shoot an arrow at

Hades while he viewed Persephone: control of Hades' heart was Aphrodite's rationale although she masked that intention when she commissioned me.

Let me not at this juncture hold back on itemizing some of the other ways my influence in the creative process has been established, be it in representational art or in sculpture. Consider Titian's nudes from Ovid's *Metamorphosis*: six paintings delivered to Philip II of Spain in the sixteenth century mirroring Zeus' golden shower of rain. I was very active over a lengthy period of time in the production of these masterpieces. In two of his famous works, "Eros and Psyche" and "The Kiss," Gustav Klimt got it right, perfectly right. On the other hand, Baroque sculptor Antonio Canova, who produced beautiful statues, misnamed a piece now in the Louvre that specifically references me, Eros: "Psyche Revived by Cupid's Kiss." Damn it all, I cried when first discovering this misnomer. Nonetheless, the work stands as a tragic reminder of my own heart's proclivity, a tragic turn of events I'm indisposed at the moment to recall in detail. Consider as well, dear reader, Rodin's "The Kiss" which is so representative of what my influence can inspire. As to Bernini's fleshy stonework (that Isla referenced when in the Rijksmuseum) evident in "The Ecstasy of Saint Teresa," that too is from much of my time hovering about his hammer and chisel.

Then there's the Farnese Eros in the Archaeological Museum of Naples, a Roman copy in marble of one by Praxiteles. It does me justice— my perfect form, my inherent charm, my irresistibility, and my absolute— I could go on. Sufficient to say it is a favourite, which supports the notion that when you're totally self-possessed, as I am, there's little need for pompous self-promotion.

Criticism? Of course I've been subject to criticism both from immortals and mortals alike, hearing negative comments like Eros is full of himself, Eros is unrestrained in singing his own praises, Eros boasts like an Olympian discus thrower, Eros congratulates himself at every turn. I make no apologies, dear reader, I make no apologies whatsoever. I simply provide those who are tuned in to my words with an updated CV and such, it can be argued, is definitely the case here. Besides, how can the god of love not express self-love? Not doing so would prove to be not only inconsistent but also illogical, a contradiction in discourse to be avoided by all means possible.

Now, Candace Troyes vis á vis Drake Cantlay. Love can lead the unsuspecting on a wild goose chase. Both Aphrodite and I are partial to the goose. A goose chase, however, was not my intention in arranging an intimate connection between these young people. To be clear, I did not inscribe Drake's name on the arrow that penetrated Candace's heart and caused her so much confusion. A minor point, really.

Matched with that of the Pickett twins, so eye-catching and fetching, Drake's rainbow riding gear does not stand out as significantly connotative. Just an oversight on my part because I am definitely not colour-blind; a simple misreading of certain obvious details due to my focusing on the way Candace returned Drake's polite smile. She just looked interested. What also led in part, a significant part, to my miscalculations was the fact I heard Cole Cantlay say to his son when leaving the dining area after the first evening meal, "The young women at our table are very attractive, the kind your mother probably had in mind to bring you around, to get you to go along with her plans."

In retrospect, dear reader, a father's innocent enough remark, passed no doubt in hindsight with humour if not ironic intent.

"Yes," Drake replied, "absolutely lovely. That Candace is a knockout, alright."

Not exactly a libido-wrought reply on Drake's part but sufficient to indicate budding interest. And later, when nosing about the Cantlays' berth, I discovered no expletives of wonder, desire, or rejection fingered on portal windows or steamy shower room mirrors. Please understand, dear reader, that my relating such details does not equate to a facile rationale for actions taken. Stated facts like these support a reasoned explanation about the circumstances surrounding my decision to let fly the gold-tipped arrow at Candace. They do not underpin anything like a sketchy excuse for having screwed up. There is a world of difference between explanation and excuse. I never stoop to sloppy self-justification. Doing that is ungodly.

It seems relevant at this point in my narrative to consider how exaltation of the divine gets practised in the rituals of ordinary mortals. Just to set the record straight, the historical record in particular: like Aphrodite, I too had my altars for veneration, that is to say, in the good old days. How could the god of love not be exalted in ceremonies of significant social and religious importance? Most notable was in the Academy in Athens and in the gymnasium in Aulis at a time when love of male beauty reached a par with that of women. Consider the statuary emerging from that time period. In ample evidence, the pairing as lovers between older men and youths in what can be defined in contemporary language as an educational coming of age. The practice was more than considered acceptable in the days of my ascendance; in fact, it was prescribed for male members in the upper echelons of sophisticated society in the era to which I allude.

As source of love in all its forms and manifestations from time immemorial I, Eros, have served in all realms, high and low, as champion of homosexuality. How could it be otherwise? Sapho had her acolytes and devotees on the island of Lesvos. Needless to say, I inspired her poetry. I was extolled as animating spirit and force for the Sacred Band Of Thebes, paired lovers transcending the tush push of brotherly affectation as they advanced as a couple into mortal combat. Sadly, I was engaged elsewhere when they were defeated in battle. As to the concerns of transgender transformation, I'll deal with the issue once the question of pronoun identification is settled, settled at least in English.

To round out the issue of romantic cross purposes, I shall at the appropriate time pull a lead-tipped arrow out of my quiver and fire it lightly at Candace whereby she will whimper slightly then right herself. She will not remain impervious to love or its expression indefinitely, but only for this misdirected version of those amorous, compulsive rushes she was afflicted with and for which I accept total responsibility.

Though self-recrimination is unbecoming and ungodly in an immortal such as I, relevant here is my alluding to Leda and the swan and the law of unintended consequences. The Trojan War, anyone? A toxophilite miscalculation according to my windy and whimsical friend

Aeolus, who is given as much to humorous jibes as he is to mercurial misdirection. He said I was guilty of firing a dart DUI, deployed under the influence, as he described it. I suppose he had a point. Admittedly, I was enduring a species of divine hangover. Too much ambrosia, too much bee bread and nectar. The fragrant juices confer longevity— immortality, if you will— on those who consume them. I'm okay with that. Always have been, right from back there when time was pregnant with potential. And true, ichor flows in my veins. The point is, that I invited myself to a bacchanal where nymphs and satyrs cavorted. Maenads entertained us with a frantic and ghastly but thoroughly enjoyable dance. All this being what contemporary cultural pundits borrowed from our ethos and termed "downtime with Dionysus." I was also somewhat vexed after an impatient Pan libeled me, proclaiming loudly that I had no musical talent whatsoever. Untrue. I have good pipes, capable of a superior lyrical expression, both soothing and sympathetic. It is universally accepted that I am an accomplished flautist. Another instance where truth was sacrificed to prejudiced perception.

Let me also inform you here, dear reader, about how I wreaked my revenge on Apollo who also saw fit to insult me, nay, not just insult, belittle me. He put me down, claiming that his was a bigger bow than mine. Sweet it is to fire a love dart at an opponent and have him suffer the consequences in total ignorance of what's up. His heart thus penetrated, Apollo attempted to romance the beautiful naiad Daphne who was absolutely repulsed by his advances because into her heart I'd launched a lead-tipped arrow, ensuring she would avoid all romantic overtures, be they godly in their origin or not. Indeed, the bigger they are, the harder they fall, and Apollo came down from on high unhinged in a state of miserable rejection. And ask yourself, dear reader, this timely question: "Was it Josephine's sexy eau de parfum or my gold-tipped arrow that induced an enraptured Napoleon to embrace disaster and defeat?"

So now, early morning in the lounge of the *Amoretto Algea*. Having wished Ruth Rudiger a good morning, Mick Malory sits with his first coffee, composing another email to his daughter. He writes of the cycling and what it demands of him despite the electric assist bike he rides; he writes of the friendly and helpful crew and of fellow guests like Professor Albrecht who is proving to be a willing and sympathetic listener. Otto Müller, the BMW guy, is extremely energetic. He and his wife Elsa bike a great deal and are keen to share their knowledge of cycling venues in Germany, like along the Rhine River, for instance, and in the Grafenberg Forest in Dusseldorf where they live. As to others among the guests, Conor St

James from table two has an aura of secrecy about him that young Benny Birtwistle seems able to demystify with his special kind of good cheer. The Jones couple from Vancouver are very nice people, sophisticated but ordinary at the same time. Dexter Pickett, father of the twins, is guarded and plays it close to the vest. Another mystery. There is general amusement in watching budding romances unfold onboard and along the Lowland byways.

Send.

Ruth Rudiger with book and coffee in the same seat she had on previous mornings greets Professor Albrecht as he approaches. Behind the professor with a second cup of coffee in hand, Mick sidles over to join the professor, sloshing, sipping, and then swallowing hastily. Pardon the alliteration, dear reader, but that is exactly how it transpires. If I take no offense, then I see no reason why you should.

"As I was getting around to explaining yesterday before emotion got the better of me," Mick says, seating himself, "it was as though some moral imperative was guiding my hand, which seemed like a positive thing at that time of my ordeal. On the other hand, I'd made of my misery a kind of ecstasy that lifted me periodically beyond the pain of loss. Not entirely, though."

"Yes, yes," Professor Albrecht agrees, "you wanted justice. Of course, this is imperative, to get justice."

"It was like this, Wolfgang. I wanted justice, yes, but I wanted more than that, I wanted revenge."

"Revenge is a different kind of justice. *Lex talionis*, retaliation, yes?"

"True enough, measure for measure," Mick says, angling his head. "But some perspective is needed here." He allows the darting, light-reflecting shapes on the ceiling to distract him for a moment, then he lowers his head and smiles.

"From the water," Professor Albrecht notes, "these bouncing spots."

Mick nods agreement and continues. "To deal with the sickness in my soul, closure was suggested as the remedy. Closure. I got it from all sides. By closure, I argued, what others meant was something aesthetic, something reflective of a beautiful life lived, whereas I firmly believed that in spite of that life, Delores' death was ugly and any closure for me had to be moral."

"I understand your reasoning," the professor quickly assures Mick. "A fine distinction, but one you needed to make, yes?"

"Yes. Regardless of the time that had passed since that unhappy day, I was still grieving. Precisely that, a moral closure to the story of her life."

"What did that require, a moral closure for your wife's life?"

"That's it. I didn't know exactly. Some kind of retribution on Flower's part? Like you mentioned, *Lex talionis*. The law of retaliation. An eye for an eye. It continued to get confusing for me. The more confusing it got, the more I wanted revenge."

"This is puzzling for me also, Mick."

"Perfectly understandable why you say that. My analyst in the second go-round of counselling, Doctor Sophia, suggested cognitive reframing as a means to resolving things. So intense was the suffering the loss of my wife caused me. Thus, psychotherapy 2.0, as my daughter termed it with a touch of irony."

"This was good?"

"Eventually. In the beginning it amounted to intensified raging against Flower. I won't go into all the details of this monster's life but I could write a book about his malfeasance. You see, I hated this so-called self-made man with a passion. As I told you already, I wanted to see him suffer in all ways possible, suffer the way he caused me to suffer."

"Yes, I remember you saying this. The very words."

"You see, I abhorred the bastard to the extent that all the words in the lexicon for hatred loaded into a single utterance failed to express the intensity of the animus that motivated my need for revenge. But I didn't want to see him dead even though I bought myself a gun and worked out certain dire scenarios."

"A gun? To shoot him?"

"A semi-automatic Glock. Crazy, right?"

"This is like desperation, Mick. Your analyst must have..."

"Yes, my analyst must have questioned my sanity. She queried me on my intentions. I had no intention of really using it on the culprit. In time, discussions with Doctor Sophia brought it all back again to my wanting to see Flower suffer. I'd come up with outrageous suggestions. If acted upon, they would have amounted to torture. I was getting perverse."

"How did this..."

"How did this make me feel? Just what my analyst asked me. Awful, it made me feel awful, despicable, to want to see another human being be subjected to such horrible tortures. How could I be more vile in my imaginings than Flower in his infamy? I have to tell you, Wolfgang, these perverse impulses were irrepressible."

"A very moving story, Mick, the pain of loss and how it can affect a man's peace of mind."

"So true. It was absolutely soul destroying to have lost my beloved Delores."

"And so, you are here now on this boat telling me of these tragic events."

"Thanks to Doctor Sophia's cognitive reframing. But enough, Wolfgang, let's enjoy our coffee."

Dear reader, compassion urges me to state the following: had Hera, goddess of marriage, been capable of shedding tears for humans, hearing of Mick Mallory's misfortune might have been such an occasion where she could not hold back. On the other hand, Hera would be at odds with Eris, if not totally mocked by her. Remember Eris, mother of entities that plague humans, the personification of hate and strife?

Once all the guests are seated at their tables, many already wearing cycling gear, Finn Bonger rings his bell and announces that during breakfast the *Amoretto Algea* will sail from Heusden to Lith and it is here the cycling will begin for the day. Following the Maas River, the route to Cuijk will cover fifty-four kilometres and pass through Ravenstein and Grave. Many sights to see.

Breakfast holds no surprises. Conversations are spirited though sighs of unrequited love still hang in the air above a couple of tables. Preparing lunch bags has become a ritual: cut meats, cheese slices, apples and oranges. The Picketts are the last to leave the dining area and like most of the guests ahead of them, they make for the upper deck, Bonnie leading and Tim bringing up the rear. He takes a long look back into the lounge.

In the lounge Ruth is talking to Candace and Isla. The perceptive observer will likely assume that whatever the subject of the conversation it likely involves a follow-up on the revelation that Drake Cantlay is gay. Such an assumption would be correct.

"I didn't mean to rush away last night," Candace says, "after you explained things, like about Drake. I felt so compromised. So foolish."

"But you did return with Isla shortly after. By then Mick Mallory and Professor Wolfgang were there as well."

"After you retired, Isla and I told them about what happened on our previous excursion in Holland. My babbling on was more or less a distraction from what I was feeling about coming on to Drake. I did feel quite foolish...like after..."

"You're good now I'd like to think," Ruth says.

"Yes. I gave it some thought and talked it over again with Isla. I'm okay knowing what I do. I just can't figure out, *we* can't figure out, what came over me so suddenly. Drake's a good looking guy, has a winning smile, he's polite, helpful. So's Finn Bonger as far as all that goes. And yet I still can't help feeling attracted to Drake. I can't explain it, Ruth. Isla's been helpful but she's got her own situation, you know, Tim Pickett."

"I'm glad you're resolved, Candace," Ruth continues, "as hard as it may still be for you, emotionally I mean. What about you, Isla?"

"Still befuddled," Isla replies. "Tim Pickett's attractive enough, but I just don't know... Like, I try not to hurt the guy's feelings. Tom Pickett's equally attractive. So why Tim?"

"Speaking of Finn," Candace adds, "did you know he's been with Captain Van der Oor on the Amoretto Algea for only a month or so."

"Much like Chef Simon," Ruth explains. "After Maastricht he's off to Paris and a new assignment. Some of these bike and barge tours are operated on an ad hoc basis as far as personnel goes. It's seasonal work."

"You know, when I asked Finn Bonger about the name of the boat," Isla says, "he just shrugged his shoulders, hadn't a clue."

"He's just hired on as a sort of DJ of cycling, really. He does know the countryside well enough and some of the history. In fact, his knowledge of local spots of interest is quite detailed."

"Yeah, like about the windmills in Heusden," Candace says.

"About *Amoretto Algea*," Isla says decidedly, "he wasn't so informed. *Algea* is not in my dictionary. Kept getting algae. I did some online research but didn't get much there either. All I could get for *Amoretto* was a reference to Cupid. You see, I wanted to include the barge, you know, this boat, in a sonnet I started a couple of nights ago."

"More going on than the cycling and the sights, eh? All kinds of material for your poetry."

"Yeah, like what's with Tim Pickett's interest in me and his twin brother's role in it all. And Finn Bonger watching Candace all the time. *Amoretto Algea*, what a name for a converted barge."

Ruth explains: "*Amoretto* comes from the Italian *amore* which comes from the Latin *amor*. Love in English. An *amoretto* is like a representation of Cupid in art; in other words, little love or in the plural *amoretti*, little loves.

"Like in that Rijksmuseum piece we were looking at," Isla says. "Makes sense. We had to distinguish between Eros and Cupid, if I remember right."

"Yes, we did."

"The etymology of the word algea is more interesting," Ruth continues in her explanation. "Ancient Greek concepts come into play here. As far as I can recall from my classical studies, years ago, the Algea are the personification of pain and suffering, spirit-like entities who bring tears of lament and sorrow. Anguish, if you will. They are the offspring of Eris, the goddess of strife."

"Put the two words together and what do you get?" Isla prompts.

"Confusion."

Ruth says, "I would answer that question this way. What you get is a fairly accurate juxtaposition of love's labours and love's losses. Eris versus Eros, the yin yang of classical contrariness."

"Right on," Isla says. "Elizabethan sonneteers were fond of using the concept in a variety of ways."

"Precisely," Ruth says, then adds, "the vicissitudes of love, eh."

"Who knows? By the end of the week I might end up with the start of a sonnet sequence."

"Starting with love at first sight. Tim Pickett and his endless sighing. Now that's a theme to develop, Isla."

"Yeah, love at first sight, or second sight, or hindsight, or sight seemingly unseen as in the case of Drake Cantlay."

Ruth again. "The ancient Greeks called the love at first sight phenomenon "mania from the gods" which I suppose we can embellish upon by calling it an induced hypnotic trance. The cause? The perception of beauty enhanced by desire to possess completely. Would that fit your experience, Candace?"

"Somewhat. Like, Drake's good looking enough, I suppose."

"Handsome enough," Isla comments, "but no Adonis."

"As an agony aunt I've dealt with questions relating to the issue of love at first sight."

"Often?"

"Very often. In scientific terms what happens is this. The brain produces dopamine and serotonin. Chemical reactions actually. They produce a euphoric state. It's like the brain goes on an endorphin high."

"So what you're saying, Ruth, is that it's not the heart that's affected, it's the brain."

"Heart palpitations can result, they're symptomatic, but the source of the sensation is the brain, yes."

"Palpitations, like I had them whenever I spotted him."

"I don't want to get too technical here so I'll just say this: When hormones are released, oxytocin brings on that feeling of being high."

"But why Tim Pickett? I offered him no encouragement at all."

"And why did I entertain such feelings for Drake?"

"Yeah, it's not like Candace used her phone to read the barcode on his arm to get personal info. And as for Tim, I saw no QR code stamped on his forehead to explain his coming on to me."

"Amusing analogies, Isla."

"Isla's always coming up with novel ways of looking at things. She can't help herself. When we were talking about the struggles of love, she starts quoting from Hamlet, "the pangs of despised love" and all that. We mentioned your husband's keenness and...well, you know."

"Yes, I know. Don't worry, dear. Ray hardly fits the role of tragic hero."

"What I said about rejection also applies to what you were going through because of Drake Cantlay."

"Is that really relevant now, Isla? How you do come up with stuff!"

"Again," Ruth intervenes, "let me recall what ancient poets, dramatists, and epic writers like Homer had to say about love and how it plays out in an individual's life. The goddess of love and lust, Aphrodite, also known as Venus, is very important, of course; she belongs in a category all her own."

"Yeah, we get Valentine's Day and the antics of Cupid."

"No disagreement there. But according to the earliest texts, love breaks down into several manifestations, each inspired by a particular god. First, there is Eros, god of love and desire, equally important as Aphrodite, if not more so, because he predates her in a very significant way. History has seen Eros evolve from an idealized version of youthful beauty to little wingy Cupid as in *amoretto* or *amoretti*."

"Eros vs Cupid again," Isla states knowingly.

"Then there is Anteros," Ruth continues, "god of reciprocal love; he complements Eros and punishes those who reject love and he deals with the madness of hormones gravitating around an irresistible image of loveliness. Pothos is the god of passion and longing for one who is absent. Hymenaios is celebrated as the god of marriage. Hedylogos inspires sweet talk. He knows my husband well. There are a few others. The Greek language today has several words for love: eros is one of them as in Eros, the god of love."

"Eros is blindfolded, right? If he is, it means love is blind."

"Sometimes he is depicted that way. Like in Piccadilly Circus, there's an Eros statue where he is depicted with a blindfold. It's actually a statue of Anteros, but that's a whole other story."

"Yeah," Isla chips in, "like the statue of Justice. She has a sword in one hand, scales in the other, and has a blindfold over her eyes which signifies that Lady Justice is impartial, unbiased. But sometimes she can't see the forest for the trees and the culprit escapes."

"A good comparison, Isla, ambivalent enough to be true."

"See, I told you what she's like."

"Yes, love may be blind. It was in your case, Candace. It often allows one to overlook the faults in the beloved and I know quite a bit about that, Candace, as no doubt you understand what I refer to. Also, love is blind can also mean that it can hit one unexpectedly, out of the blue, without apparent reason."

"Does love is blind equate to love at first sight?'

"A reasonable enough equation, Candace. Love is a many splendored thing, as the old song has it, which is another way of saying love is multi-faceted."

"So, Ruth, would you say that Candace is— what's that expression? Lovesick?"

"Love sickness is that biological reaction I was telling you both about. You've experienced the symptoms, Candace, heart palpitations, loss of normal functionality, and so on. Basically, an emotional state difficult to get a grip on."

"You hear a lot about Platonic love."

"Yes, affection for an individual without sexual intensity, none at all in fact. Consider it a deep and abiding friendship. Gender differences are negligible. According to Plato, it's a kind of love that touches on wisdom, truth and beauty. You two seem to exemplify the idea."

"I don't know about the wisdom part, Ruth," Isla says, "we're still young enough to screw up."

"With guys, then, it gets them beyond bromance, is that right?"

"'Man crushing' is the more contemporary term, Candace. Get with it, girl. Raise your level of social awareness."

"To tell you the truth, I don't know how my lovely cousin here keeps up with what's in and what's out. Memes and things. Buzzwords. She can always go one better. Sorry, Ruth, for interrupting."

"No problem, it all fits. Now Plato would argue that the love we're talking about is spiritual."

"So in all of this, where does Tim Pickett come in?"

"Right out of the blue."

"In our constant search for understanding and self-knowledge, we question the randomness of an encounter, why love hits when it does, its spontaneity. Theorists on the subject say that in the folds of human grey matter, love comes after beauty. In other words, sexual attraction and desire lead to romantic love and subsequent entanglements. Love can last a lifetime given the right elements."

"In marriage, you mean?"

"Yes, possibly, but not only under those conditions."

"My parents' marriage lacked the requisite conditions," Isla states. "It was doomed right from the start."

"The ancient Greeks, as I was explaining, came up with their answers to questions of love. Foremost is the arrow that Eros shoots into the heart of unsuspecting individuals. Fascinating stuff, I find."

Bravo, bravo I say. I've known for some time that Ruth Rudiger, counsellor turned agony aunt, was educated, erudite, informed, well trained in the arts and sciences of explanation and analysis, but her ability to recall so handily so much information about me and my cohorts is astounding. Her name rhymes with truth. I must in some way be inspiring her. I respect her for not mentioning other extant interpretations of what my captured poses mean. For instance, a blindfold Eros indicates lust. Really? That when I sleep, under a tree, suppressed sensuality is the result. Really? My holding a torch downward represents death. Death of infatuation more likely, its transience, its brevity. A globe sometimes, universality implied. That one I can condone.

The right moment has arrived. I pull from my quiver a lead-tipped arrow and let loose. Candace shivers. To say she looks stunned is to overstate her reaction. At minimum, she looks as if she's just enjoyed a good burp, one that she welcomes wholeheartedly. A hesitation of slight duration follows after which she rises quickly and says, "Let's introduce a little gaiety into our lives, shall we?" And that said, she leads Isla and Ruth out to join the others.

The *Amoretto Algea* continues its course along the Maas River where stretches of sandy shoreline mark distances covered. The barge progresses at a steady rate through low lying areas of verdant farmland, dotted here and there with towers and spires that puncture the overcast skies and break up the flatness of the surrounding terrain. Small groups of guests bide their time on the upper deck, take notice every now and then of passing river traffic, and exchange comments about windmills near and far. By mid-morning, the *Amoretto Algea* enters the Rijkswaterstraat Sluis in Lith and stirs up interest among the onlookers. Once through the lock, the barge cozies up to the jetty and comes to a rest. Here the fifty-four kilometre ride for the day begins, destination Cuijk.

The pattern established on previous mornings for setting out is followed. Conor St James pedals off on his own. Finn Bonger takes the lead position at the head of the group and Tom Pickett volunteers once more to ride sweep. Places in line are, as usual by now, "fit in where you want." Windy conditions prevail but the enthusiasm of the cyclists to keep together and pedal on determinedly remains high.

Grey tinged cumulus clouds piled high in the sky, voluptuously shaped and mounted, Baroque to the discerning eye, complete the scene perfectly. The clouds reflect how a master like Peter Paul Rubens might have rounded off his Flemish landscape, stood back, and congratulated himself. Visit the Rijksmuseum, dear reader, and you will get the picture many times over. The temperature this outing is agreeable, not too hot, not too cool.

The group keeps to a set pace along dikes and well-marked pathways that traverse open farmland where mooing cows and braying sheep and bleating goats and barking dogs announce their passing. Ubiquitous are the odours of fecund productivity. After an hour and a half of non-stop cycling, Finn Bonger guides the group along the cobbled lanes of Megen to arrive at a location where the town tourist bureau is open for "the gathering of information" as he so eloquently puts it. Bike stanchions are available in the parking square and are quickly filled. Bonger announces a forty-five minute break, "time enough for some exploring or chomping down on sandwiches." He considers the stop a lunch break or coffee break or whatever individuals determine for themselves. Cafés are in the immediate area and within easy walking distance. "Lock bikes and take panniers" are his last instructions.

The group begins to disperse. I hover momentarily above the Giles family. They decide to go walking about in pursuit of some storefront that caught Benny's attention as they cycled by. Lizzy and Nigel seem delighted to be indulging their son's interest in things outside the range of his normal curiosity. After all, this trip was for him.

Otto and Elsa Müller enter the tourist bureau and I leave them in there poking about.

The Picketts?

"Take a turn at riding sweep," I hear Bonnie encourage Tim. "Who'd know the difference? Besides, it'll take your mind off futile pursuits." The family of four disappears from my purlieu and don't reappear until just before departing time. I have no idea what they get up to.

My real interest lies in how Candace is handling things. During the cycling, she placed herself ahead of Isla and immediately behind Finn Bonger. He directs the two of them along with Drake and his father to a café called De Poort, which lies down a block and around a corner, and promises to accept Drake's offer of whatever drink he might like once he's finished with inquiries in the tourist centre. Candace and Isla are most agreeable.

Following this ensemble and finding another table under awnings at De Poort are Ruth Rudiger, Angela Jones, Mick Mallory, and Professor Wolfgang.

"Husbands?" the professor asks when no husbands show up.

"JJ and Ray have gone looking for a bank or a bank machine, whatever comes first."

"A small town is Megen, *ja*. But they may have luck."

"Listen, folks, drinks are on me," Mick Malory declares. "All good with that?"

Apparently so.

Approximately an hour later, along the route between Megen and Ravenstein, Benny complains that he can't go any more, that the bike is not what it was like before.

He stops pedaling in a panic and causes his parents visible concern.

"Not good," he cries. "Not good. Not good. Not good."

Ray Rudiger, who has been riding in close vicinity, comes up to assist the boy and yells for the sweep to signal Bonger. All cycling comes to a halt. I hover above the scene, watching Rudiger inspect the bike. He concludes that the problem with Benny's bike occurred because the cable linking battery to the electric assist mechanism has been disconnected, and naturally nothing happens when Benny shifts positions on the handlebars or when he changes gears. The problem likely occurred because of the shaking of the bike along the cobble streets. Problem solved, Rudiger announces, and the ride can continue. Bonger congratulates him for a job well done, as do Nigel, Lizzy, and Benny himself.

A logical question arises at this point in the days' outing: which of the Twins is riding sweep? Tom or Tim? Slightly put off by the possibility of their having switched places in the line without my noticing, I hover about for a moment or two of speculation, then inspire myself with a superb idea. The propitious moment lies ahead.

I repeat: what Ruth told Candace and Isla has a great deal of merit.

Roughly following the meandering Maas, riders from the *Amoretto Algea* continue along designated cycling paths through tracts of rich farmland from Megen to Ravenstein and beyond that to Grave, a fortified city that grew in importance during the Napoleonic era.

"Keeping the desired pace," Finn Bonger said before the group started up again, "will allow for extra time at the next scheduled stop. It is an atypical spot for cyclists to find a bit of downtime and is interesting in its own right for a good number of reasons."

"Mamils. Mamils. Mamils," Benny Birtwistle calls out when a group of lycra-clad seniors zoom by in the opposite direction. He stops momentarily, as do those following him.

"What was the boy shouting?" Angela asks her husband before pushing off again.

"A quintet of cyclists passed us at Mach one," JJ explains. "Benny was warning us in that funny way he has of expressing excitement."

Half-way between Ravenstein and Grave, Finn Bonger slows the pace of the group, and after signaling, takes a left hand turn off the narrow Zuijdenhoutstraat pavement, the cyclists following in line without bunching up too much. Tall shade trees line each side of the long cinder drive into what he proudly announces as "the farm café." Finn informs all that they have a good half-hour stop here before pushing on to Cuijk, an hour or so away. WC facilities are available for those in need. The purchase of a piece of pastry or a beverage would serve as a token of appreciation to the hosts. Service is inside. And the delicious pies.

Bikes get stationed along the drive and in an area adjacent to one of the barns. Grazing cattle with large curious eyes loiter about a fenced-in pasture, one of many that lie beyond the farm precinct. Picnic benches and tables are situated around a brick patio and these the cyclists make for with eager, stretching steps. Groups form in a random fashion with those in need of the washroom toing and froing.

The Picketts set themselves up around a picnic table. The twins are looking very twin-like, but a marked difference at this point is how eagerly Tim, still standing, casts about looking for Isla. Who else would it be but Tim? This prompts another bout of fraternal mockery from Tom who gets up and puts a muscular arm around his brother's shoulder. Bonnie and Dexter break out in derisive laughter, Tom joining them. Their laughter brings to mind the old saw about the last laugh being the loudest.

Or is it this way: he who laughs last laughs best?

Be that as it may, dear reader, and for the moment consider the image of the Discobolus, a bronze statue of a discus thrower created by Myron in 450 BC. Got it? Now picture Michelangelo's masterful sculpture, David contemplating his next move. Put either or both figures in cleats or cycling shorts and you have a determined Tim Pickett tossing his helmet up and down.

In another comfortable situation on the patio, Candace and Isla are with the Cantlays, JJ and Angela Jones. Their conversation turns on cycling and how it has gained widespread acceptance in North America. Isla says she plans to join a riding club when back in New York. From what she has heard, miles of bike routes criss-cross the city. JJ provides a few details about the riding club he and Angela belong to and about the various goodwill cycling events in which they've participated. Notable is the gran fondo going from Vancouver to Whistler. A September event. Angela says the Chilliwack to Hope gran fondo is easier as it is somewhat flatter. Not to be left out, Drake mentions how Ottawa has provided cycling enthusiasts with innumerable routes around the capital. Cole Cantlay asks what their opinions are on electric assist bicycles and nobody in the group hesitates in providing one.

Elsewhere, Benny clucks as he gazes about a wired-in chicken coop that runs along two sides of the building that gives access to the WC. Laughter of a different order ensues. Nigel ruffles his son's hair and then hands him a piece of chocolate.

At another table Mick Mallory sits with the Rudigers and the Müllers and, while finishing off a piece of pie, listens in on their talk about travel plans after the Amoretto

Algea excursion concludes. Ray and Ruth Rudiger will spend a couple of days in Maastricht then make their way to Paris. The Müllers will return to Germany and get back to work. And there are domestic considerations: Otto has his recalcitrant son, Hans Dieter, for a week.

With the bottom of his water jug, Mick vaguely traces the stem of a single rose forming part of the nature-themed print on the tablecloth that covers their table; then he says he'll return home and maybe write a book, either about travel or about love or possibly about both at the same time. In memory of his wife, Delores, who was quite literary.

At this point, Otto Müller asks, "Did you know that Herr Professor Wolfgang is writing a book on the German philosopher Fredrich Nietzsche?"

"No, I did not know that. He's talked about Nietzsche to me but has not mentioned he was writing a book on him."

"*Herr* Professor Wolfgang is very modest, *ja*."

"Coq of the walk," Ray interjects, pointing down with a wavering index finger.

"What a lovely rooster," Elsa declares, and rustles in her pannier to pull out her phone. Snapping a couple of shots, she adds, "His comb, *ja*, is like the red of the panniers."

"A delightful display of colour," Ruth agrees. "Like the cocky little fellow's just wandered off an impressionist's canvas."

"He's quite used to people," Mick says, breaking off a bit of pie crust and tossing it to the strutting bird.

"Lucky bastard, to be roaming freely among us. But then, he can return at will to all his girlfriends secure in the cozy harem over there."

"Oh, Ray!" Ruth chides, then turns to the others. "It's the same old same old with him."

"What she said," Ray says and grins widely.

"Now where did Wolfgang get off to?" Mick wants to know.

"Herr Bonger told him that inside the barn is the nose and motor section of a downed Spitfire," Otto says. "From the war. He is very curious about it."

"I think I'll join him as soon as I've finished feeding this insatiable puffed-up bird."

"Perhaps we should get Hans Dieter some chickens." Elsa's suggestion seemingly drops out of the blue. Her tiny snicker grows into an infectious laugh which captures the attention of those around her.

"A new bicycle maybe is better, *Liebchen*," Otto offers, pulling to the side of his forehead a damp shock of blond hair. His blue eyes remain intense. "Hans Dieter is not a happy boy," he goes on to say, "not like Benny."

Benny, who has been freewheeling about, calls for his mother and father to follow him inside. "Lots of stuff," he says, "lots and lots of stuff." Benny is absolutely correct. Inside the main building there is a hodgepodge of collectibles on display, eclectic memorabilia from local sources and from far afield.

"Time to go, Benny," Lizzy says and guides her son out and back to his bike.

An hour later, the cyclists reach the *Amoretto Algea* moored along the central quay that serves all manner of river craft plying the Maas. The usual method for loading the bikes takes place, Captain Van de Oor giving directions from his usual perch. Upon arriving safely and secure in the knowledge that "no serious incident," as Lizzy says to Nigel who is guiding Benny onboard ahead of him, "detracted from the enjoyment of the day," the guests go about their usual ways, some immediately to their quarters for showers, some to the lounge or upper deck for post-outing drinks.

The evening meal is served at the usual time and, as usual, Finn Bonger rings his bell to get the attention of all the guests now gathered in the dining area and seated at their assigned tables. He compliments the group for how successful the cycling went, which raises a round of applause and Ray Rudiger's yelling out, "We couldn't have done it without you Finn, but then again maybe we could have." When the laughter peters out, Finn goes on to provide information about the city of Cuijk that he claims is significant in a number of ways, from prehistoric archaeological discoveries to modern industrial successes. It was once an important Roman settlement and the central hub for a connecting road system with a bridge across to the other shore. The name derives from the bend in the river. Immediately across Maasboulevard, Finn continues, stands Saint Martin church constructed during the Gothic revival. It is worth a visit. Equally worthy of a visit is the Ceuclum Museum which is housed in the adjacent tower. On display within are Bronze Age pottery and many artifacts from succeeding eras, Celtic, Roman, Gallo-Roman and so on. A wonderful view of the city and of the Maas Valley can be had from the top of the high tower.

"If you're up to the climb," Ray Rudiger shouts out, "which I am not."

"Now," Finn says and then pauses until the snickering subsides, "please enjoy the wonderful salmon dish Chef Simon has prepared for you."

"Bish, bash, bosh, real good nosh."

"Cut it out, dear," Ruth chides Ray. "You're only so funny."

When Finn Bonger and Dirk van Kesteren finish cleaning up the last of the tables, Bonnie Pickett asks for the use of the playing cards and poker chips. Ray Rudiger, Cole and Drake Cantlay have agreed to join her and Dexter in playing a little Blackjack.

Cole declares the following: "This is not normally how we spend our evenings. Gambling is not in our repertoire of pastimes."

While shuffling the cards, Bonnie Pickett explains how the game works. Both Cole and Drake nod. It's not that complicated a game she states encouragingly and nods.

As I heard Lizzy Birtwistle say on one occasion, "A nod is as good as a wink."

The rest set out to visit the church, museum, and tower. These are JJ and Angela Jones, Ruth Rudiger, Mick Mallory, Professor Wolfgang, Otto and Elsa Müller. Accompanying Nigel, Lizzy, and Benny is Conor St James. Benny insists he tag along and he complies readily leaving Benny little time to fuss.

Before Candace and Isla leave for the tower, Finn Bonger asks them if they might prefer to join him, Chef Simon, and Dirk van Kesteren for a drink at a local brasserie a short distance away.

Isla responds first to the invitation. "That would be great, Finn. Love to. But you made the museum and its finds so interesting, I've just got to check things out there."

"My cousin here," Candace points out, "is interested in everything and that includes pottery shards, old coins, and arrowheads. Besides, the view from the top of the tower is to die for, isn't it?"

"Yes, it is worth climbing the many stairs. Another evening, perhaps," Finn concedes.

"Maybe we could meet up after visiting the tower," Candace offers.

"Brasserie de Poorten," Finn responds and smiles, "down the boulevard to the right and around a corner."

And where are Tim and Tom Pickett in all of this? Watching from the sidelines but listening intently. When Candace and Isla head across Maasboulevard, they follow.

At this juncture in the evening, dear reader, I leave most of the Amoretto Algea visitors poking through the various displays in the Ceuclum Museum. Pottery shards, old coins, and arrowheads. I've seen them all from all over the continent.

Benny wants to get to the top of the tower but runs out of breath and likewise numbers to count after racing up the many circular stairs to the base of the second level. Lizzy and Nigel are winded as well and are unwilling to proceed any higher.

After a cursory viewing of exhibits, Candace says she wants to get to the top and encourages Isla to follow her, which she does without too much resistance. They pass the Giles family resting and continue climbing up the winding staircase to reach the next level. From here they must make their way up a set of two ladders, the final requirement in reaching the viewing deck at the top of the tower.

Candace leads off, Isla in toe, and behind her, Tim Pickett following closely. He's indeed hard on her heels— to describe the configuration of their ascent in delicate terms. Bringing up the rear of this not-so-delicate order of hands, arms, legs and bottoms, Tom voices a few lewd comments about what the hell are he and his brother up to and how Tim is really making an ass of himself. Nonetheless, Tim willingly endures his brother's sneers and jeers in dedicated pursuit of his heart's need.

Conor St James, who alone has reached the pinnacle and the viewing platform, is occupied in taking photos from such a high vantage point. I leave him there for the moment to carry on doing what he is doing.

Let me, dear reader, at this point in the sequence amplify the effects of the split screen. On the right of the viewing area, Candace and Isla pointing across a vast panorama running from north to south, the *Amoretto Algea* made fast along the quay in the foreground and across the river areas of green stretching into the tree-lined horizon. In the middle, as it were, Conor St James taking everything in. On the left, the Pickett twins, distracted momentarily by the triple spires of Saint Martin's Church. When they begin to circle around towards the young women, I understand that the propitious moment has finally arrived. I reach into my quiver but before I can extract my chosen arrow, Benny Giles pops up and blocks my line of sight. He locates Conor St James and happily hustles over to join him. With Benny's inconvenient appearance, the propitious moment evaporates. And so, dear reader, the only consolation I can offer you on this occasion is my promise to follow through on action that is unquestionably warranted when dealing with these unresolved affairs of the heart. In the meantime, I usher you back to earth.

At eleven-twenty P.M. of the fourth night of the *Amoretto Algea* trek to Maastricht, Captain Jan Van der Oor meets with Finn Bonger, Chef Simon Oliver, and Dirk van Kesteren in the lounge. The trio has just returned from the Brasserie de Poorten. The captain says they'll forgo the ritual involving Irish whiskey as no doubt they have had a few good measures of spirited drink for one night.

"The hangover is a poor travelling companion," he says with authority. "And so, I ask how it goes with that *pijn in de kont*, Ray Rudiger?"

Dirk answers, "Still playing at being— what do you call it? A smart ass. He tells me how a guy who called him a lightweight, cut-price belligerent didn't fare so well in the end. I don't know what half of what he said means."

"It means some bloke called him a wanker for some reason and he defied him."

"Rudiger thinks he's a rock star," Finn says. "I don't know how the wife puts up with his sexual intimations."

"She's cool," Dirk says.

"The Picketts still strike me as an odd bunch. The wife's pretty fast with the playing cards. Very impressive. One of the twins is trying to seduce Isla Troyes, but without too much success. Some of the activity in the hallway could be written into act one of a French farce."

"It must not disturb the sleeping guests," the captain insists.

"I'll see to it," Finn says, nodding his head.

"Finn, Dirk tells me you're soft on the other bird," Chef Simon says. "It's the truth, innit?"

"Impossible not to be."

"Just taking the piss, mate," Chef Simon says and yucks it up a little. "But what is the old *Amoretto Algea* anyway, Captain? The Love Boat?"

Day Five
dead man's hand

Cuijk to Arcen:

The lounge in the *Amoretto Algea*, early the fifth day of the bike and barge excursion, Amsterdam to Maastricht. Ruth Rudiger with book and coffee sits where she did previously.

"No Wolfgang?" Ruth asks when Mick Malory stops and offers her a good morning.

"Last night he said he'd had a good day's exercise and if sleep carried him a little longer into the morning, he'd accept it most willingly."

"On this trip, Ray said he'd sleep in whenever he could. When he worked, that was never the case at all. It was all business. And early."

"Quite the character is your husband. A real joker. Comes out with some pretty snappy comments."

"Hasty utterances. Humorous intent, but not always so funny. *Ejaculatio praecox* of the tongue."

"Latin, right?" Mick Mallory prompts. "I take it you mean not thinking before letting the tongue waggle."

"Close enough. I studied the classics way back. Latin courses were mandatory."

"I underwent something similar before university. A waste, really, because I wasn't going to be a doctor or a lawyer."

"Is that where you met your wife, at university?"

"Yes, that's where I met Delores. I'm still missing her greatly. Counselling had some benefits for me but..." Mick trails off as he looks intently at his coffee cup.

"Counselling has its limits," Ruth says. "I understand that. I couldn't help overhearing some of what you were discussing with the professor. I thought I might last night on the upper deck, you know, talk about it with you. But then Candace and Isla returned in an up mood."

"Quite the adventure they had on the *Iphigenia*," Mick notes and grimaces. "Family tragedy, but they're dealing with it." After taking a sip from his cup, he continues. "As for me, it's been helpful talking to Wolfgang. Kind of like extended therapy."

"Well, sit here and engage in another session. I'm a good listener."

"Why not? You know," Mick says, seating himself, "Delores would have liked you, I'm pretty sure of that. She would really have loved being part of this biking thing. And meeting new people. All the different personalities. Isla reminds me a lot of my daughter."

"How so?"

"When it comes to the imagination. How she expresses herself."

"As in the poet part of her personality."

"Yea, that's it. And she cycles well, Isla does. Like my daughter. And for that matter, like Delores."

"I suppose you can take some comfort there, Mick."

"Sure. And in the cycling. Being part of something beyond myself."

"That's excellent."

"You see, when I met Delores, she was into biking big time. Very athletic. Delores was..."

"Do go on, Mick. I'd love to hear about Delores."

"When I met her, she was well on her way to earning a BA. She'd planned on teaching drama in high school, but she decided eventually to go into nursing."

"A noble calling."

"It was for her, yes, but I think she would have been a superb teacher. She had wide ranging and diversified interests, you know, was cultured, into art, and music, even what our kids were listening to when they got to that age."

"Yes, that age. I know what you mean."

"There was so much more to Delores than just being savvy or 'with it,' as we used to say. Her personality, the witty banter, the mauve beret stylishly aslant her short, bobbed hair that seemed to quiver when she laughed and the come-hither look. Delores had big brown eyes, and with the simplest of touches, she could make them, I don't know, seem like the most beautiful eyes in the world."

"Lovely memories, Mick."

"It was nothing short of love at first sight for me. I was absolutely knocked for a loop when I first laid eyes on her. In one of the local student pubs. Weak kneed. Heart pounding in my ears. You understand what I mean?

"I have an idea."

"She had a quirky sense of humour that anyone who met her enjoyed. I miss it. I miss her for so much more than that, even now after all the time that has passed since her unfortunate death."

"But you're resolved, are you?"

"More or less. You know, it was painfully difficult trying to get rid of her things. I left the chore to my daughter. And so, the house got emptier. But for a period of time, Delores assumed the characteristics of a revenant, a frequent spectral visitant, and I gladly went along with the phenomenon."

"A house with an absent loved one can bulge with emptiness."

"Right on, Ruth. That's it exactly. You feel across the pillow to your right and find that nothing there is responsive to your desire. The fabric remains cold to your touch. Nothing is reciprocated. Indeed, those strange nights on the edge of the bed, your trembling fingers moulding to your face, awake at all hours, and through the cracks staring blankly into the semi-dark.”

“One is the loneliest number, eh.”

“I remember that song from back in the day.”

“Very catchy, if alone. Tell me, did therapy not ease that kind of anxiety? That sense of complete loneliness?”

“Well, I became a little more self-reliant, I guess you could say.”

“How so?”

“Leonard Cohen’s “Dance Me to the End of Love” was Delores’ favourite among many beloved songs of his. Hearing it together always invoked memories of our wedding night when my heart began beating like a metronome set to some musical signature born of primal rhythms.”

“I know that song as well, Mick, but I can’t say it brought on similar memories of any night like yours.” Here Ruth sniggers, looks at Mick with amusement shining in her eyes, and then adds, “Not with Ray, anyway. I understand the symptoms you describe so graphically, however.”

“An exaggeration, right? But not too much over the top. I’d put on the song every once in a while, and, instinctively, dance around the kitchen partnered with a broom when sleep escaped me, or like that one time when I broke out of a dream certain that I’d heard enchanting strains from melancholy violins."

"Did this kind of behaviour work its way into discussions with your therapist?"

"Not exactly. Vaguely, maybe. On the whole, though, I have to admit that therapy did help. And travel. I took the trip to Greece that Delores and I had planned for an anniversary celebration."

"So basically, the time spent in therapy proved beneficial for you. Is that right, Mick?"

"More or less. I had two stretches of prescribed professional consultation, the first with a grief counsellor called Athena and the second with a psychologist therapist called Sophia. All about understanding grief for what it is and getting on with living."

"Healthy acceptance of events beyond one's control," Ruth offers, "and ultimately reintegration."

"Pretty much. Sophie guided me through 'cognitive reframing,' what she called a useful theoretical way of considering a problem."

"I'm familiar with what cognitive reframing entails."

"Sophie used the word 'rewind' several times in her explanation of the theory, drawing on the old trope of the half-full versus the half-empty view of reality."

"Got it."

"To tell you the truth, Ruth, I think I'd been doing cognitive reframing in my own way right from the get-go. As to the idea of rewind, I'd done rewinds over and over again. I made every effort to visualize what happened by the shores of the Trent River where Delores was incapacitated. I analyzed repeatedly just exactly how it could possibly have come about, her actions before the wave that felled her and after it struck, the actions of the others and their impotence, the devastation of a life lying on the sand in mockery of the woman I loved, the departing ambulance wailing imminent death."

"Perfectly understandable, Mick. But you did eventually come around. Reframing is aspirational in its intention to change how a patient feels and not just thinks."

"That's pretty much what Sophia said but not exactly in those words."

"An interesting aspect of cognitive reframing theory is the use of analogies and stories, even myths, to change the thinking of the afflicted patient, to have him or her distinguish grief from trauma. I often find that myths can clarify matters when I'm in the process of helping individuals work through their problems."

"Right on, Ruth. I think it did in my case. I did travel back in a sense. I mean to the land where these applicable myths originated."

"Greece."

"Exactly."

"And now here you are, getting on with it, as you say."

"Right, right."

"The story of one's life as a narrative with beginning, middle, and end, as opposed to reliving over and over again one disturbing chapter."

"That about sums it up, Ruth. As Wolfgang put it just yesterday, one's life is a work in progress."

After sipping more of his coffee, and savouring what he sipped, Mick states in a rather decided way, "I feel lucky to have made the professor's acquaintance. The same with you, Ruth."

"Much appreciated, Mick. Very kind of you to say that. Wolfgang would agree, I'm sure."

"Now," Mick starts, indicating the book that lies in Ruth's lap, "I'm curious about what you're reading. What is it?"

"A psychology study called *Values*," Ruth answers, picking the book up. "I like to keep abreast of new research in the field even though I've actually been retired from the counselling business for some time now."

"I do, too, try to keep up, especially when it comes to electric vehicles. What have you discovered more than what Doctor Freud gave us?"

"A way of looking at what determines an individual's world view and how he or she responds to life. For instance, someone like you, if what I've gleaned from my reading is accurate, holds 'intrinsic' values. In other words, you are empathetic, self-accepting;

you relish intimacy, enjoy friendship, and offer a helping hand to those less fortunate in society. In this description, I'm placing you outside your response to the tragedy you suffered as a loving husband, if you see what I mean."

"That's only half of it, right?"

"Right. Someone exhibiting 'extrinsic' values is concerned with status, image, power and wealth and is capable of rude and aggressive behaviour. Insecurity can lead to compulsive behaviour. Very needy. Likes to be the centre of attention. My husband Ray exemplifies the type perfectly."

"Like I said, he's the kind of character you can't help but take notice of. Hey, I heard the two of you are celebrating forty years of marriage."

"We are. But I have to confess that life with him has not been easy. He's always been a bit of a womanizer. On the other hand, even though he can be extremely prurient, he doesn't hang about louche hotels playing Casanova."

"Love is blind."

"That's what they say. Ironic, isn't it?"

"Would you miss him if...?"

"I probably would. But not as much as you miss your Delores. But I wouldn't be alone in missing good, old Ray Rudiger."

"You know, Ruth, even now on the boat at night, I see Delores doing her hair, which she always kept short. Back then, when we were together, I'd be amused at how loud her head would be crackling with little charges of light."

"Visual memories linger. And the sounds associated with them."

"The memory of her scent lingers too, as does that of the perfume she preferred, a subtle fragrance contained in a heart-shaped, brass-topped bottle called Essence."

Wow! Hearing Mick Mallory's continuing tale of tears for lost love brings to mind yet again how I endured the misery of being without my beloved Psyche. A short spell of abstinence for sure. But, oh, the intensity of that raging sense of betrayal compounded by that of loss, even in an immortal.

Just for the record, I consider myself an Olympian regardless of the lesser status others residing at the summit of the mountain attribute to me. Truth be told, and I will get to that, make no mistake about it, I was around before any of them rose to the heights of high position and haughty disposition.

When engaged in enterprises touching on the affairs of mortals, I offer nothing resembling a meditation on the human condition with its polar highs and lows, its transcendence and its existential angst, no, not one iota. I leave that to Apollo in the celestial sphere and his wealthy acolyte stand-ins, who, when consulted, deign to decree from a stance of fee-for-favours-rendered. Indeed, I leave that as well to the philosophers and metaphysical theorists; the psychologists and psychiatrists; the sociologists and socialists; MD's, witchdoctors, and all practitioners of hieratic quackery; and every unspecified know-it-all operating under a shingle of dubious authenticity, prescribing solutions to problems from pseudo-professional points of view, including a possible maiden aunt with a degree in animal husbandry. I even leave it to the likes of Ruth Rudiger who, as we have just witnessed, is exceptionally well-equipped to assist the benighted. However impoverished in that domain I admit being, I do reveal smatterings of insight gleaned from centuries of observation concerning the vicissitudes of love in all recorded manifestations from the obsessive compulsion of amour fou to the steadfast dignity of amour éternel. And I deliver without being sententious or given to pompous moralizing or offering to the willing ear aphoristic maxims of memorable but useless content. Furthermore, I abhor stumbling inadvertently across tautological fault lines in any of my communications. But then there was Psyche's indiscretion.

Ironically, the more humanlike, the more banal the Olympians became in the minds of pundits and commentators: consider Zeus and his insatiable lust, his endless amorous incursions into the private domain of nymphs, princesses, and other mortal wenches, virtual one-sided assaults in the sense that the victims were often ignorant of the power of the force assailed against them in whatever form it took, bull, swan, impenetrable light.

The question of the numinous light of the immortals cannot be avoided, and I'll weave that fact into the story that Canova, previously alluded to, so wonderfully carved into his block of marble. As you shall see, dear reader, that episode in my long story is worth knowing and merits being told. As to the brilliant light of divinity, that of Zeus in particular, I am loathe to define it as the beatific vision which the high and mighty proponents of Christianity have determined to be the endgame for its powerless and subservient practitioners. Saul of Tarsus claimed he was blinded by the light but doubt arises as to the veracity of that claim judging by what he got up to after the fact. The point is this: Olympian light and that of its lesser immortals is too much for human eyesight. Blinding. That's how it is understood and I'm okay with that because I really do know and my own story will attest to that while highlighting the thematic relevance of the kiss.

Gods are shapeshifters, protean, capricious, and capable of bringing about change in unsuspecting mortals, often as a punishment for offenses taken. Censure. Opprobrium. Punishment. In many ways, we mirror human foibles, aspirations, frailties:

ambition, jealousy, vanity, cupidity (I am not fond of that word but it works in the present context), revenge.

Zeus, then, and the ineffable brilliance of his glorious light: not only was the Theban Princess, Semele, raped by Zeus, she was blinded by him, and more than just being blinded, she was totally consumed in flames and got burned to a crisp. The upshot of that peculiar coupling was the materialization of my good buddy, Dionysus, who was born of Zeus' thigh. Just imagine the postpartum party.

Zeus had his endless love affairs. But let it be understood that Aphrodite slept around as well and not only with immortals. How could she not, being the goddess of beauty and love and, might I add, sexual proclivity bolstered with enthusiastic readiness. To their credit, neither Zeus nor Aphrodite were guilty of instituting the fig leaf as cover for pudendal or phallic exposure. A popular interpretation of my origins is that I am Aphrodite's son by Ares: absolute perversion of fact, truth decay at its worst. I predate both of them. In fact, my arrows initiated their romantic entanglement. That the god of war and the goddess of beauty could have produced a smaller, softer, chubbier me with miniscule wings to fit into the Roman pantheon is nothing short of ridiculous. Cupid, my ass. Talk about today's snowflake generation!

A necessary note here about wings on statues and replicas of ancient Greek gods and goddesses: again, a mere human perception derived from the observation of birds in flight, a metaphor at best, useful in depicting rapid movement. Mine, for instance.

Canova's masterpiece depicts with exquisite precision how Psyche is revived by my kiss. Discard the flagrant use of the fig leaf. As the chorus of a well-known song has it, everybody knows. The statue dramatizes my descent from the empyrean zenith of my retreat where a sphere of inexhaustible fire burns. I'm sculpted as returning to earth without my wings being singed, like a bird of prey hovering over its wide-mouthed fledglings. The kiss is crucial, dear reader, in understanding the reason for my discontent and how certain events fell into place, making things whole again. Here is how it all shakes down in this plot of one envious, vengeful goddess and the conniving of two devious and equally envious sisters.

Long story short, part the first. Psyche's beauty inspires her peers with immense admiration to the point of venerating her, a mere mortal, as though a goddess. She incurs the wrath of Aphrodite who flies into a jealous rage, commissioning me to do her dirty work which involves condemning the girl to marry a despicable monster. "Because of arrogance," Aphrodite announces, "let her be cursed to endure a burning passion for the ugliest specimen of humanity." That curse is not to be, however. When I behold Psyche, her beauty impassions me beyond what binds me to my association with Aphrodite. It is as though I've pricked myself with one of my own arrows. I see fit to have Zephyr carry Psyche to a luxurious mountain hideaway where all her needs are met and where we love by night, the understanding being that I can never reveal to her my true identity as the god of love in all his glorious light. Brilliance makes demands and curiosity has its costs. Twice I warn my night-time wife to overcome the temptation that the need to know arouses. Covetous sisters convince Psyche she indeed needs to know what she does not, namely, who exactly her secretive consort is. The plot to discover the truth entails her carrying towards our marriage bed not only a candle to light up the night but also a knife, lest what she finds is the ugly reality of the curse. Once she lays eyes on my youthful beauty, she is consumed with regret. Drippings from the candle arouse me from sleep to discover how I have been burned, betrayed by the one I love. "Without trust, there is no love," I cry, fleeing the scene and finding refuge in Aphrodite's domain.

Part the second in this tale of love lost and love regained. Distraught beyond all measures, Psyche searches me out. Fruitless are her endless efforts to find me. Contrite, she appeals to Aphrodite for assistance. "But of course I will help you," the gloating goddess promises. Aphrodite is as strict in her reprisals as I am, but in the case of Psyche, she definitely stretches a desire for revenge beyond what is reasonable even for a pampered and petulant goddess. Hers is a profound and unforgiving jealousy. And so, Aphrodite's conditions, austere in the extreme, if I am to be regained as husband: complete four tasks, the most difficult of which is to enter the underworld and bring back for Aphrodite, and for her alone, a box of Persephone's beauty cream. Done! Psyche successfully completes her challenges but not without a little help from her friends. But alas, insecurity, curiosity, and vanity compel her to open the box and with that action she falls into a deep and binding sleep. Psyche is mortal after all; she is human, all too human. In my lament, I bring her before Olympian Zeus and make my plea. Zeus in his munificence gives her nectar and ambrosia which render her immortal, a goddess in her own right of the animating force that moves the spirit and nourishes the soul. She abides still in our luxurious mountain hideaway. Periodically we wander together of an evening through Elysian Fields. Our pleasure is increased tenfold when our daughter Hedone joins us there. By the way, dear reader, I still bear the scar on my shoulder from having been burned by Psyche but I hold zero resentment. Love is blind and for a time that is all that she knew of love. The kiss, much as the sculptor Canova depicted it, is forever on our lips.

In considering all the incidents that make up that enduring prototypical tale of boy gets girl, boy loses girl, boy gets girl back, to borrow from contemporary literary criticism, a distinction has to be drawn between what Mick Mallory suffered and what yours truly did. Mick Mallory, sadly, does not get his girl back whereas I did. Recently, I participated in a discussion with two of my close compatriots, Anteros, god of reciprocal love, and Hymenaios, god of marriage, but the most I could do or say to assuage their concerns about how Mick's story evolved was to flutter my wings (the equivalent of a mortal's shoulder shrug) and then raise three fingers to suggest it was all in the hands of the Fates.

At this juncture, dear reader, let me direct your attention back to the early gathering of guests on the fifth day of the *Amoretto Algea* adventure. I need not burden you with all the details regarding how the morning ritual unfolds, it unfolds in much the same ways as it did on previous mornings. All arrive in the dining area, queue up, load plates for breakfast and lunch, sit in their usual seats and possibly discuss between slurps of coffee and mouthfuls of sausage and egg what to anticipate in the outing that Finn Bonger is arranging for the day.

"The bicycles will all be unloaded by nine o'clock," he announces with his usual morning enthusiasm once all are in their places. "We depart at nine ten for a fifty-three kilometre trek which will take us through Boxmeer, Afferden, Well, and Broekhuizen before reaching our final destination. All lovely Dutch towns. Also, we go back and forth across the Maas. Those of you remaining onboard, enjoy your day, and we will see you at four in Arcen."

Ready and waiting for Finn's call that all the bike batteries are secure in place and that setting out is imminent, JJ and Angela join Otto and Elsa Müller near the ramp on the upper deck. They engage in pleasant chit-chat.

"Such brilliant sunshine is very encouraging," Angela says and finds murmured agreement.

Then JJ mentions how impressed he is with the way business enterprises are conducted on such an elaborate scale. "It's interesting to see the variety of vessels cruising up and down the Maas," he goes on to say, "long flat barges carrying varied cargo like sand, gravel, machinery, and then there are tankers transporting who knows what."

Otto explains: "This river and the numerous similar waterways running in every direction, and the canals, ja, are typical of many western European countries. They are long-established commercial and industrial routes that nature and human ingenuity formed together for the benefit of everyone. If you visit Antwerp or Rotterdam or Hamburg you would be amazed."

"Some of the smaller barges look quite homey," Angela says, "curtains in windows, even vehicles suspended in place or in parking slots at the stern. Very cool."

"All set," Finn Bonger finally calls from down on the quay whereupon the cyclists take to their bikes and prepare for the challenges of another outing. Those remaining with the Amoretto Algea are Dexter and Bonnie Pickett, Lizzy Giles, and Professor Albrecht. From positions on the aft section of the upper deck, these four call out encouragingly to the cyclists.

Coaxed by one of the Pickett twins, Drake Cantlay volunteers to ride sweep.

"It's like riding shotgun because you get a pretty good shot of everyone's butt." A howl of a laugh follows.

Drake shrugs. He accepts the yellow vest and secures the walkie-talkie unit handed him. Slipping the vest on, he asks, "Which one are you?"

"Tim."

"I thought the one called Tom rode sweep."

"We both rode sweep. Him, then me."

"I see."

"A couple of things to understand about the switching. One, it was like a fake handoff in football. Intended to deceive, but in our case just to get a laugh out of the confusion some might have had about who was who."

"Like in that old routine of who's on first?"

"Yeah, that's right, man."

"Did it work?"

"What do you mean, work?"

"Did your switching positions cause confusion?"

"Worked with you, didn't it?"

"Evidently. What was the other thing?" Drake asks, shaking his head. "You mentioned two things."

"The other thing was me riding there so I could get my mind off that girl's ass. The one from your table. The brunette."

"Did it help?"

"No, just added to my own confusion."

True to his word about leaving at ten after nine, Finn Bonger shepherds the cyclists out of the Maaskade parking lot and heads them down the dual bike path leading away from Cuijk. Except for the minor change in the position of sweep, the outing this day rolls along in typical fashion with the route through flatlands following the geographic ins and outs of the Maas. By ten fifteen Finn Bonger has the riders filing down Steenstrat in Boxmeer. Coming to a stop by a conveniently located bike stand in the town centre, he reminds them to lock up and take their panniers with them. They have a forty-five minute break. He recommends two spots for coffee, the Café

Rijk, which he points to, and across from it, the Hotel Bar Generaal. Both have comfortable outdoor accommodation and both serve excellent coffee as well as any other beverage of preference.

Attaching both their helmets to the handlebars of his bike, Nigel Giles ruffles Benny's mop of hair and then together they head off along Steenstrat. Benny starts off with a pannier in each hand but father, his roly-poly sidekick, relieves him of half his load.

"Not heavy. Not Heavy. Not heavy."

The Pickett twins malinger by the parked bikes when the group moves off.

"Drake fell for it," Tim says. "But know what, I think he's gay. You might not pick up on it right away but I think that's the case."

"So no problem, then, right?"

"No problem as long as she's responsive."

"How can she resist?"

"She seems to have so far. It's been, like, three days, man, and you haven't made a decisive move in her direction."

"She seemed interested in the gay guy. He's a nice enough guy. Besides, you're no further ahead with the other one, Isla, in spite of all your ridiculous fiddling and wiggling about and talk of heartache. Ma doesn't think she's much to look at. Same with the old man. Same with me, bro. Your behaviour's been embarrassing, really."

"She's got perfect proportions."

"Talk about perfect proportions, that Candace chick's got it all. She's called Candy. I appreciate that. But…"

"So you know how it is. How frustrating."

"Just how frustrating is it?"

"Well, let me fill you in. Again."

Although I find humour in their give and take, I decide at this point it's time to leave the Pickett twins and their asinine conversation. Before gliding away, I do catch marble-mouthed Tim complaining about the pain in his erogenous zone for which he can find no socially condoned release.

"So I heard, bro." Tom's jibe is the last of their dialogue I take in before drifting along Steenstrat in pursuit of the others.

I find Mick Mallory, Cole and Drake Cantlay under the extensive awning at the Café Rijk. When Finn Bonger wanders up, Mick Mallory insists he join them. They want his opinion of electric bikes, a subject that's come up around their table.

"When not leading a group like ours," Finn answers, "I ride a regular bike. My older, married sister owns an electric cargo bike. Two young kids."

"What about Conor St James?" Drake asks. "What does he ride?"

"He brought his own bike with him, a very expensive one, Tour de France quality. Specialized."

"Likes to do his own thing," Drake says.

"Not part of the group." Cole says.

"No mystery there, guys. Conor's very much an individual. He likes to work independently. He loves competitive cycling, especially time trials. Considers his time with us as a kind of training. He belongs to a club in the UK. Has a brother in Ireland just as committed to competitive cycling as he is."

"So no electric bike for him," Mick says. "Best for folks like us."

"Agreed," Cole Cantlay says.

Under another Café Rijk Canopy are Elsa Müller, Ruth Rudiger and Angela Jones, finishing off their cappuccinos. At an adjacent table, Ray Rudiger, Otto Müller, and sitting half-way between the two tables is JJ confident, one would expect judging from his position, he can contribute to both conversations when called on to do so. Otto takes a last gulp of the Pilsner he ordered as does Ray but with manifestly more gusto.

"I find it so nice," Angela is saying, "how well all the guests on the *Amoretto Algea* have come together. I didn't think that would be possible. All so different. All from different places. So little disagreement."

"Part of the appeal," Ruth suggests. "As advertised."

"We Germans, not so bad, ja."

"Not at all, Elsa," JJ asserts quickly, assuming an almost stentorian projection, "not at all. You know, I'm thinking that given enough days, seven in our case, everybody will mix with everybody else in a friendly way."

In what seems like an attempt to recognize the notion of amicability being discussed or to confirm the facile bonhomie he enjoys with JJ Jones, Ray Rudiger says with some noticeable conviction, "I tell you folks, whenever you hear JJ pronounce on some issue in that deep voice of his, you'd think you were listening to former Prime Minister Brian Mulroney delivering a speech. You just want to believe, don't you?"

"Mulroney, yes," Angela says, "but not always. With JJ, almost all the time."

JJ responds, "Let me say this about that."

What JJ says here I've heard before, so I'll leave him saying it and leave you, dear reader, guessing.

Across at the Generaal, I zero in on Candace and Isla sitting and sipping coffee.

"Like leaky blood sausage," Isla notes and giggles.

"What?"

"Your mascara's running down your cheek."

When Candace returns from using the facilities, she says the interior of the building is quite extensive and looks to have enough space for a stage and dance floor.

"Probably used for receptions and the like. Washroom clean?"

"Spotless," Candace answers and then sits down again. "I wanted to ask but forgot to until just now. What were you saying to Lizzy on the deck before we left? Whatever it was, it seemed to light up her face."

"You know how she quotes a lot of old sayings. A tempest in a teapot, for example. I was playing around with expressions involving the Dutch. Like explaining the difference between Dutch uncle and Dutch courage. One is getting solid advice, I told her, the other taking a drink before dealing with something challenging. She cracked up."

"Good for Lizzy. As for me, I need to fill up with Dutch courage. I've just got to say it again, Ray Rudiger is a jerk."

"Yeah, a real jerk-off."

"Look at him over there gawking, pretending to be interested in what they're discussing."

"Compulsive. Probably can't help himself."

"He follows my every move with intense scrutiny. It's like he's trying to see right through me."

"Yeah, spooky."

"Scoping me all the time, from near and far. Like a stalker."

"Somehow you've created a thirst in him that only you can slake, a hunger only you can satisfy. I'm working those images into the poem I'm composing. I've found the word I was seeking, to rhyme with delicious."

"First, where does delicious fit in?"

"You're delicious, as far as he's concerned. You'll see how it all comes together when I get the poem completed, when I come up with a satisfactory closing couplet."

"What's the word?"

"Lubricious, which means oily or intimating sexual desire."

"So, like, you're suggesting that Ray Rudiger is lubricious."

"It works. Not only that, lubricity rhymes with felicity although...."

"What about lascivious? Doesn't the word mean lusty or something like that?"

"It does but it has one too many syllables. A similar word is salacious which denotes the obscene or pornographic. It rhymes with ungracious."

"Ungracious! How about creep which rhymes with peep? How do you come up with this stuff?"

"Phone," Isla says. "About all that, Ruth was very objective last night concerning Ray."

"You know, I hate to speak ill of the man, but he really puts me off. He's an intrusion. Know what I mean?"

"He longs to be noticed with more than just the batting of eyelids. Your eyelids. That's what I think."

"He's married, for heaven's sake," Candace emphasizes. "He and Ruth are supposed to be celebrating their long marriage."

"Poor Ruth. I don't know what she could ever have seen in him. He reminds me of those gargoyles you see on medieval cathedrals and churches. Supposed to ward off evil spirits."

"Work that into your poem, would you. Or Caliban, like before. I'm thinking, even computer generated imagery, like, could not improve his demeanour. And those ugly tattoos on his arms. Playing cards and dice and a mishmash of flowery designs. Repulsive, really."

"Beauty and the Beast. That's the Rudigers. And you, too."

"Duck, Isla, here come the twins."

"At least they don't go around showing off any ridiculous tattoos. Do they have any?"

"None that we've seen at least."

"Nothing like Caliban's."

"Whose?"

"Rudiger's. Those ghastly spiderwebs of his that spread down the calves. They attract nothing but criticism. Or they should, as far as I'm concerned."

At ten forty-five, Finn rounds up the cyclists from their different venues and leads them out of Boxmeer, Drake Cantlay once again at the rear of the group. They ride along the Maasstraat as far as the Afferden–Sambeek crossing and by eleven fifteen all bikes have been run on to the ferry and parked along the port and starboard railings. Finn Bonger pays the fee for all members of the group. There is time enough to take a photo or two, which some do (Angela, Elsa), or grab a snack from a pannier (Ray Rudiger), but little time for fraternizing or cozying up to a target of amorous speculation (sorry, Tim!). There is hardly time for passing a comment about waterfowl (Finn to Ruth) or how cloud formations give definition to the blue sky overhead (Isla to Candace). There is just enough time for the whisperings of innuendo that pass across the deck of the ferry like the susurrations of the breeze.

By eleven thirty the group has formed another single file, this one on the east shore of the Maas and continues the ride towards Afferden. Over the next two hours or so, routes bordering the Maas take them through open country and small villages into the vicinity of Well. At one thirty they stop by the entrance to Kasteel Well.

After bikes are parked on both sides of the Kasteellaan Road and panniers taken, Finn Bonger gathers the cyclists together and explains: "Kasteel Well is now the property of a college in the USA. It caters to students from abroad, mostly from America, interested in expanding their knowledge of European culture. Educational excursions throughout Europe on extended weekends are part of the program."

"When was the castle built?" JJ asks.

"I believe it is from the fourteenth century. It has two what you call moats, inner and outer and a courtyard by the round brick tower. There are gardens at the back with beautiful flower beds that some of you might like to inspect. Also fountains. Also ruins. Follow the path either way. We have twenty minutes to look and enjoy."

"Dutch dictator," Ray Rudiger calls out, dropping his pannier and folding his arms.

"Twenty minutes only," Finn continues. "Then we must ride on. Our route this afternoon will take us back to the west shore of the Maas."

"So why the hell did we cross to this side?" Ray wants to know. He looks around for an answer but gets none. "Just a rhetorical question, folks, that's all."

The group breaks up into small clutches that start to amble across the brick bridge spanning the outer moat, some to the right, some to the left. Seeing that the twins go off to the right, as does Ray Rudiger, Candace and Isla go off to the left and stop where it is convenient to sit and rest. They take delight in feeding bits of bread pulled from unfinished sandwiches to the swans scooting about in the outer moat.

I hold up here and allow myself a little happy reminiscence about how much Aphrodite loves her birds, doves in particular but also sparrows and swans. In effect, a moment or two of downtime for me from the constant hovering and eavesdropping, not that I couldn't sustain my endeavours ad infinitum should that be my wish. The time Finn Bonger grants his group of cyclists grants me the opportunity, dear reader, to instruct you further regarding my relationship with Aphrodite. Ages ago, it is believed by some, she advised me about being too frivolous, if not too frivolous, then too whimsical, if not too whimsical, then out and out malicious. The error lies in the identity of the one to whom she addressed these remarks. She anticipated well the frivolous, whimsical, and sometimes malicious antics not of yours truly but those of her little bosom pal, stupid Cupid. Also, I did not, and still do not, contest the belief that she is my adopted mother. Truth is, I played along with the pseudo adoption as a concession to Zeus to keep power politics to a minimum. Recollect, informed reader, how Isla Troyes had the whole relationship sorted out correctly when in the Rijksmuseum with Candace.

Although some of the *Amoretto Algea* group will likely have hustled to complete the circuit around the Kasteel Well grounds, and some apparently did, they need not have rushed or have felt bound by the twenty minutes allowed by Finn Bonger. The last to arrive back at the driveway is Tim Pickett. In his extended right hand he carries a yellow tulip as though he were participating in a ceremony. When he sees that the group has formed a semi-circle around an upturned bike with Finn Bonger fiddling with it, he hands the flower to Tom who laughs and quickly discards it at the base of a large tree, one or two marking the entrance like giant, green-topped Cyclopes.

"She's got a flat tire," Tom says to Tim as they move in.

"Who's got a flat tire? Not Isla, surely."

"No, not Isla. Angela, the woman with the flowery cycling gear."

"In no time at all, Finn will have it fixed," Ruth informs the twins. "He must get used to incidents like this. He comes prepared. Drake's a good help."

The incident delays the group's setting out by a good twenty minutes time, Finn explains to those close enough to hear, that might have been better spent at their next scheduled stop. To make up for the lost time, they will take the Koninginnebruge across the Maas rather than the ferry which operates further up the river. After the flat tire is repaired, Drake's work for the most part, Finn leads the cyclists out from Kasteel Well towards the bridge. In a long, straight single file they cross to the west side and, taking the Veerweg road that roughly follows the bends in the Maas, head for Broekhuisen, the next town in their schedule. They make good time through open country and along shaded roadways. Along one straight section, they encounter several elderly couples on elaborate e-bikes. Bulging saddle bags bounce rhythmically as they pass. Quick greetings are exchanged.

"Pole," Cole Cantlay calls out, echoing the calls ahead of him. And like those ahead of him, he slows down to pass black and white lane markers. Benny Giles is behind him.

"Pole. Pole. Pole." Benny readily shouts out to his father who is close behind and slowing down.

Shortly after, with Otto standing by his bike indicating a left hand turn past the Het Maashotel and the Café 't Tolhuisje, it's down an incline to the Arcen-Broekhuizen ferry slip.

"What?" Ray Rudiger shouts loud enough for everyone to hear. "Another bloody ferry."

"It just reached the other side," JJ observes. "We'll be away again before you know it. Finn's has this all timed out."

"He rides roughshod over us."

"Ray's not used to having others make decisions for him," Ruth explains to JJ and Angela.

"What she said," Ray agrees, indicating Ruth. "I still think the guy's got it in for me."

"Don't you think he has reason to, dear?"

Ruth's matter of fact question induces Ray to suck his lips into a trumpet shape through which he blows out a series of disapproving notes. JJ and Angela pull back, seemingly much amused.

The *Amoretto Algea* cyclists now lined up in orderly fashion at the terminal are not the only ones waiting to make the crossing to the east side of the Maas. Bikes are evident everywhere. People are everywhere. Picnic tables dotting the surrounding terrain are fully occupied and mark the area as a recreational stopover for cyclists. Umbrellaed café terrasses add further levels of accommodation. Tree boles topped with sculptures inspire curiosity. They do so with Isla and Candace who park their bikes and wander over to regard what looks like a work of metal contorted into the shape of an airy creature with bent wings. Concluding what they do about the sculpture, Candace turns back, Isla following a moment later. Together they return to their place in line just behind Finn Bonger.

"Whoa! Whoa! Whoa! Holy shit!" Tom Pickett bellows rapid fire.

He is absolutely unconcerned about disturbing the serenity of the scene with his obscenities.

"What the fuck just hit me?"

"What do you mean, hit you?" Tim asks.

"Something hit me.'

"Nothing hit you, man," Tim insists. "You're just imagining things."

"No, no, it's real," Tom counters, clenching a fist and pounding his chest. "In my gut, sorta, and limbs. Like an electric shock. Lost my balance. Like getting crushed by a blocking fullback."

Tom stumbles toward Tim and in doing so knocks his bike over and then his brother's bike. Hushed amusement arises from the ranks surrounding them as they right the bikes. Isla and Candace snicker. Ray Rudiger's loud guffaw increases the hilarity in those observing the twins' confusion.

"Get it together, man, you're embarrassing yourself," Tim says, knocking Tom on the shoulder. "And me."

"The way you did all the family with your moaning and groaning," Tom says defensively, "and your endless hankering for the so-called girl of your dreams. But I kinda see now why you went on."

"You do?"

"I do. She's lovely, isn't she? Very desirable."

"Who you talking about? Candace?"

"Isla, that's who. I'm all screwed up. I mean... I can't see straight."

"How many fingers?"

"Two. No, three."

"Right, three."

"She must be a witch or something. But I gotta..."

"You're jonesing, aren't you?"

"What?"

"Longing to be with her. You are, I can tell. You're just like me, man, just like me. Definitely. You're pining, just like me."

"But I get it now, bro. I really get it."

Indeed he gets it. I made sure of that when the perfect opportunity presented itself. As Isla and Candace turned back from inspecting the sculpture, Tom Pickett had them in his sights. And I had him in mine.

As you know, dear reader, chaos is in my DNA and I make no apology for bringing it on when I am moved to do so. I have a fondness for my place of origin and like to perpetuate its relevance, and I make no apology there either. I acknowledge chaos as a necessary and fundamental principle of my operations in the space-time continuum, and I make no apology about that as well. Like an agent provocateur on a mission, my arrow can disturb how a mortal normally conducts affairs. In this case, I've arranged for a double dose of amused distraction for all the *Amoretto Algea* guests. It's what I can do, get a kick out of doing, and make no apology about seeing it done.

So, one of my gold-tipped arrows penetrating the breast? Yes, precisely. The heart pounds, the ears ring, etcetera, etcetera, etcetera, and an irrepressible, overwhelming, magnificent confusion arises in the core of one's being. Thus, Tom Pickett, in a whirly-gig world just like his twin. Tom Pickett who previously scoffed at my handiwork.

As JJ predicted, in no time at all the ferry arrives from the east bank of the Maas, unloads on the west bank and then, loading up again with cyclists, crosses back to the east bank. Within fifteen minutes of scurrying off the ferry, the Amoretto Algea gang are locking up bikes in the parking space behind the Hertog Jan brewery. Finn Bonger has designated a forty-five minute break.

"That's it?" Ray Rudiger calls out as he detaches his pannier. "A mere forty-five minutes?"

"It's too late to do the tour of the brewery," Finn announces, "but not too late to sample the brew. Think of our break as down time with bottoms up."

"What do you think he means by bottoms up?" Tom Pickett asks Tim Pickett when the applause for Finn's announcement peters out.

"Don't know," Tim answers. "What do you think he means by bottoms up?"

"Don't know. That's why I asked you, bro."

"Yeah, right."

"So, right here, then," Tom says, running his bike along a fence and securing it.

It appears the twins have been exchanging remarks as they rode along shoulder to shoulder. Exchanging barbs, perhaps. Whatever the medium of exchange, locked in an unusual kind of fraternal debate is likely a more accurate description of how they have been engaging each other.

"You're in no condition to throw down, man, here or anywhere else," Tim insists.

And the debate continues. If a reader, who is cognizant of thematic imagery, were to toss a football into the mix, an equally metaphorical disappointment would no doubt be the result.

"Come on. Don't crap out on me, bro," Tom challenges, forming a fist with his right hand. "Rock, paper, scissors!"

"Best of three," Tim says after a moment's consideration. He sounds agreeable enough. He raises and lowers his right hand in quick movements as though trying to shake up an incontrovertible truth before releasing it.

"Roshambo," Drake explains to Otto and Elsa who are watching the goings-on, puzzled about what the twins are doing with their hands actually means.

"It's an unsophisticated method we have of determining who wins or who gets first choice in some matter. A way of resolving a friendly disagreement or argument."

"Is amusing, *ja*?" Elsa says, smiles, and turns with Otto to follow the others, Finn Bonger leading the way with Candace and Isla right on his heels.

"Okay, three out of five!"

One cannot help noticing a long flow pipe stretching across an open area from the brewery to the café. Inside, a shiny brass pipe continues the flow of brews to service the taps at the bar. It is a brightly lit bar with decorative jugs hanging above it and behind it are cabinets replete with a range of bottled choices, all locally produced. The atmosphere is pub-like, warm and inviting. Ample seating is available and that suits the

Amoretto Algea cyclists perfectly as they find comfortable accommodation in this corner and that. Service is immediate and friendly and the time allotted for the stopover passes quickly.

When Finn Bonger excuses himself from their table and walks over to the bar to talk to a server he appears to know well, Candace makes the sign of the heart with the index fingers and thumbs of both hands. Isla smiles approvingly.

As well you know, dear readers, love is not always self-effectuating: hence my input. But in the vibes occurring between Candace Troyes and Finn Bonger, the attraction is self-effectuating and therefore needs no action of mine. We'll see how things between them unfold over the next three nights.

Before leaving the Hertog Jan establishment, Ray Rudiger enjoins JJ to visit the men's washroom. "It's a must see even if it is not a must use. Very colourful and for us at our age a reminder of our limitations. Labels mark each of the urinals with a given brand of brew available here in this joint. Choose your bottle, choose your pissoir."

The *Amoretto Algea* is docked alongside a jetty on the south side of Arcen. The cyclists are required to dismount, secure their panniers, and leave their bikes with Finn Bonger and Dirk van Kesteren to load onboard, then each must negotiate a ramp leading up at an angle to the entrance of the barge. The last in line to follow the procedure are Ruth Rudiger and Tom Pickett.

"Nice town, Arcen," Ruth comments. "Didn't take us too long to get here from the Hertog Jan pub."

"No, not too long," Tom agrees, dropping his pannier. "You're Ruth, right? I was told you are a good source to talk to about romance and stuff. I don't mean anything kinky, though."

"Which one are you? Tim or Tom?"

"Tom. I'm Tom."

"Romance and stuff? But nothing to do with la vie en rose kind of stuff. What's on your mind, Tom?"

"What I need to know is, like, without acting like an idiot the way my brother has been doing, or being too direct and be put down embarrassed, what's the best way to let someone know you're interested in them?"

"You mean, interested in her. And her in question is Isla Troyes. True?"

"True. I'm overwhelmed by her. Fascinated. It's like...it's like nothing I've experienced before. Driving me mad."

"I understand."

"There's a kind of glow about her. Know what I mean?

Something pure."

"Yes, I know what you mean."

"So, like, I was wondering, a bouquet of white roses?"

"Why white?"

"Because white is supposed to represent purity. Right? Besides, my brother says red means...well, I'm not sure. He's got nowhere with her. We're both taken with Isla, you see."

"That's become obvious in the last few hours. White versus red. Sounds like you two are having your own war of roses."

"We're competitive. Have been since we were kids, way back. But nothing like this. Hit out of the blue."

"Tom, I think you should see Elsa Müller, Otto's wife. She runs a florist shop in Dusseldorf. She'd be up on symbolism, flower arrangements, and bouquets. She's easy to talk to. She might recommend something helpful. Anything I might tell you would lead to...well... further confusion."

Tom Pickett wastes little time getting in touch with Elsa Müller. She recommends that before dinner he visit La Belle Fleur, a high-profile florist shop on the main drag of Arcen that the group cycled by earlier en route to the *Amoretto Algea*. She expresses an amused sense of appreciation in the form a wide smile when Tom immediately sets off.

Dinner on day five of the *Amoretto Algea* adventure proceeds in the usual way, all the guests engrossed in their usual kind of table talk while digging into another of Chef Simon's culinary delights. There is, however, no presentation of a bouquet of roses to anyone, which is not unusual at all. When all is said and done, and table five gets cleared and wiped clean, Kirk van Kesteren hands Bonnie Pickett the aluminum case she requested. Joining her and Dexter in a poker game are Mick Mallory, Ray Rudiger, and JJ.

"I've been meaning to tell you, fella," Bonnie says to Ray, "you're inviting bad luck big time."

"Yeah, you're a dead man," says Dexter. His words sound ominous. They come across like a threat as he raps a clenched fist on the table top a few times.

"Why's that?" Ray Rudiger asks, sneering incredulously.

"You've got the dead man's poker hand," Bonnie says and shakes her head. She continues shuffling the cards while Dexter organizes the chips around the table.

"You mean this?" Ray challenges, pointing to his upper arm.

"Yup. Black aces, black eights. Your five of diamonds is negligible."

"I know the story," Ray states, rubbing his arm. "I'm contrarian by nature and consider it good luck. At bottom, it's just a tattoo, for Christ's sake."

"Serious players think of it as bad luck," Bonnie says.

"I'm not a serious player," Ray contends, counting his chips.

"That's obvious," Dexter says. "One man's goose is another man's gander."

"Wrong. That's not how the saying goes."

"Well, fella, how about your goose is cooked?" Bonnie snaps.

"Looks like they're just setting you up," JJ says, lifting his chin in Ray's direction. "Get you off your game."

"Cut the cards, Ray!" Dexter says gruffly.

"Yeah, and ante up, fella."

Day Six
not suitable material

Arcen to Roermond:

The lounge in the *Amoretto Algea*. As is his wont, Mick Malory sits with his early morning coffee writing another email to his daughter, cc to his son. Ruth Rudiger has not yet appeared nor has Professor Wolfgang.

"Another day to look forward to on this fabulous odyssey of mine. It is physically demanding but not without rewards of various kinds; it also provides an opportunity to gain greater perspective on our family tragedy. Soon the professor will appear and engage me in our continuing discussion about your beloved mother's untimely death and what my response to it has been. I don't hold back. I let it all hang out. Episodic, largely. Morning fare for the most part. I open up with another fellow traveller called Ruth who, like the professor, listens well and is very understanding about the vicissitudes of life and love. Talking with virtual strangers provides greater objectivity, if you see what I mean. It's sort of like being in therapy again but with more distancing, even more than what Greece granted me when I was last there. Not exactly an exorcism of the emotional demons that hounded me for so long, although I have got into that with both of them. I'd describe our conversations in these early morning sessions as more like a psychological levelling out that has certain cathartic effects. I feel good about getting on that bike each day and riding my brains out or, to put it more crudely, riding my ass off.

"Professor Wolfgang Albrecht is a really interesting guy. I've readily connected with him since that first evening meal. Wolfgang walks with a slight limp and wears colourful kerchiefs. Very European, the scarves thing. A large white moustache overhanging his upper lip and bushy eyebrows give him a somewhat wild appearance despite the wire rimmed glasses that signal a kind of cultured dignity, at least that's what I see when listening to him or when he listens to me. Observant, dark brown eyes sparkle with interest. However, he does not look overly bookish, which he is, of course, bookish, being a philosophy professor. He's to write a book on Nietzsche. His voice is deep and a little raspy and portends both authority and conviction, but Wolfgang is anything but overbearing. His conversational style is very informal, like being tuned into Beethoven on an easy-listening radio station. As well as being an expert on existential philosophers— Nietzsche, Heidegger, Sartre, Camus et al— he's a Thomas Mann aficionado. I know so little about that author that I feel unable to ask Wolfgang intelligent questions. The man's a movie buff but asking him what he thinks of the movie they made of Mann's *Death in Venice* is not too profound. He did give me his impressions though. He liked it. And as to existential philosophy, he did give me a primer on Sartre's *en soi - pour soi* and Camus' Absurd, and also a few pointers on existential psychology and how it is organized to help individuals such as me with the story I have to tell. Insightful.

"Ruth Rudiger. I may as well tell you about her as well. She's Canadian, from Calgary and into cycling. Once a high school counsellor, she now writes a lovelorn column which, she tells me, she takes very seriously in that it's all about helping people sort things out in their lives. She's definitely personable, and it seems everybody on the Amoretto Algea knows her and has talked at length with her. Her husband, Ray, is a character and it seems everybody onboard has had dealings with him in one form or another, not all positive. The Rudigers are celebrating forty years of marriage but Ray seems indifferent as to how Ruth is enjoying the bike and barge experience. Has his own agenda which does not reflect very well on a long-lasting, loving relationship. In one of his little asides, Ray described Ruth this way to me: 'She's like an external drive, capable of holding tons of business related facts and figures all to our mutual benefit as a well-to-do family. Not only that, she has a list of all the misdemeanors known to man committed by man, that man, more often than not, being me.'

Ruth proves herself very philosophical about husband Ray. She allows that first impressions may be accurate enough but only to a certain degree. True, Ray loves to be in the limelight, she confesses, and can be obnoxiously loud about it. However, she states emphatically, first impressions can be very limiting in what they reveal about the man behind the appearances, the good aspects of his character, his generosity not only in terms financial support for recognized charities and for other needy organizations and but also in terms of time volunteered in the service of youth groups and sports or cultural events for all ages. In other words, Ruth's contention is that husband Ray is much more than he pretends to be, like the vociferous bossy type given to sexual innuendo. As to Ruth herself, she's a very patient and sympathetic woman. In that regard, she reminds me a lot of your mother.

"Must close off. The professor is working his way over from the coffee machine."

Before greeting Mick, Wolfgang indulges in a prolonged yawn. It transitions into the reason why he is later than usual this morning, the crux of it being he endured a fitful sleep because of the commotion in the hallway he heard during the night. He punctuates his explanation with a raised eyebrow and a sly smile.

"We talked about how the pain of loss affects a man's peace of mind," he adds, "just so with a man's loss of sleep."

"A restless night, then," Mick says sympathetically.

"I make of it a joke now."

"Ruth's late today as well," Mick adds, casting a searching eye about the dining area.

"This is a bright woman, Ruth. She knows the ideas of Kierkegaard and..."

"Right, like those we discussed here and there, truth is subjectivity and so on."

"With Kierkegaard we begin and get to Nietzsche and then to Heidegger and to the meaning of being in the world. Ruth, she understands— *ach*, what is the word?"

"Intuitively?"

"Yes, intuitively. She asked about Heidegger and his involvement with National Socialism."

"So called, right?"

"Just so. Heidegger did not backtrack, *ja*. It is thought he considered his political involvement close to being the greatest stupidity of his life."

"That's something, at least."

"Although support for him is divided, some hold that his affiliation with the Nazis was antithetical to his philosophy."

"Is that Ruth's point?"

"*Ja*, she is insightful," Wolfgang replies. "And that may be the case, what she implies. However, I would suggest to you that the apparent contradiction in Heidegger's life be summed up as personal error. This is how he described it."

"Ruth's erudite, well informed. We talked yesterday, she and I. She knows all about cognitive reframing and grasped immediately how it guided me out of the depths of my discontent and my despair about living without Delores."

"You told me how you did transcend your need for revenge against Flower. This is good."

"Revenge, yeah, it possessed me like a demon. But I did get beyond the need to avenge her tragic death. That's true. The circumstances I told you about drained me emotionally and bent me mentally out of shape to the point of ethical crisis. I definitely needed help, which, fortunately, I received."

"You discovered for yourself what being in the world means for you in the face of what cannot be changed."

"That about sums it up, Professor. The gnawing urge gave way eventually to the definite conviction that Flower was nothing but an instrument of fate. Delores' death, Flower's part in it, and my response to both had been written up like a dictum irrespective of any moral order I understood.

Events were orchestrated, beyond my paltry will or sense of duty, to fall into place the way they did."

"Heidegger would acknowledge this as truth."

"Maybe so, but I did feel cheated by fate, never having the opportunity to murmur bedside words of comfort or of hope for imminent recovery."

"This too must be acknowledged, *ja*."

"Oh, yeah. Flower's fall from grace, if ever in my mind 'grace' were associated with his name, was an outcome that time arranged according to its own whims and caprices or by dint of some elemental force of natural justice."

"*Ach*, here is Ruth coming. But you must tell me before the end of our excursion what became of Flower and what you call his fall from grace."

"In a word, Nemesis."

"Retribution, *ja*."

"That's it exactly. As one pubic notice on his fate put it: Silas T. Flower, not suitable material for the role of tragic hero. The details of just how this is so, Wolfgang, can keep until later."

With Ruth's arrival, unusually late this morning, the line begins to form for the breakfast offerings. Once all the guests are seated, Finn Bonger begins his announcements.

"Today we leave Arcen, pass through Venlo, have a longer stop in Kessel, and in the late afternoon we get to Roermond where there are many fine restaurants for you. The route today, like in the previous days, will follow the Meuse as much as possible. Also, we will go back and forth across the river a couple of times."

"Why back and forth again?" Ray Rudiger asks, wielding a fork back and forth over his plate.

"We follow the most scenic route is why. And we visit the most interesting towns. For example, Venlo is important historically. It is also architecturally interesting, as you shall see on our ride."

"Finn, could you explain summat's been puzzling me and Benny," Nigel Giles calls out. He rubs his son's head affectionately.

"Of course."

"Right, then. The river is called the Maas, innit? Also the Meuse. What's the difference?"

"Maas is Dutch. Meuse is from the French and Latin. I think. It refers to how the river meanders. It has many bends and turns."

"The English word maze probably derives from the same roots," Ruth adds and gets a grateful look from Benny.

"So, about Roermond," Finn continues, "this evening you are responsible for your own dinners."

Murmurs.

"Yes, Angela. Oh, I forgot. Has anyone found a ring? Silver. Angela cannot find a silver ring of hers."

"No? No one?"

"And speaking of losing or misplacing things," Ray Rudiger says in a typically insistent voice, "I'm minus a travel card. Anyone find it? It's blue. It's special. Has my name on it. Anyone?"

"No? No one, Mister Rudiger. Sorry. Okay, we set out at nine."

Access to and from the quay where the *Amoretto Algea* rests is by way of a long, slightly inclined, brick-paved driveway that forms part of a riverside park and recreational area. Finn Bonger stands by his bike at the top of the run counting the cyclists as they approach the road out of Arcen. Today the count is eighteen, with Conor St James already departed and Dexter Pickett again remaining with the barge because of his injury. Once again Drake Cantlay has offered to serve as sweep. Bright sunshine and moderate tailwinds encourage the cyclists to pedal along at a steady pace.

Shortly after ten o'clock, Finn Bonger arranges a quick stop for the group at the Het Vorst Fruit market.

"Available for purchase is a variety of offerings, from assorted locally produced cheeses to fruit and vegetables, honey and jams, curios and bric-a-brac."

Almost all the group takes to the inside, setting bikes in an arrangement that puts me in mind of the foremost line in a phalanx of ancient warriors, this one all chrome and vibrant colour. Benny and his father remain by the bikes. Mother has promised the lad a surprise. While waiting, Benny arranges the back wheel of each bike perfectly in line, making sure that the valve of each tire is aligned in exactly the same position below each back fender. That, dear readers, is concentration of the first order and definitely deserving of a surprise.

The cycling continues, never deviating too far from the Meuse, and by ten forty-five the group is coasting along Parade, a popular thoroughfare in central Venlo. Finn Bonger halts the pedaling where Parade intersects Klaasstraat, an equally busy cobbled lane. Modest commercial interests are evident on both sides of the strip but innumerable boutiques, cafés, pubs, and eateries dominate: they mark the area as the reserve of pedestrians and cyclists. Outdoor seating under umbrellas and awnings is ubiquitous.

"This coffee break," Finn declares, "will last until everyone is ready to go again. Lock bikes and take panniers."

Tables and chairs from the Koffiepauze Café are available in the center of the junction and attract the interest of many in the group. The Giles family begins walking up Klaasstraat, Benny bouncing ahead.

"Man, there are bikes everywhere in this town," Tim Pickett observes, pointing in all directions. He then pulls out a chair for his mother, Bonnie, and one for himself.

"Where's Isla?" Tom wants to know, standing arms akimbo.

"Strolling off with Candace up there," Tim answers.

"You two still competing for the attention of that little plain Jane?" Bonnie teases, waving insistently at a waitress. "At least the other gal has some real sex appeal."

"Yeah, right, Ma," Tim responds. "Ruth Rudiger and that professor guy are with them. And when I see that old fellow pedaling along and keeping up just fine, I figure Dad should be here with us."

"Your father has his own agenda and don't you forget it. He cleaned up last night at cards. Just try and appreciate that. Cleaned Rudiger out and enjoyed doing it."

"Gets me all heated up," Tom says.

"What?"

"Isla, Ma. Always it's Isla."

"So the cold shoulder she keeps giving you should help cool you down," Bonnie says and cackles gleefully.

"Ma, I don't think the girl's frigid the way you say," Tom argues and finds agreement with Tim. "You're just used to the casino gals. She's not like that."

"Shameless. Both of you. You're just not up to it, boys, not like on campus. You and your useless bouquets of sentimental claptrap."

"How can someone so cool be so hot?" Tom's question comes across like a lament as he stands there holding the back of his chair.

"Stop whining!" Bonnie says. "It's unbecoming a grown man."

"Mind if I join you," Ray Rudiger asks, sliding a chair over from another table.

"Feel free," Bonnie says, motioning for Tom to sit down.

"Thank you," Ray says, an ambiguous smile anchoring his apparent gratitude. "I couldn't help but hear your concerns regarding the young women in our group. Maybe they're more interested in hooking up with a mature type, a man of the world such as me. Ever give that possibility any thought, boys?"

"You gotta be kidding, fella," Bonnie says.

"Not so much," Ray counters, and after the waitress takes their order and heads back into the café, he says. "Well, *que sera, sera,* as the song goes."

"Good luck, old man," Bonnie says. "Too bad you wasted a lot of it up last night playing poker."

"Easy come, easy go."

"I see you've got your tattoo covered today. What happened, we spook you?"

"Dead man's hand, give me a break," Ray counters. "I may have lost a few bucks last night, but that's the extent of it. Nothing fateful about it at all as far as I can see."

"Fate plays some strange hands, fella," Bonnie says lifting an eyebrow. "Doubling down rarely works as a bluff."

"Whatever. Did you notice any of those interesting buildings we passed getting to this spot?" Ray is beginning to look as though he's had enough of Bonnie Pickett's advice for the present.

"Interesting, if you're interested in looking," Bonnie says. "Do you know if there's a casino in Maastricht?"

Tim and Tom shrug their shoulders. Ray shakes his head and looks over to the adjacent table where Finn Bonger is engaged with the Cantlays, JJ and Angela Jones.

"What would you say, Finn," JJ asks, "ours a typical group?"

"Pretty much. People from different countries. We get a lot of Germans and Americans. Canadians too."

"All good reviews, I should think," Cole offers.

"Not always, but I've only been with the *Amoretto Algea* a short time. A recent review described us a not being sympathetic to all the guests' concerns. It's simple, really, people lose things or misplace them and eventually find them. No need for alarm bells ringing or calling in the authorities."

"All above suspicion, of course, you and the rest of the crew."

"Absolutely. The Argentinian group we had two trips ago were not too praising of our efforts to keep them happy. They thought us suspicious."

"Really?"

"Really. They were something else. Not at all typical like you people. A collection of wealthy middle-aged men and their trophy wives, eight in total, all showing off."

"Ostentatious, were they?" JJ asks.

"If that means parading around demanding this and that, then, yeah, they were what you said."

"Sounds like you were dealing with gross expectation and assumed privilege. I've had dealings with people like that."

"The young ladies were in their late twenties and early thirties. Beautiful, but somehow not real, not like Candace Troyes in our group. That's real beauty."

"Agreed," Drake says nodding.

"Meretricious hags, were they?" Ray Rudiger chimes in, having abandoned the Pickett table and intending to join this one. The scraping of his chair legs across the cobbles gets an unfavourable reaction from both JJ and Cole.

"According to Chef Simon," Finn continues, "the alfa type in the group was a wanker, making all kinds of demands about the meals they preferred with no understanding of how procurements are made on an excursion like this."

"I don't think you want to be doing that," Cole says, "making special requests of Chef

Simon. He has his way of delivering delicious meals."

"Chef Simon also has a way with words. He called the wives a sorority of saucy vixens."

"That's rich," Ray comments and then snickers. "Saucy vixens sounds appetizing. Titbits you'd want to work your gums around."

"Captain Van der Oor warned us during our meeting the first night out. In his peculiar way of expressing things, he defined them as a type of groupthink propped up by uniformity."

"That's saying something," JJ observes.

"What really bugged me about the men was their attempts to prove their vitality and their virility as if the extent of each hadn't been established publicly already."

"What you mean is beauty was masking truth," Drake says.

"I suppose that's what I'm saying, considering age and its physical limitations regardless of enhancement or remedy.

"They were caught trying to be what they were not," Drake continues knowingly. "Both the men and the women."

"Right on."

"So what was the issue that brought the unfavourable review?" JJ asks. "I'm sure you all kept your opinions to yourselves."

"One of the ladies complained that somebody had stolen her necklace. She was a bit of a tease, this one, a come-on if you catch my drift. She pointed her finger at Dirk, then accused me in private of covering up for him. I found myself in a delicate situation. A couple of days later, her husband found the necklace in the bottom of her pannier.”

“I was thinking about what you said this morning, Finn, about a lost ring and my travel card, also presumably lost.”

“You found it?”

“No, I didn’t. But I have my suspicions about these missing articles. Conor St James, he’s always on the boat by the time we get there after our cycling for the day. Who knows how much time he has to freewheel about, like in the rooms. You said at the start of the excursion that locking our rooms was optional, that each day they were serviced by crew, namely Dirk van Kesteren.”

“So, you think maybe Conor is a thief?”

“Could be.”

“Well, then it follows that you must also suspect Dirk.” Finn suggests. “But hear me, Dirk’s above suspicion.”

“What about Pickett?” Ray says. “He’s missed another day of cycling. Could be him.”

“Where are you going with this, Ray?” JJ asks, evincing a species of tolerant disdain. His deep voice deepens.

“Trying to get to the truth,” Ray answers, and then turning his attention to the

Picketts, he calls out, "Your father a thief, boys?"

"He may be a little standoffish but, man, he ain't no thief," Tim says.

"That's exactly right, bro. In his line of work, he deals with a lot of losers. Don't consider yourself special in his eyes. Got it?"

"Do yourself a favour, Ray," Bonnie chimes in, "and check the bottom of your pannier." She punctuates her remark with her staccato cackle.

Occupying another of the Koffiepauze Café tables are Mick Mallory and the Müller couple.

"Wolfgang was impatient," Elsa says to Mick, "when Otto said he looked like Friedrich Nietzsche. I think the expression you have in English is put off, *ja*?"

"I had no idea. I mean that he resembled Friedrich Nietzsche."

"Very much so," Otto says and snorts.

"And no idea that he was put off in being thought of as resembling Nietzsche. He's talked to me about Nietzsche and other philosophers."

"To you he listens patiently," Otto continues after another impatient snort. "To us he complains about such modern conveniences as the internet. *Kacke und Dreck*, he says about the content. All crap, *ja*? Keep up all the nonsense language, he says, and by the end of the century, we'll be grunting again to see our basic needs met, like cavemen."

"He's helped me gain greater insight about sorting things out in my life. He asks probing questions, then lets me ramble. Or rant, as the case may be."

"Rant?"

"Rant means talking angrily about something that bothers you."

Elsa says: "*Herr* Professor, he can rant, *ja*. Did you ever imagine that you would be witness to the destruction of human civilization as we understand it, even with all its shortcomings? *Herr* Professor puts to me this kind of question."

"He's right in the sense that our generation bears responsibility in many ways for the upheaval of the world around us. 'Life refuses to accommodate wishful thinking' he's said to me on more than one occasion. I get what he means by that in the general sense of necessary remedial actions, but with me it has more to do with personal redirection."

"We bear responsibility, *ja*," Otto says, "but not necessarily all the guilt. Did he mention Nietzsche's *Amor fati* to you?

"Not yet, no."

"Perhaps he will. Now, please, Mick, let me get your coffee."

"And I will take a picture of you and Otto," Elsa says, "together at coffee, *ja*, and then of all our *Amoretto Algea* people at these tables."

The time is ten forty-five. Finn calls the group together and outlines the route they will take until their next scheduled stop in Kessel. Crossing the river to the west side is how they will start. Stretches along the Legioenweg bikeway make for excellent cycling. Nice views of historic towns. Beautiful country.

While the group crosses the bridge and cycles its way from Venlo to Kessel, I'll pass on to you, patient reader, while I hover along over them, other significant information regarding the august assembly of Olympians and how I, Eros, operate as god of love and passionate desire, in other words, my modus operandi.

In communicating with mortals, we gods and goddesses use the language of those that recognize us, that follow what we say and do. Most useful is English because of its range and adaptability. Among the Romance languages, French is the most precise. We can express ourselves well enough in German. As to the rest, our instruction is, go get a translation. Greek? Of course, but classical, that of Demosthenes and the great tragedians, not the more vulgar demotic vernacular.

Latin? Only in the unlikely event of consorting with ecclesiastics relying on churchy argot. Mostly, it's basic English, my attempts with the iambic pentameter Shakespeare employed in his great tragedies having left me breathless, so to say. In using English, I make every effort to avoid splitting infinitives or ending a sentence with a preposition. Believe me when I say that I abhor mixing metaphors. As to the awkwardness resulting from non sequiturs, I've had little criticism. And it is I who made asking rhetorical questions popular with eminent speakers, especially the mortal ones. My peers have jeered at me for being wordy, especially Apollo, the so-called source of intellectual light, who believes he's cornered the market on eloquence (being the patron of poets and musicians and such, although resentment arises when he shoulders Calliope and others of the Muse Sisterhood out of the way as he does when it suits him). But I'm indifferent to criticism. Bombastic? Me? No, absolutely not. Loquacious, rather, thank you very much. Recall the great accomplishment of Doctor Samuel Johnson, an enlightenment scholar of great intellectual acumen and perseverance; intending precision, clarity of definition, and consistent spelling, he developed the dictionary for everyday use. Was his work inspired by Apollo? If so, then Apollo should use a dictionary when stymied by something I've articulated or the phrase I've employed to make a point. I've cajoled him about that frequently. Truth be told, he's quite capable of getting very hot-headed when things don't go his way. No pun intended. Admittedly, certain words are buried in my memory; lack of salient vocabulary is not a shortcoming of mine when communicating with my esteemed and learned reader. I just have to dig a little deeper sometimes to find *le mot juste*, as picky French linguists demand.

A further word or two about words. I've also been accused of considering myself an etymological rock star, to borrow a label from contemporary lingo. None can deny that I influence language, psychological terminology, and social entertainments with terms like erogenous, erotica, and erotic. As to the influence of my daughter, Hedone, her name has been associated with pleasure, enjoyment, delight; cognates include hedonism and hedonistic. True, philosophers bandied about the meaning of her reality, from the Stoics and Epicurus to Aristotle, the latter giving her meaning a five star rating if balanced with nature and if the result of reason and virtue. Aphrodite got aphrodisiac and not much more. Never mind about cupidity for the time being.

Regardless of how my peers view my linguistic manipulations, I must admit that we all perform our various roles to the benefit of those residing in our wide estate, namely, in what is understood as the West. As to the Orient and what it encompasses, we agreed among ourselves to leave its denizens to their own devices, that is to say, to their own demi-gods and full-on divinities.

I think it both timely and poignant at this stage in my narrative, dear reader, to draw a couple of themes together. To this end, let me work with two authoritative sources in explaining the workings of fate in the affairs of mortal beings. I'll leave the immortals and the consequences of their actions to the Olympian court. Nonetheless, reconsider for a moment Prometheus' lot. What was the tragic flaw in his character? Excessive concern for humanity? Remember how in doing what he did for the benefit of mere mortals he really pissed off Zeus. Prometheus had to know what suffering he would have to endure in that he possessed foresight. In his case, call it retribution on the divine scale.

There are many commentators with a lot to say about destiny in the human sphere but the two I have chosen with good reason for your edification, dear reader, are credited with the kind of provenance that only centuries of respect provide, millennia, in effect, buttressed with knowledge of both truth and beauty. The point is this: how Olympian gods and goddess see that the stipulations of the Fates get carried out. With this in mind, take into account the way mortals frequently make choices that bring on dire consequences. Who, then, am I referencing? Heraclitus and, of course, Aristotle.

Heraclitus of Ephesus, a renowned pre-Socratic philosopher, introduced the notion of eternal flux, inexorable change, the world as constant becoming. More germane to our present concern, however, is his belief that a person's fate is determined by his character, be he or she the subject of a prophecy or the victim of a curse. This motif has received widespread dramatic treatment, initially in the ancient world of my ascendance and then down through subsequent ages. Although he finds fault with some of the speculative positions in Heraclitus' world view, when it comes to an individual's fate and how time and place have it play out, Aristotle of necessity stands on the ground established earlier by Heraclitus. Character is indeed fate.

Aristotle models his prescriptive ideas on Sophocles' *Oedipus Rex*. In an attempt to avoid the prophecy that he would kill his father and marry his mother, prideful Oedipus takes action that ironically leads him to commit the very crimes he wishes to avoid. In the unfolding of events he comes to the realization he cannot escape a fate dictated by divine decree. Hubris, excessive pride in Oedipus' case, at work.

Aristotle's formulation: an individual, neither particularly virtuous nor villainous, takes action that results in misfortune, personal and communal. The cause of the fall from grace, a flaw or frailty in character deemed excessive. Peripeteia (reversal) and anagnorisis (recognition) play their part and lead ultimately to catharsis.

I ask you, dear reader, would these considerations apply to anyone described in our continuing bike and barge narrative?

And among the group, would Bonnie Pickett take bets either way?

By twelve-thirty, the *Amoretto Algea* cyclists have parked their bikes in an extensive set of stalls and, toting helmets and red panniers, dispersed around the grounds of the Kasteel Kassel, the renovated medieval castle converted to an upscale restaurant that houses a large patio providing panoramic views of the Meuse Valley. According to Finn, the place got and continues to get mixed reviews as far as preservation goes, although it is highly praised as a venue for weddings, receptions, and other social events. At night spectacular lighting gives the castle an otherworldly appearance. Cole, Drake, and the Pickett twins, encouraged by Finn Bonger, have opted to explore the interior. If they don't reappear until just before leaving, that will suit me just fine. On this the sixth day of the bike and barge excursion, I'm beginning to tire of keeping abreast of every character and every conversation in which he or she participates. All the gods and goddesses have their gardens and their downtime. And so do I, as mentioned already at the castle in Well.

The others in the *Amoretto Algea* group wander through the park-like grounds that surround the castle and make for the cobbled path that hangs over the high bank of the Meuse. Finn suggests it is an excellent spot with many benches to rest on and have lunch. The views are impressive.

Bonnie Pickett, having chosen a suitable bench, invites Finn to join her. He's been strolling along the walkway with JJ and Angela who stop to take photos. Ray Rudiger, coming from the opposite direction, stops, listens in for a moment, then arranges himself on a bench next to Bonnie's.

"Hey, Bonnie," Ray calls out, "forget about picking Finn's brain. I can tell you anything you need to know about electric bikes."

"So you're good for something, are you?" Bonnie responds briskly, her voice husky on the verge of a disparaging cackle.

"Good for a lot of things," Ray answers and then swigs from the water bottle that he pulls out of his pannier. "Tim or Tom, one of them anyway, told me you're a dealer in a casino. That right? You never mentioned that, did you?"

"That's right. Like they say, keep your cards close to the vest."

"Where?"

"Where what?"

"Where are you employed keeping your cards close to the vest?"

"Lately I'm at the Steel Pier Casino in Atlantic City."

"Never heard of it."

"There's lots you haven't heard of."

"Like what?"

"Like I'm known by pit bosses as Quick Draw Larson."

"Larson?"

"Larson's my maiden name. Used for certain purposes that I won't get into with you."

"You were quick on the draw when you and Dexter took me for a bundle last night."

"Maybe you just allowed yourself to be played. Get a little sympathy along the way from JJ and the others. Looks like you got a gambling problem. I've seen it before. Can be tragic."

"Tragic?"

"I use the term loosely."

"I don't do tragedy except for when I take Ruth to the opera."

"Heavy. By the way, I'm also known as Busty Pickett but not because of the size of my boobs." Saying this, Bonnie lets out a high-pitched staccato laugh that rises to a crescendo. "I got Blackjack, and you got busted, fella. Get the picture?"

"You sound like a tommy gun going off."

"Bobblehead!"

"Husband call you that, Busty Pickett?"

"Got his own way of saying things."

"What's your husband do?" Finn Bonger asks. He's been in the middle of the antagonistic dialogue, apparently trying to infuse a softer word.

"Dexter runs a pawn shop in Atlantic City. Calls his place No Compunction Junction. Very successful. Knows quality when he comes across it." Another burst of raucous laughter from Bonnie.

Like Finn and JJ, Angela has been listening to the back and forth, a slow-motion bobblehead in her own right. She asks Bonnie how she got started as a dealer.

"Long story short. Money, honey. As a little girl, I was taken with my mother's wedding dress which hung at the back of her closet. Maybe I was six or seven. At any rate, I put the dress on, the high-heeled shoes, the gloves, grabbed the little bejewelled purse, and went out for a walk, dragging the train behind me. Passers-by thought it cute, or that I'd costumed up for begging, or whatever. A small lorem ipsum of an impoverished mother, getting nickels, dimes and quarters in my hand and stuffing them in the little embroidered purse with the pearly white handle. By the time my mother rescued me and her dress, I'd amassed a small fortune. Well, eight dollars and seventy-five cents in silver was a small fortune for a kid my age at the time. The point is, I got used to the idea of easy money."

"Same with your husband?" Ray asks.

"Same."

"And the twins? They're at college, right?" JJ asks.

"Right. Football. Got athletic scholarships. Another form of free money. When they were young, their grandmother nicknamed them Tom Thumb and Tiny Tim. She thought she had a sense of humour. Ironic, how they turned out."

"They're behaving rather oddly, don't you find?" Angela observes. "As their mother, maybe you—?

"You got that right, alright. They're involved in a cupcake romance. Neither one of the bubbleheads can entice the cake out of the cup, if you see what I'm getting at. They don't know what's hit them, and neither do I nor their father."

"Ah, yes, Isla Troyes," Ray Rudiger notes.

Speaking of Isla Troyes, she and Candace sit on a bench further along the walkway eating sandwiches. Between them and the Bonnie Pickett bench are redheaded Nigel and young Benny who has engaged his father in what appears to be an endless game of rock, scissors, paper.

"Roshambo. Roshambo. Roshambo."

"You like the sound of that word, yeah?"

"Roshambo. Roshambo. Roshambo."

"Brilliant game, innit? Keep track of wins for me, son."

Let us leave them to their game, dear reader, and return our attention to Candace and Isla and their chatter. Be assured, conversation on this bench, though perhaps on a repeat theme, could not possibly be as repetitive in substance as the previous one.

"As I was saying, they're like an intrusion without borders," Isla states with a firm nod of her head.

"Thankfully they wanted to see inside the castle, otherwise we'd be subject to laments about rejection and descriptions of what burning fervour is like."

"You know all about that firsthand, don't you?"

"Not anymore," Candace says and then after a moment's thought adds, "I can control my feelings for Finn. That's the difference."

"When it comes to the twins' antics and come-ons, they're like a grown-up human version of kittens in a paper bag, all quick smacks and crinkling tumbles. Not too sophisticated."

"Nothing new, then."

"Well, last night when you were being entertained by Finn, Tom comes up to me smelling like a rose garden. He said he walked all over Arcen looking for the florist shop Elsa Müller told him about. Came back with a bunch of white roses but his mother took them for herself with the father's approval. Shame."

"An odd couple," Candace says, "Bonnie and Dexter. Somehow, they deserve each other."

"Strange enough, but not like the Rudigers. Imagine, forty years married to that son of a bitch. In one of our little private moments, Ruth said that even when she admits to being wrong, she's wrong."

"Why?" Candace asks.

"For being wrong in the first place," Isla explains. "Ironic, in that her husband is 'unfaithful' as she phrases it using air quotes, but she admits putting up with it with the understanding that lust motivates him to look beyond the familial threshold, especially after her breast operation. Cancer.”

“Shame on him.”

“Ruth admits that he’s frail in some obvious ways, the gambling, for example, or the sexual innuendo and the always wanting to be in the limelight, but that he’s essentially a really generous person. Does a lot of charity work.”

“Charity begins at home. Isn’t that what your sister always kept saying?”

“Yes, she got that right.”

“Worthy of one if your sonnets,” Candace concludes. “Events here.”

“Everything in due time,” Isla states with expressed certainty and then adds, “Ruth let it slip that today is actually their wedding anniversary. You can only hope that Ray pulls in his horns long enough to arrange for a nice dinner out this evening to celebrate the event.”

“That would be something to celebrate, him catering to her, I mean. Just don’t drag the poor woman though the outlet mall looking for the latest in sportswear.”

“It’s massive, the outlet mall. Got something for everyone. Even me.”

“And me,” Candace agrees.

Then Isla poses the inevitable question, “So, what’s Finn like?”

"Carved like a Greek god," is her inevitable answer.

I can accept that. Finn Bonger is indeed a physical specimen worthy of note, worthy of comparison to a god like me. He is also an all-round good guy.

When the *Amoretto Algea* cyclists gather together again, this all-around good guy announces that the WC facilities on site are open to the public. For those in need—bottom block, back of the parking area. At this point, Elsa Müller insists on taking photos of the castle from the lower perspective of the courtyard, then photos of couples and family units, and then the whole group lined up by their bikes. JJ and Angela decide to follow suit. More pics of everyone antsy to get going. By one-thirty, all are well on their way to leaving the castle behind in the rear-view mirrors of memory. Dorpstrrat takes them out of town and a short time later they're crossing the Meuse again via the Veerpont Kessel-Beesel.

Lizzy Birtwistle is smiling benevolently as she watches Benny beating out a tattoo on the guardrail of the ferry in a Benny-inspired iambic pentameter rhythm. Nigel is with him, more or less. Otto and Elsa are also watching Benny. As if moved in sympathy, Elsa taps Lizzy on the shoulder. "You and your husband are so patient with your boy."

"He's a good lad. Fit as a butcher's dog, he is."

"You love him very much, *ja*."

"Love. That's the long and short of it, innit?"

"His condition, you understand it, yes?" Otto asks.

"Quite a bit. Benny's OCD."

"Obsessive compulsive disorder," Nigel explains. "The Pickett twins taught him rock, paper, scissors. He's put his MP3 player aside and taken to playing the game with me. At times he's overwhelmed by the repetition of it. But I indulge him, yeah? He's way ahead of me in the scoring and can't be tricked."

"Ruth Rudiger and I have talked about Benny's condition," Lizzy says. "She was a high school counsellor at one time. Very understanding, so she is."

"Helped you, *ja*?"

"Yes, she's a dear, so she is."

Once across the river and back on the east shore, Finn picks up the lead with Drake Cantlay still playing sweep. Skirting the village of Beesel, the group follows country roads and well-used bike paths, frequently meeting locals coming and going at speeds commensurate with age and type of bike. Midway between Beesel and Roermond Finn directs the pack into the Petrushoeve Camping reception area declaring the pause in the cycling will last a half hour.

"A well-deserved pit stop," Finn says, wiping his brow, "before pushing on to our final destination for the day. Cold drinks are available here. Tips for using the WC are always appreciated."

Some of the cyclists wander around on foot, stretching, others ride their bikes casually through the campsites checking things out, while others plant themselves on seats placed conveniently on the reception area patio. Pretty well everyone is sucking back on iced tea or other purchased drinks. In one shaded corner, Mick Mallory and Cole Cantlay discuss the differences between vacationers, campers, and travellers and seem to be generating a lot of laughter. In another shaded corner where redolent red roses hang about posing possibilities, Otto and Elsa are now with Ruth Rudiger who, until their arrival, had been sitting alone smiling at the day. Perhaps she is reminiscing about what might have been had I, Eros, been drawn into her life forty years ago.

"Fragrant roses and their poses," Ruth says, and nods at the couple. "Uplifting."

"The scent lifts the spirits, *ja*," Elsa agrees.

"We hear, Ruth, that you are well informed," Otto states with an inquisitive look on his face.

"Informed about what? Roses?"

"The problems of difficult children," Otto answers speculatively.

"*Ja*," Elsa says, "maybe not serious psychological disorders, but the emotions and also normal social behaviour."

"You've been watching Benny Birtwistle and—"

"Yes, of course, but not to make complaints. Nein, nein. To study how well his parents accommodate his behaviour. And how they respond to his needs. To see if we can learn what is helpful."

"In what way, helpful?"

"My son is…"

"*Liebchen*," Elsa interjects, "allow me to explain. Otto was married before. He has a teenage son. Hans Dieter is his name. He lives with his mother and her new family. He does not have the curious habits Benny has, but he is difficult to talk to when we are permitted to see him. School for him is difficult. His only interest is videogames. He—"

"Wait, Elsa, wait," Ruth cuts in. "Tell me about his friends."

"He has no friends. He says nobody loves him. Not Otto. Not the stepfather. Not the mother."

"Hans Dieter says his mother favours the little girls who are now so important in her life. This leads to depression."

"There are many demands on us," Elsa adds, "financial, emotional, and so on. But Otto and I are responsible people."

"Of course you are," Ruth assures them. "I can't suggest anything other than the need for greater understanding of the boy's situation and the declaration that you love him, especially you, Otto. Things will improve for all of you with time."

"Yes?"

"Yes. Let me tell you a story similar to yours. It may provide you with insight and a path forward."

"Please, yes, do so," Otto says. Again he is emphatic.

With time pressing before Finn Bonger summons the group to depart, dear reader, let me provide you with an edited version of the story Ruth tells Otto and Elsa Müller. The Young family lives on the same block as the Rudigers in southwest Calgary. Brendan Young was Ray's protégé: he guided him in his career as an oil field trouble-shooter. He travelled widely and often, but he could not, unfortunately, deal realistically with evolving familial troubles. Young admitted having absolutely no patience for the intransigence of his music-obsessed son, Elliot. Ongoing domestic disputes intensified over the years with antipathy verging at one point on hostile rejection of the so-called recalcitrant teenager. Elinore, an equally conflicted wife and mother, threatened separation; this caused greater anxiety for Brendan who turned to alcohol for the understanding that eluded him on the home front. Brendan's sojourn in Montreal, business mixed with pleasure, led him towards greater understanding of Elliot's situation through familiarity with the tragic story of poet Émile Nelligan, who, as a nineteen-year-old, enjoyed a successful entry into the artistic community of Montreal in the last decade of the nineteenth century, and then fell victim to madness. With reflection and greater understanding came empathy and paternal declarations of love, all leading to acceptance of Elliot for who he was and not for what his father wanted him to be. A satisfying resolution, dear reader, and quite acceptable for the Müllers to consider, or as Ruth put it to them, mull over. A denouement to a familiar enough narrative that required no darts of mine at any time.

Roermond, five p.m., dining area of the *Amoretto Algea*, the barge docked at the Cruise Terminal by the N280 overpass, all guests present and accounted for. Before the guests leave "to eat out" (as determined by the schedule), Finn provides for those interested, and there are some, a few facts about Roermond as an historically significant site of early civilizations and, he declares, "for too long in the centre of brutal combat, Celtic, Roman, and just about every territorial European war of the last two millennia whether it involved Spain, France, or Germany. An earthquake in 1992 caused extensive damage to the city, almost as much as was evident by the end of World War II. Roermond is now a popular tourist destination for a number of reasons, one being its waterpark, but being so close to rivers, canals and waterways, there is always the danger of flooding. But not this evening."

"Is there a casino in town?" Bonnie Pickett asks when the snicker subsides.

"There is. Joe's Casino, which is small and intimate. It's between here and the outlet mall."

"I heard that the outlet mall is like a city within a city," Candace calls out.

"A good description. There are more than two hundred shops within the mall and many cafés and restaurants."

"Great."

"Brilliant."

"For those of you more interested in the old city, there are many sights to see. Grand churches, historical buildings like city hall called Stadhuis, important monuments. Start your explorations in Markt Square. A variety of restaurants are there and also on Roerkade, which is the street that follows along the Roer River. If you remember, Roermond is where the rivers Maas and Roer join."

"Any maps available?" Conor St James asks.

"Maps of the central area are available from our reception desk. Okay, Dirk, bring it in now."

What Dirk brings in is a bouquet of roses. He presents it ceremoniously to Ruth Rudiger who rises from her chair at table one. She is completely taken aback but in her surprise manages to thank Dirk who slowly retreats to where Chef Simon stands waiting. Ray Rudiger is completely nonplussed. He rises and awkwardly attempts to smell the roses.

"This was delivered to the Rudigers by request to mark their fortieth wedding anniversary, which is today. From a local Roermond florist shop. Congratulations, Ruth and Ray."

Much applause and resounding congratulations.

"And now Chef Simon and Dirk, proceed."

With Captain Van der Oor looking on with approval by the entrance, they indeed proceed, but in measured steps, Chef Simon carrying a large candle-lit cake and Dirk behind him carrying a large tray with all the accoutrements necessary for serving stacked neatly on it. They place their burdens on the crew's table to a wild burst of applause.

"Let me read what's on the cake," Finn says. "Happy Fortieth Anniversary, Mom and Dad."

More applause. When Ray pecks Ruth on the cheek, cheers rise and the clapping increases in volume. He takes a bow, several in fact, and then leads her over to the designated table where together they blow out the candles. He picks up a long knife. After a moment's hesitation, he hands the knife to Ruth and begins removing the spent candles. Smiling, Ruth cuts into the cake.

"This surprise," Finn explains, as he takes a plate with a creamy wedge of cake on it, "was organized in advance by their daughter back in Canada. Her name is Amber. Very loving of her. Very capable."

I leave it to you, dear reader, to imagine how this little impromptu (shall we call it) celebration unfolds. Comments abound, mostly congratulatory in content. Ray bathes in the adulation while Ruth is more modest in her thankful responses. Benny is allowed two pieces of cake. In half an hour the assembly disperses.

As you well know by now, omnipresence is not numbered among my attributes. You can only assume with me that Ray will wine and dine Ruth appropriately this evening, perhaps asking others like JJ and Angela to join them. In all likelihood, he will not order the hamburger he has been babbling about craving "like a good piece of ass" as he so crudely put it to JJ in an aside that I happened to catch. Certain it is that Candace has induced Finn to guide her and Isla around the gigantic outlet mall. I leave all the other guests to their own hungers and the decisions they take as to how to satisfy them. Given all the possibilities I have for eavesdropping and all the directions I can follow, I opt to hover along with Cole and Drake Cantlay as I have not paid them much attention lately.

After limited exploration of Sint Christoffel Kathedraal, a small art gallery, and few other sights of interest, Cole and Drake re-enter Markt Square to settle down under an umbrella at the Brasserie Central to enjoy large mugs of local brew and hot, spicy hamburgers. They want to catch the colourfully costumed, life-size sculptures that tour around the Stadhuis clock tower but they're hours late as noon has come and gone and by noon tomorrow they'll be well on their way to Maastricht. Their conversation does not exhaust my patience the way that of some of the others I've listened to can, nor does it entertain me to the point of launching me into a bout of raucous laughter. Jocularity and cunning wit appear not to be in their DNA. They are first to arrive back at the barge. At this juncture, I take flight for Olympus, not to check in, no, I operate totally independently, but just to see who the poor victim is that Aphrodite plans on seducing or prompting her sidekick to prick to her advantage. Thus, I can plan my next moves. Tomorrow is the last day of the *Amoretto Algea* excursion.

Timely it is, then, to clarify for your benefit, dear reader, a matter that over a number of centuries has been of great concern to me. Since day one with you on the *Amoretto Algea*, I have referenced this concern. Simple intimation can be limiting. With the passage of time, over which I have no control, the image of the god of love and desire, me, in effect, ruggedly handsome and attractive in the absolute physical sense right from the inception, evolved into a child-like, misbehaving, dandified urchin with wings that would fail to arrest the fall of a sparrow. True, blame for mischievous behaviours and assorted indiscretions with which the god of passionate emotions is associated might conceivably go easier with a child, but it's all fake, counterfeit, and nothing but a sham substitution of the cute for the godly, the peewee for the grand. A total mischaracterization of long established fundamentals: that's how any observer with a logical outlook would view it. How ridiculous that a snotty-faced hang-about could win the heart, even inadvertently, of a beauty like Psyche. How absurd that such a diminutive creature with nothing of any size or length to boast of could father the demigoddess Hedone, who is clearly my daughter. Visualize that farcical encounter. It would be all micromanagement, to say the least, nothing but a tiny tosser, to borrow from Chef Simon's repertoire of pejoratives. A little bit of bint on the side? Nay, a scandal worthy of contemporary tabloid sensationalism.

The abuse of my identity, my majesty, is ubiquitous. On the fourteenth of February, pint-sized Cupid stars as the darling of the month, triggering romantic remembrance or amorous attachments, lovey-dovey style. Bogus! He gets far too much coverage in the movies and other media outlets. Since the silver screen came on the scene and debuted epics chronicling my Olympian peers and their exploits, only once was I accurately portrayed when Aphrodite directed me to help her champion, Jason. Thankfully, no mention of Cupid there. On the other hand, he gets more attention in contemporary songs than is warranted, but, thankfully, it's not always favourable. In one lyric he is repeatedly called stupid. A most appropriate epithet. Stupid Cupid. Moreover, there are lamentable lines about young love and high school pacts involving tragically doomed teenagers à la Romeo and Juliet. His doing, no question. What also piques me to no end, in fact I abhor the practice, is how comic book composers arrogate my name. Laughable results. Disjointed plots. In this age of superheroes, none can hold a candle to our pantheon of demigods, Hercules, for instance, and a recent film production cataloguing his exploits left me somewhat pleased. One last point: it is not a great credit to common sense that writers and commentators never described me as wearing a long flowing cape. Awkward.

Let there be no more talk of Cupid. I, Eros, insist.

Day Seven
you think, therefore I am

Roermond to Maastricht:

It is the penultimate morning in the *Amoretto Algea* lounge for Mick Mallory and Professor Wolfgang and their mutually beneficial conversations. In the background, the kitchen chatter between Chef Simon and Dirk van Kesteren rises and falls over the clatter and clang of their usual breakfast preparation.

"So, Mick, you left off saying just how your return to Greece helped you put things in perspective," Wolfgang says, stirring his coffee, then reaching down and placing his spoon just so on the edge of the low-slung table. "You experienced the misery of many months without your cherished Delores. You must tell me more."

"My trip to Crete helped me in that I could entertain taking on an adventure like this one, you know, touring around the Netherlands. And socializing with interesting people. Well, with people like you."

"Of course, you would say such a thing to me and I thank you. What most did you notice in returning?"

"The changes are what struck me most. I wandered around retracing former steps in the various historical quarters of Chania. It was as though a metamorphosis on the grand scale had happened."

"Like foreshadowing, *ja*?"

"I suppose you could say that. I had to remind myself that forty years had passed since I was first there. The vaulted lanes of Topanas district, where established families lived for generations, were largely commercial by this time and a little more meretricious in their appearances and come-ons."

"The juxtaposition of old with new. Contrast like this I know well."

"I consumed my first giro at a new souvlaki joint on Halidon Street and followed it up with a beer in Venizelou Square."

"Of course."

"I toasted Delores more than once, her memory having accompanied me along the colourful alleyways lying within the original Venetian walls. Terracotta, ochre, rust, sepia, sea blue— a phoenix had definitely risen out of the ashes and rubble of Nazi bomb sites."

"Like with you?"

"Right, right. I get your meaning. Transformation."

"*Ach*, I know well Venizelou Square. Rows of tables spilling out onto the flagstones from cafés and tavernas. People everywhere, coming and going, all along the quays. Anna and I have been among them."

"Insistent waiters bounding in and out," Mick adds, shaking his head, "and everything going on in time to plucky bouzouki music."

"*Kakophonisch*, we say in German. Cacophonous, I think for you, Mick."

"Exactly. As to other changes, a few differences in the commercial signage here and there, but much of it still reflects the services offered by ancient Olympian deities having escaped their twilight. For instance, Rooms to Rent Aphrodite, Hermes Scooters, and Sea Adventures Poseidon."

We don't age, of course, we immortals, it's just that our stories are getting old, worn out with use, and just as frequently chipped away by abuse in the modern media, especially with CGI enhancement blowing special effects out of proportion, all in the name of entertainment. However, I am not anticipating any massive and violent collapse of the divine order like Gotterdammerung, no twilight of the gods bursting into absolute disorder. No, nothing like that. So, dear reader, rest assured my work, such as it is, will continue.

At this juncture in the *Amoretto Algae* narrative, I've decided to present the truth regarding my birthright as the offspring of

Chaos and Gaia; to put to rest diverse apocryphal genealogies regarding my personal history; and to elucidate and legitimize my legacy. Do bear with me.

Early theorizing about my being as the god of desire and all its associated emotions and impulses is based on the idea that love equates to seeking wholeness, one half of the self constantly attempting reunion with the other. Consider the details of that proposition, that is to say, bifurcation to fork myself. I thought it absolutely ridiculous when first I heard it. Made me laugh. Much to my consternation, however, modern speculation posits this far-fetched notion as worthy of pursuit, linking philosophy, genetics, and astrophysics. Interesting possibility for specialists in the esoteric dream fields but equally ridiculous as my being upstaged by Cupid, a situation I have deconstructed for you, or to put it more graphically, smashed to smithereens for you, smithereens appropriately understood as small pieces which is a most fitting description considering Cupid's size and his near invisible attachments.

Many other versions of what transpired in the flight of time's arrow through the universe regarding my origins came to fruition. One later tradition has me as the son of Aphrodite by Zeus. Or Hermes. Or Ares. Take your pick, dear reader. If Ares, then it follows that Deimos (fear), Phobos (panic), and Harmonia (harmony) are my siblings. Interesting possibility, but no, absolutely not. I am singular and coeval with time itself. At any rate as I mentioned earlier, the Bitch of Beauty slept around, which is only natural, considering her own origins, inclinations, and seductive intentions. Very coy of Aphrodite not to reveal which immortal god had the advantage. Regardless of paternal input, so to say, and even though there is a majority belief that Aphrodite may be my mother, that's far from the truth and I reject such a claim outright. Olympian politics aside, theory debunked, thank you very much.

Qualification, here, dear reader. Beliefs develop within a region and over time. The promiscuity of Zeus reflects the wide-spread understanding that all the spoils of war belong to the conquering king, and these include matrons and virgin daughters. Such is the essential paradox that defines Zeus as the father god, polygamous progenitor that he is thought to be. Zeus can be a mean-spirited, puffed-up cockerel at times, even donning swan wings in making inordinate physical advances on an unsuspecting victim. I owe this self-promoting and importuning rapist no filial devotion whatsoever. In fact, I get a charge out of witnessing Zeus and Hera having it out about his infidelities, many that I myself inspired.

All that said, dear reader, I bring you back instantly to the early morning coffee klatch in the *Amoretto Algea* lounge.

"Understood," the professor says regarding the commercialization by mortals of the Olympian pantheon of immortals still widely evident in the land of my original recognition as significantly godly. After a moment's pause, he asks, "So, what happened to Flower? This you must also tell me."

"Well, it's like this, Professor..."

"*Ach*, here is Ruth coming. Let's welcome her."

And that's exactly what Mick and Wolfgang do as Ruth makes her way over from the you-brew-it coffee machine and greets them. With book and coffee, she arranges herself comfortably in one of the lounge sectionals.

"I've been reading an article," Ruth begins, holding up a magazine entitled *Redefining the Soul*, "about how love is like quantum entanglement. Professor? Mick? Any thoughts?"

"Is that the theory," Mick asks speculatively, "where humans survive by conniving an alternate life in an alternate universe?"

"Maybe. I can't decide. A bit too scientific for me to grasp fully."

Professor Wolfgang raises a finger and comments, "I understand quantum entanglement to be how two subatomic particles, even though they are lightyears apart, are linked closely together."

"As in everything is everything," Ruth says.

"The interconnectedness connection," Mick says in response to Ruth. Wobbling his head, he appears amused as to how he came out with that statement.

"Okay," Ruth picks up again, "love, as with quantum entanglement, is like a binding force in the universe. Two people remain harmoniously connected despite the distance that can separate them. It's all mutuality."

"Like soul mates," Mick offers. "Delores and I were soul mates. I have no doubt about that."

"Introduce quantum entanglement into the equation," Wolfgang says and then pauses for a speculative moment, but continues with, "and it would mean soul mates binding in a higher-dimensional spacetime."

"I didn't take the idea that far," Ruth says. "I was just wondering if there was a connection (that word again) to Aristophanes' theory of a primitive half of the soul seeking the other half. In other words, equating love to seeking wholeness."

"This brings the quantum entanglement idea from astrophysics and a multi-dimensional universe down to early philosophical speculation, *ja*."

"Right."

"Then again, attributing following in love to some idiopathic source leaves too much to idle speculation."

"Idiopathic?"

"Idiopathic essentially means you're unable to identify the source. Say in medicine, a blood clot on the lungs and you don't know what caused it."

"Right, right."

"But in any attempt to achieve clarity about all the dimensions of love, you can't disregard the biological effects."

"If we go further with these ideas," Wolfgang suggests, "we must look more closely at what Einstein had to say."

"That would take me way beyond my paygrade. I'll just live with the memory of Delores, who was my better half, as they like to say, and seek harmony with what's left of me."

Soon enough, the line forms for breakfast offerings. When all the guests are settled at their tables, Finn Bonger tinkles the bell for the morning announcement. The cycling route from Roermond to Maastricht will cover approximately forty-two kilometres with a break of an hour or so in Thorn, which is known as the white village. Near Born, the group will rejoin the *Amoretto Algea* and motor into Maastricht.

"What time do we set out this morning?" Nigel Birtwistle asks.

"We leave from the boat at nine-fifteen."

"Any news about my ring, Finn?" Angela asks.

"Yes, yes, I almost forgot. An envelope was discovered on the reception desk early this morning by Chef Simon. In it was a ring, probably yours, and a pearl necklace. Yours too?"

"Haven't looked to see if it's missing, but I do have one with me."

"Also, Dexter Pickett found your blue card, Ray, under a table on the upper deck. Late last night."

"That's convenient, isn't it?" Ray Rudiger shouts out. "I wonder how I could ever have dropped it in such a high visibility spot. Makes you think, doesn't it, folks?"

"Please see Captain Van der Oor to claim these items," Finn says, nodding his head at Ray and then not at Ray. "Enjoy your breakfast, folks. And you, too, Ray."

Snickers.

"The last day of cycling awaits you all," Finn adds. "Make the best of it. The weather is promising."

The business of breakfast continues the way it did on previous mornings, the preparation of lunches included. Arranging sandwiches, fruit, and other comestibles for a midday meal on the road brings a nostalgic word from this one and that one about how they'll miss the daily ritual of bagging a lunch, something they did when they were kids.

As good as his word, Finn leads the cyclists off at precisely nine-fifteen. Mick Mallory has volunteered to ride sweep for the last ride and he dons the yellow vest smiling. As for Conor St James, he is long gone. The day is warm, sunny. Hornerweg bridge takes them across the waters of the marine park and the Lateraalkanaal into the rural areas of Limburg province. Hay fields and horses, those are the predominant distractions along this section of the route. A scheduled stop at a renowned bakery in Heel occurs just after ten o'clock. By eleven the group is pedaling along the cobbled streets in the "white village" of Thon and comes to a full stop in the parking lot of Saint Michael's Church, site of the former Imperial Abbey. After hearing Finn's brief commentary on the church, which he describes as "an interesting fusion of Baroque, Gothic Revival, and women power," the group settles into familiar patterns.

Lock bikes, secure helmets, and take panniers: Finn's standing order is followed to a T.

Benny Birtwistle recognizes Conor St James' Specialized in the bike stand and looks around expectantly. He spots him coming through the gates of the graveyard adjacent to the church and emitting loud ululated notes of expectation, he waves him over. After exchanging a few words with the boy, Conor St James mounts his bike and quickly disappears. Bouncing rhythmically,

Benny heads mother and father up a side alley that leads away from the dark Gothic portal of the church.

Otto and Elsa enter the graveyard and I leave them there to their observations and meditations, which I expect will be nothing but respectful. The majority of the group, and that includes Tim and Tom Pickett, follows Finn into the church and I abandon them all on the threshold as I have been in this fabled sanctuary on several occasions, both before and after the restoration. I hover back to where Candace and Isla are still hanging around by their bikes, seemingly undecided as to how to spend the time they have at their disposal. They turn and immediately walk out of the parking lot when they see the Pickett twins pile out of the church as though in a mad rush to embrace their destiny.

Well, that's exactly what awaits them as they stand there in the shadow of the church with the spirits of empowered aristocratic women from times past darting about them. The twins look absolutely dumbfounded, more so, in fact, than what has been habitual with them over the last few days. It is at this precise moment that I reach into my quiver and withdraw a lead-pointed arrow, fit it to my bow, and let fly at Tim. It goes straight to the mark. I quickly repeat the action with Tom as my target and get the same result. Risible the way the twins shimmy and shake as a single individual might, like mirror images split apart and reunited under favourable auspices, or like in a rehearsal for a Vaudeville song and dance routine, voices muted altogether, steps uncertain, no one leading and no one following. However, the twins are free, free at last from the bondage in which I caught and held them. When the whimsical dance is done, Tim and Tom Pickett do a volte-face and re-enter the church. Will they offer prayers of thanksgiving? Hard to say, even for me. Not my area of expertise. And not my concern.

At this juncture, I decide to catch up with Candace and Isla. I follow them as they saunter around a few of the cobbled streets of the white village taking an occasional photograph. After sufficient exploring, they arrange themselves at an outside table at De Pannekoekenbakker on Hoogstraat and order iced tea.

"Last day of cycling," Candace says, after the server brings the drinks. "It's been really good."

"Right," Isla agrees. "I'd do it all again as long as...Well, you know what I'm thinking. I just could not deal with the twins when they came out of the church. Bad enough on the boat the way they're acting. The big louts make the limited space seem even smaller."

"At least they're our age, more or less" Candace points out. "Not like you know who with that calculating stare of his. Even at breakfast when Finn was explaining about today's ride, the old letch was giving me the once over. You know that thing he does, the two fingers pointing from the eyes that means I'm watching you. Did it a lot with Finn at the beginning. Probably thinks he's being subtle. Or mysterious."

"He's not really that threatening, though, is he? Not like that creep last year."

"Not really," Candace answers. "Yeah, last year... those two deaths in the family. Two murders, I still can't believe it. Like, they put a whole different complexion on the adventure. Still mystifying somehow."

"That was then and this is now," Isla states with conviction, "and I still can't understand how Ruth perseveres. Imagine, forty years with Ray."

"Ruth's strong," Canace says. "Has character. Ray's not really hateful but I'm close to hating him anyway."

"Yeah, Ruth will survive because she's smart and resourceful. Life has a way of just carrying on. Now you, will you miss Finn when it's all over?"

"I don't think it's ever all over."

"Let me write that down."

I leave the young ladies to their discussion of the future and what life may hold for each of them and turn my attention elsewhere. Wondering what has become of the Birtwistle family, I flit over past the graveyard and buzz up the lane that passes the church; it gives on to an open area where a few commercial interests are located. At the De Wijngaard Café I spy Mick Mallory,

Cole and Drake Cantlay, and Wolfgang Albrecht. The professor is holding forth on the history of the Imperial Abbe, so named, he points out, under the aegis of the Holy Roman Empire. Dating from tenth century construction, he goes on, the site underwent numerous transformations, from nunnery with legitimate religious observances to a convent of financial convenience for her ladyship and other female aristocrats of high nobility to a medieval tax haven. I am perfectly aware of the history of Thorn where windows at one time were covered in and houses were painted uniformly white to avoid the payment of taxes; so when Benny Birtwistle, emerging with his parents from the nearby Het land van Thorn history museum, loudly greets the professor and interrupts his donnish seminar, I applaud the boy. He holds up the fridge magnet bought in the museum and repeats in that wonderful echolalia rhythm of his that what he saw in there is "brilliant, brilliant, brilliant." Before joining his mother in heading back to the bikes, he engages his father in a game of Roshambo.

Shortly after mid-day, the cyclists have crossed the border into Belgium, their destination the city of Maaseik. Following picturesque rural bike lanes, they parallel as much as possible the waterways to the east that feed off the Meuse.

"Any Konik horses in these parts?" Ray Rudiger asks when the group bunches up at a junction.

"And they are?" Cole Cantlay wants to know.

"Smallish, semi-feral horses. Supposed to roam freely in parts of Europe."

"Ja, this is so," the professors agrees. "Polish. Grey colour with interesting markings."

"I was just wondering because we've seen a lot of horses today."

"Konik horses around here?" Finn Bonger says, "not that I know of."

"But we have seen lots of mamils," Bonnie Pickett pipes up, "in small herds going this way and that. Grey beards with very colourful markings. A lot like you, Ray, only sleeker and faster on the uptake."

"Mamils?" from Cole Cantlay. "Did I miss something at some point?"

"Mamils are middle aged men in Lycra pedaling their asses off," Bonnie explains, then lets out one of her staccato laughs just as Finn Bonger leads off again.

Keeping the pace set by Finn, the cyclists make their way through a recreational area dedicated to water sports, a virtual aquatic playland. Comments fly over heads and get captured by the wind. After skirting the Spaanjerd marina with its display of yachts, big and small, they pick up the Maasdijk bike path that leads eventually into Maaseik.

At a shaded corner of the central Marktplein in the Belgian city, Finn in typical fashion advises all to lock bikes and secure panniers. The allotted time is an hour. Departure for Born is at one forty-five.

In a place of prominence in the centre of the square stands a nineteenth century statue of artists Jan and Hubert Van Eyck. The native sons of Maaseik look regal in their imposing hats and flowing garb which are reflective of the times when they achieved wide recognition as masters. My favourite perch, if perch I may call it— not that I really need one as I can hover indefinitely— is atop the statue. It is a position from which I can survey the square and keep track of the doings of those who come and go talking of Michelangelo and of early Renaissance art as practiced by the Van Eyck brothers. Although situating my esteemed self on the heads of these renowned artists limits eavesdropping, it does provide perspective and three-sixty degree viewing. Not my first observation post. Before alighting there today, I listen to inquiries made of Finn as to where interest and needs may be met.

As might be expected, dear reader, the *Amoretto Algea* contingent divides into recognizable subgroups that take to ambling about, drawn to whatever might be of cultural significance to them in addition to a Belgian pint which some, like Otto Müller and Ray Rudiger, declare as culturally significant in the absolute sense when in

Belgium. There is a preponderance of green awnings along each side of the square and in each of the corners. Also cultural, but local in nature. Around the perimeter of the heavily treed square is a variety of businesses, from sports outlets to apothecaries to cafés. The square also serves as an auto park.

Mick Mallory and Professor Wolfgang, after exchanging a few words with Finn, have started in the direction of the archaeological museum. The Cantlays go looking for a bank or a bank machine. The Birtwistles are directed by Finn to De Potter which serves ice cream delights at a reasonable price. There are other options to satisfy Benny's cravings, he informs them, but they go with the first suggestion. Candace and Isla make off in another direction. In all likelihood, Finn will be joining them if past is indeed prologue. The Bienvenue will do. As for the Picketts, they just suddenly disappear and I leave them to their own amusements. The Rudigers and Joneses have made their way through the square with only a cursory word about the statue and now sit under a green awning at the Pannekokenbakkerij Maaseik in the southwest corner of the square. Below me at the base of the Van Eyck statue, Otto and Elsa Müller munch on the sandwiches they prepared earlier. Talk of how in returning home they will deal with Hans Dieter is desultory at best.

At this juncture, Conor St James, riding through the square, stops, parks his

Specialized, and studies the Van Eyck statue. He consults the small reference book he pulls from his pannier. When Otto greets him, Conor apologizes for not noticing that he and Elsa are sitting there. He asks if they would like him to take their picture at the statue of the famous artists. They agree and Elsa hands him a phone, briefly explaining its workings. Snap, and then snap again, and as quick as a flash, Conor St James is gone.

Packing up their panniers, the Müllers saunter over to the southwest corner of the square. I opt to hover along with them. I appreciate how they are welcomed by JJ who offers to buy them a drink. They willingly join in. The topics of conversation, prompted by both JJ and Ray, range from the fused architecture evident around the square to a preference for Belgian brew over that of the Dutch to laments regarding the approaching end of the boat and bike tour. I've heard this all before, so I leave the six of them at their table under the green awning at the Pannekokenbakkerij Maaseik. Back on my perch, I spend what remains of the hour distracted by a wedding party mulling about what is conceivably a reception hall or a civic centre, possibly, where all the significant players wear white running shoes, even the bride and the individual I presume is the groom. Love with style. Must be the French influence.

No gold-pointed arrow necessary in this scene I determine although for a moment I am tempted to dig into my quiver and do something to alleviate the forlorn look on one of the groom's attendants. Save the dart, I instruct myself, and I do.

Shortly after two p.m., our cyclists have crossed back into the Netherlands and, following the bike path along the Julianakanaal, they pass the Schipperskerk to arrive at the *Amoretto Algea* which is moored at one of the jetties in the area of the Born Locks System. Innumerable photos are taken of the group preparing to board the boat by those most interested in having what could be called tangible memories or visible proof that they themselves, now that it's close to over, actually endured the rigours of the daily cycling or maybe both at the same time. All climb up the ramp once the bikes are loaded and shortly thereafter the *Amoretto Algea* is enroute to a final southbound destination before heading back to Amsterdam the following day with a new lot of adventurers. Not on board are Tim and Tom Pickett who convinced Finn Bonger to guide them in cycling all the way into Maastricht.

Some of the guests relax in the lounge having changed from their cycling gear or performed other commonplace post cycling rituals. Before too much time has passed since boarding, Bonnie is dealing cards. With her playing poker are Dexter, JJ, Ray Rudiger, and Drake Cantlay who has learned quickly when to hold them and when to fold them and when to go all in. One would think Bonnie would take a holiday from shuffling cards and taking peoples' money, but no, apparently it's what she's most comfortable with when not tearing strips off her twin bobblehead sons or complaining about the paucity of hot water for showering which she did when ordering a glass of Chardonnay from Dirk.

On the upper deck, pockets of conversation are within my hearing once I've tuned in— the sights of the day and how bodies and limbs are feeling after the cycling, that kind of thing— but what interests me most is the continuing conversation between Mick Mallory and Wolfgang Albrecht. Like the professor, I desire to know how the story of Mick's misfortune concludes. With a bang or with a whimper? What I overhear of their initial talk is how good the pint of Amstel tastes.

"*Prosit*," Wolfgang says, raising his mug. "It is agreeable, yes?"

"Very," Mick says and clinks his glass with Wolfgang's. "So, bottoms up, eh!"

"A grace beyond description, the first gulp," the professor says, licking his lips after downing a large draught. "*Lecker, ja.* Very tasty."

"It's almost as if the first mouthful makes all the physical effort worth it."

"Just as you say."

"Less of a struggle each day out," Mick says. "Ha, I don't mean downing the beer. I mean I'm finding that the cycling makes for a kind of physical and mental balance."

"Interior balance, yes? Calmness."

"I suppose there are ways in which equanimity and equilibrium are connected. As I suggested earlier, I'm able to accept what life has presented to me, whether it's accepting Delores' unfortunate death as the workings of fate or participating in a bike and barge experience in the Lowlands. All part of the recovery process."

"This brings me to ask," Wolfgang states rather pointedly after taking down another gulp, "if you were successful in getting justice."

"There is resolution of a sort in terms of lost love and the regrets that follow the loss," Mick says and swigs from his mug. He looks about. He watches the treed landscape go by as the barge runs steady as she goes down the canal. Then a spot of open country comes into view.

"Justice in any form does not return the loved one to the one who is bereaved," Wolfgang prompts when Mick turns back to him.

"The wild emotional reactions that took over my life needed attention, which I received. But was I successful in getting justice? Depends on how you define justice. And how you define success."

"So, revenge per se was not part of your recovery, your attaining equilibrium?"

"I heard it said that a man intending revenge needs to dig two graves, one for his victim and one for himself."

"But you never got that far with your shovel, *ja*."

"That's right.

"So, inform me, please, what happened to the culprit, this fellow Silas Flower?"

"Like I said earlier, Nemesis took him by his mop of hair and gave him a damn good shake down. Know what I mean?"

"*Ja, ja*. Nemesis, the goddess of retribution."

"Inevitable. Irresistible, no matter your wealth or position of power. The details of the come-uppance Flower suffered are interesting."

"How so?"

Mick looks out across the port side of the barge again. A cityscape is slowly passing and holds his attention for a prolonged moment. Wolfgang lifts his mug as though in a gesture of encouragement.

"I'll tell you how so. The Furies followed the lead that Nemesis gave them," Mick says and smiles.

"What mean you, the Furies?" Wolfgang asks, and then, as though chuckling to himself, he adds, "They are part of the Canadian justice system?"

"Metaphorically speaking, yes, you could say that. I appreciate the humour, Wolfgang. The Furies idea is my daughter's. You know, the symbolic correspondences in the Greek myths. She's a teacher. She shares my antipathy for Flower and all he represents."

"I understand. What the ancient Greeks conceptualized in their myths, I know of these things. How they personified every human dimension— love, fear, ambition, greed, excess. Nietzsche, yes? He had much to say about myths and society. Apollo versus Dionysus and so on."

"To be more precise about our Canadian furies," Mick explains, "three women of the Sorority took Silas Flower down in the courts."

"The Sorority?"

"The Sorority is an assembly of Canadian women seeking retribution for rape, sexual assault, and sundry other grievances. Also known as Suffragettes 2.0. In this case, the three women embodied the vigorous and demanding potency of the Furies."

"*Ach, ja*, I remember now, the Sorority, from the news."

"Civil and criminal suits gained momentum and eventually crushed Flower," Mick goes on after taking a gulp of beer and licking his lips. "In the wake of a series of financial setbacks, serious ones at that, he committed suicide. The setting was a hunting camp by Echo Lake in Northern Ontario that Flower once owned. A witness described Flower as projecting the gazed rapture of a tormented soul. Something like that. He reported hearing Flower cry "Eris, my love!" These were the last words the man uttered before he pulled the trigger. Eris was the name of his twin sister."

"And so, an ignominious death."

"Exactly. I ask myself often if history will pardon Flower the way it continues to give a pass to highly placed, disreputable characters, prominent politicians foremost among them? History does repeat itself and often, but not often enough it wipes plausible deniability off the public slate."

"So, my friend, you are one with yourself, yes?"

"One with myself, yeah, that's pretty much the case. Fate is as fate delivers, you could say."

"Good. We mentioned Nietzsche, a moment ago, *ja*."

"You did, in connection with the Greek myths."

"Nietzsche has much to say about fate. He professed *amor fati*."

"Which translates from the Latin as love of fate, if I'm not mistaken."

"Just so. A declaration of acceptance. But more than that. He means love absolutely. He puts it in words such as this: "not forward, not backward, not in all eternity, not merely bear what is necessary, still less conceal it, but love it.""

"Yeah, I follow that, difficult though it definitely is to embrace completely."

"Among the early philosophers, Nietzsche felt closest to Heraclitus, *ja*."

I just love the way Professor Wolfgang includes these little stereotypical add-ins when speaking in English, these little interjections in German like *ach* and *ja*!

Be that as it may, dear reader, at this point it is incumbent upon me to amplify Mick's allusion to the Furies. An elucidation, yes, call it that, while the *Amoretto Algea* continues to motor down the Julianakanaal allowing views of varied landscapes—patchwork pastures, bisected towns, industrial sites and installations.

So, the Furies, those inexorable dark forces chasing sinners, are also known as the Erinyes. Later in their careers as moral authoritarians, so the reports have it, they turned protectors of merciful supplication. Alecto, the relentless one, pursued and whipped with her scourge those guilty of moral crimes. Megaera, the jealous one, meted out punishment for theft, infidelity, and the forswearing of oaths. Tisiphone, also known as vengeful destruction, tormented murderers.

Here, let me assure you, Mick's declaration about vengeance requiring the digging of two graves is accurate. If the subject interests you, dear reader, research the workings of Alecto, who is the personification of implacable anger, and how vengeance can be ambivalent in its effects. The story of Orestes and the Furies exemplifies only too well how a double-edged sword cuts two ways.

As the *Amoretto Algea* progresses toward the junction of the Julianakanaal and the Meuse north of Maastricht, let me add a few more facts to substantiate claims about my involvement in the affairs of the heart. Also in need of extrapolation on my part is how I communicate with mortals or with those among them exhibiting not only interest in but also fascination with my accomplishments, mortals like you, dear and patient reader. I am very capable of saying relevant things or delivering relevant commentary; it is just that I don't always find an ear worthy of hearing what I have to say, if you take my meaning. You may be inclined as an informed and educated reader to reject all that I have claimed on behalf of the immortals, me, Eros, not the least among them. Fine. Such is your choice but never forget we evolved in accordance with your progression out of ignorance in an awkward attempt to comprehend the world around you and your place in it.

I lose patience with people in contemporary settings who throw around the word myth as synonymous with lie, untruth, fake. Let me be perfectly clear on this point: myth is the very foundation of our existence and, by logical extension, yours. I could go on ad infinitum on this subject but I leave you at this point with the thought that myths, when understood for what they are in real terms, are universal and continue to serve the truths, such as they may be, of any given national culture. The American Dream, for instance.

Let me come back to first principles and well-founded postulations. I exist due to the vast imagination of mortals, their endless self-absorption, and the desire to dominate not only their environment but one another as well. In other words, I exist because you do. It's simple logic. To state the case in the service of truth, let me borrow from the Cartesian rhapsody of ideas and note in a trope worthy of gift card spin: you think, therefore I am. This inconvenient truth is based on a categorical syllogism, not a conditional one; if any condition be in play, it's to do with your ability, dear reader, to follow logic. Never forget that I exist because you do. I repeat: You think, therefore I am.

Employing the most effective point of view, let me extrapolate further. Surely, you've realized by now that we immortals are subject to the same temptations that mortals are subject to in every way. After all, they brought us into being, didn't they? I cannot emphasize enough that we are an enhanced version of what they are. I'll put it this way. We immortals evolved in lockstep with them; the more sophisticated they became, so with us. They granted us substance, personality, powers, and through us they began to understand themselves more thoroughly and the world they inhabited.

Mutual dependency. They created us to explain what they didn't understand, which is the central paradox that defines our existence. We gods and goddesses hung out in the green room of possibility, eventually taking possession of centre stage where we were allowed to control all the plots, to manage all entrances and exits, to determine all curtain calls. Enough said on the subject for now. In the meantime, let's get to Maastricht.

The Maas flows through Maastricht dividing the city into east and west districts. Conor St James, Finn Bonger, and the Pickett twins are resting on the quay under a shade tree, one of many that line the Maaspromenade. When the *Amoretto Algea* approaches and cozies up to the quay, Finn Bonger rouses himself and prepares to assist in mooring operations. Stretched out between two bridges connecting east and west, the Sint Servaasbrug and the Wihelminabrug, a series of jetties serve as ad hoc berths for touring barges like that under the command of Captain Van der Oor. Once all is secured, Dirk runs the four bikes up the ramp and arranges them with the other bikes on the platform behind the wheelhouse. A small group of guests cheer Finn and the others onboard, Candace, Isla, and Benny Birtwistle foremost among them. Mick Mallory and Wolfgang Albrecht look on, smiling indulgently.

In his evening address to the guests, Finn Bonger invites Chef Simon to describe what he has prepared for the last meal. Aproned in white and wearing his chef's hat, Simon Oliver steps forth and stands by the coffee machine. By him is Captain Van der Oor in official uniform and nearby is Dirk, red faced.

"*Blinde Vink* is a traditional Dutch dish, yeah," the chef explains. What goes into it is ground beef seasoned to perfection and wrapped in a delicately pressed veal cutlet. For this meal as well, legumes doused in a special sauce complementary to the meat. Potatoes, carrots, onions, apples, beans. All are baked with tender love and presented to you in the same way. Desert is a surprise, innit, Dirk?"

"As long as it's not another apple strudel," Ray Rudiger shouts out from his perch at table one. "That would be a surprise alright."

A few snickers and a guffaw or two at Ray's attempt at humour.

"You are the surprise here, mate, but less of a one than at the start," Chef Simon says and then, turning back to the group, he adds, "*Bon appétit* everyone."

Much applause and many a voiced thank you.

When Chef Simon retreats to the kitchen followed by Dirk, Finn Bonger takes over again. "Some of you are off early in the morning, and so on behalf of Captain Van der Oor and all of us crew, I thank you for your enthusiastic participation in the *Amoretto Algea* adventure. You will be missed. One of the best groups ever. Do enjoy your last evening with us."

"I bet you say that to all your departing guests," Ray Rudiger shouts out. His comment gets a modest chuckle.

"I'll also wager you'll be happy to see the last of me, Finn," Ray says, and showboat that he is, he takes a bill from his wallet and places it on the table with a bit of a bang.

"I'll take both those bets, Ray," Bonnie Picketts says and gets a loud appreciative response.

"Finn might not say he's happy to see you go, but I will," Dexter Pickett declares.

"And that's a sure bet," Bonnie adds.

Guffaws mixed in with the applause. Banter.

"Ladies and gentlemen," Finn says with slightly increased volume, "cherished guests, please enjoy your meal."

And so begins the last supper.

Here, dear readers, I re-introduce for your edification my myriorama and its shifting foci. The benefit of that? You are provided with a contrapuntal discussion of the future in four-five time. In other words, we'll listen in on what the four guests at each of the five tables are saying about their plans for the next day and the days subsequent to that.

"It's back to Amsterdam for us. Always wanted a city cruise."

"Then there's the gran fondo to prepare for."

"Blind pig, I think."

"Back to the butcher shop for us lot."

"But plans can change."

"Wherever you go, see the sculptures in the Rijksmuseum."

"What she said."

"Ruth said to check out Piccadilly Circus when we get to London."

"Don't play with your legumes."

"Tim and Tom have invited us out for a drink. What do you think of that?"

"Delicious. What did he call it?"

"The Venus de Milo in the Louvre. Must see it."

"Yeah, a brother in Dublin."

"You people and your goddamn museums."

"*Ja*, a book on Friedrich Nietzsche."

"Me, too."

"Sure. Let's join them."

"*Blinde Vink*, I think."

"Language, please."

"We hope to be with Hans Dieter when we get back."

"A sister in Scotland."

"The goddess of love and beauty."

"Tell you the truth, though, I don't mind checking the shapely bitch out myself."

"Direct to Edinburgh from Eindhoven."

"Randonneur."

"What's it called?"

"The redlight district, ever been?"

"In for a penny, in for a pound."

"The name? No Compunction Junction."

"It's called *Vlaflip*."

"After the Parthenon in Athens, the island of Milos."

"Blackjack table and college football."

"*Vlaflip. Vlaflip. Vlaflip.*"

"Tasty, innit?"

Gore is not my province. Gore belongs to the more warlike of my esteemed peers. You are familiar, of course, with Ares and Ate. But to the question: how did the body land where it did, bloody and broken? Be assured, dear readers, I accept responsibility for what might be called a catastrophe. My doing, absolutely. The result, unfortunately, was not at all what I had envisaged when I initiated the action.

The opportunity to take aim presented itself in a timely fashion. Judge me if you must, dear reader, but I definitely had motive. As to the means, I have that in spades with sharp points, as you very well know.

Consider the statue in London's Piccadilly Circus, a statue of none other than me, Eros, as understood now in the popular imagination. Forget Anteros for the time being. But really, what's in a name? The point is, that statue captures the dramatic moment I wish to describe for you. Beautifully depicted, I am hovering above the fountain, wings spread wide as though encompassing the world, having launched the dart with deft purposefulness. With that in mind, picture me hovering over the scene on the *Amoretto Algea*, guests on the upper deck enjoying nightcaps and exchanging email addresses. Ray Rudiger stands alone at the top of the ramp scanning the Maaspromenade.

As Gertrude Stein once pronounced, there's no there, there. There certainly is a there, there when it comes to Raymond Rudiger and has been there ever since he boarded the barge seven days ago: and there she comes. Candace Troyes, caught in the glow of evening light like an apparition emerging from the farthest reaches of the wistful imagination. Her carriage is playfully alluring, a dance evincing rhythmic sultriness and finishing school comportment. She moves like a provocation, unintended as such but consequential in its effects. She puts me in mind of my daughter Hedone and her sensual grappling with the laws of gravity. Behind Candace are the Pickett twins on either side of Isla who is carrying a bouquet of red and white roses.

Here is where I make my play. Understand, I am not a fan of Raymond Rudiger and plan to mess him about before he leaves in the morning, not in any violent way, not from any superior moralistic viewpoint, just sufficiently so that he be made to experience the kind of unrequited love he has caused in the lives of others. For instance, his wife, Ruth. I am immensely fond of her. A fan, in effect. Admittedly, Anteros is exerting his influence on me at this moment. I intend Ray Rudiger to experience intensely the pangs of love, the agony of unfulfilled desire, not simply flirt with the notion as he has been doing since appearing on the *Amoretto Algea*. Candace Troyes will have absolutely nothing to do with the old letch. She will disappear from his gawking and lascivious observations forever.

Focus, dear reader, focus. Rudiger lying in a heap that only a practicing contortionist could achieve, one with a bent for the macabre. The expression on his bloodied face remains a confusion of delight and bewilderment.

Candace Troyes. Stunning, an absolute beauty. Voluptuous. Remember, she is drop dead gorgeous. An unfortunate turn of phrase, considering the present circumstances. Now roll back the scene to a critical moment before Rudiger's unfortunate plunge. Refocus on him standing at the top of the ramp watching her approach. He looks to be preparing an overture to a fond farewell, or what is conceivably a fond farewell à la Ray Rudiger.

I pull an arrow from my quiver, set it in my bow, draw back, and let fly. In this launching and landing of my dart, I grant

Rudiger the apple of his eye, Candace Troyes — apologies here to William Tell.

The sensation of being hit in the heart is real. Recall Hesiod's description. Recall how Tim Pickett attempted to explain the unexplainable, and Tom following hard on his heels. Candace also had her fiery moment when I caught her contemplating Drake Cantlay. In Rudiger's case, like that of those mentioned, a magnificent confusion arises in his being, a total jolt to the system. He endures a sensual barrage, the eyes beholding a vision of beauty never before experienced. The heart pounds, the ears ring, the scent of roses fills the nose. The irrepressible, overwhelming feelings for the object of his attention disorient him completely. His sense of balance is affected. There is no equilibrium whatsoever in his reaching out to her and absolutely no grace.

At the top of the ramp he trips, does what can only be described as a swan song, and lands awkwardly on the metal pier, his head-over-heels aerobatics a sad display of inauspicious late middle-aged fantasy. A messy result.

Candace lets out a shriek that could under other circumstances awaken the dead. A crowd forms, comments pass. Ruth is inconsolable once the truth is irrevocably established. Outrageous incomprehension.

"Get Captain Van der Oor," Finn Bonger directs Dirk van Kesteren. "He'll call the authorities."

It strikes me that Finn Bonger is responding to a premonition, judging by the way he is surveying his immediate surroundings, as though the subtle movement of ambient air he detects has some bearing on what just happened to Rudiger. Again, I laud his instinctual response to something beyond the ordinary. More power to him, I say again. But I had not anticipated Ray Rudiger's fatefully lethal fall from grace.

"What the hell happened?" JJ wants to know.

Looking over the scene, Chef Simon says, "Time for the fat lady, yeah?"

"Was he pushed?" Otto Müller asks in an unlikely form of rhetorical question.

"Was Conor St James responsible? He was closest to him."

"How about Dexter Pickett? No love lost there."

"Finn Bonger?"

No, Raymond Rudiger was not pushed. And no, none mentioned was responsible.

Authorities come, assess the situation, question the crew and all the guests. The medical examiner attributes Rudiger's fall and death to a cardiac arrest but I assure you, dear readers, it was an aesthetic arrest, a fatal shot of scopophilia that killed him.

As Isla comments to Candace just after the body is removed from the pier: "His frailties were not commensurate with such an ignoble end. He wasn't that flawed."

Was Rudiger ever conscious of his excesses, did he regret them in any way? Most of all, did he recklessly believe that he was not bound by the vows of love? Did he at any time have an awakening as to just who and what he was? I doubt that in witnessing his demise too many onboard the *Amoretto Algea*, guests or crew, would experience a cathartic reaction to the drastic spectacle he inadvertently presented to them. In all likelihood, no peripeteia, no anagnorisis, and no catharsis. Apologies here to Aristotle.

I make no claims to being perfectly consistent, just consistent enough within the general parameters set for immortals since time immemorial. In the flight of time's arrow, we are an experiment in human consciousness just as they are an experiment in evolution's attempt to become self-conscious.

Time's arrow. I like the concept. Though fanciful, it does appeal to my sense of destiny.

All metaphorical, all this. The arrow is symbolic, as is the shot to the heart. Likewise, the whole archer thing attributed to me. A moot point, some would point out. Arguing the metaphysics of my existence and my aims would be purely academic because common tropes evolve into established truths when abstract considerations are rendered concrete. To parse to pieces the phenomenon that defines my raison d'être is to trudge again through the preserves of paradox. I accept the fact that I am representative, naught but a shadow figure in the game the three Fates play. Therefore I bid you, dear reader, hold as truth what you must. Just appreciate while I still have your attention the effects of my action.

I intend to retreat into another narrative, one less horrifying, less bloody, and less lethal in its denouement, perhaps one where chance has some shoulder room. All in due course. In the meantime, please understand that desire will never fade among mortals, thus my longevity, my immortality. The power of Zeus will fade from memory, or be relegated to lower echelons of literature, though his lust will not, nor the desires and longing that feed it. So, as to immortality, forget it. Eternal life is a phantom concept: we will cease to exist with the death of the last mortal. As to Raymond Rudiger, he was absolutely mortal.

The *Amoretto Algea* is virtually still as it lies in its birth along the Maastricht quays between the Sint Servaasbrug and the Wihelminabrug bridges. No one is about except for captain and crew. Guests have retired for the night, in all likelihood heavy with solemn regret for the misfortune suffered by the Rudigers. Ruth Rudiger is shaken but has found it possible to mix philosophical acceptance for what has passed with the kind solicitation given her by JJ and Angela Jones. They offer to remain with her until her daughter arrives from Canada. They will also help her deal with the imposing paperwork and all other official matters pertaining to the mysterious death of her husband.

"Still a *pijn in de kont*," Captain Jan Van der Oor declares. He reaches across to the bar, grasps a bottle of whiskey, and sets it on the table with a bang. Dirk van Kesteren quickly procures glasses.

"A pain in the ass, they come and go," Finn Bonger says, "but never with as much flair as Raymond Rudiger. The last supper was lively, now all is subdued onboard."

"Gentlemen," the captain says after pouring the whiskey, "I've said it before and I say it again, unsympathetic guests come with the territory. But even now Rudiger is proving to be a bigger nuisance than any before."

"All the tears," Dirk says.

"All the cups of tea, yeah."

"All the questions from the police. So much red tape. Legal inquiries. Insurance concerns. Inconveniences. Adjutant Marten is a real *pijn in de kont*. But he gives us leave to carry on tomorrow with the new guests."

"Who kicks the bucket on holidays? Only a tosser like Rudiger would think of doing something like that. Shame, innit?"

"This is my fifth excursion with you, Captain, but this is the first time I've really experienced something out of the ordinary.

Like a premonition. An omen." Finn Bonger's voice is firm, directed.

"Her name is Candace, your omen, yeah? She's leaving you broken hearted. That should be premonition enough for you, mate."

"I have her email address, also her address in New York City. It's never over until it's over. Isn't that what some Greek philosopher like Aristotle pronounced centuries ago?"

"Not likely, mate. You're just taking the piss before I wish you all adieu?"

"Socrates, maybe?" Finn Bonger prompts and smiles. "This is how it plays out. Candace and Isla take the early train to Brussels to take the Chunnel to London. London ain't that far away."

No, London is not that far away at all. Nor Piccadilly Circus. I'll betake me there after a last word to you, my dear, patient, and longsuffering reader.

Certain observations have led me to wonder where mortals are headed, given the influence of and their dependence on AI, and these days the inducements of social media giants that reduce even the most upright of senior citizens to portray themselves as idiotic, prancing marionettes controlled by the fingers of big business and political manipulators. Big Brother is rubbing his hands in anticipation. In contemplating these facts, I am tempted to launch arrows at everyone everywhere on the planet and turn activities like those seen on the *Amoretto Algea* into a raging universal bacchanal but, fortunately for all, I'm more restrained than that. This appraisal is based on the assumption that by the end of the present century, mortals will still exist on this planet, and we divinities along with them, and on the congruent assumption that mortals will not have wiped themselves out due a correlation of factors, and we divinities along with them. I am very sceptical about ultimate outcomes and you, gentle reader, should be too. No mystery there.

A footnote: Isla's poetry. How will she deal with the demise of Raymond Rudiger, aka, Candace Troyes' Caliban? Apotheosis? Or ellipsis? My bet is on the latter…

The End

Reed Stirling books also published by BWL Publishing Inc.

Shades of Persephone
Lighting the Lamp
Sejour Saint Louis
The Palimpsest Murders

Reed Stirling lives in Cowichan Bay, BC, and writes when he is not painting landscapes or travelling or hanging out at The Drumroaster in Cobble Hill, a popular local café where metaphor and metaphysics clash daily. He is presently completing work on a sixth novel. His shorter fiction has appeared in a variety of venues, both online and in hard copy, among which *The Nashwaak Review, Fickle Muses, Filling Station, Fictuary, and StepAway Magazine*